SEVEN DEADLY THINGS

A HENRY & SPARROW NOVEL

A D FOX

SPARTILLUS

A D FOX

A D Fox © 2021

SEVEN DEADLY THINGS

Published worldwide by Spartillus.
This edition published in 2021.

Copyright © 2021 A D Fox

The right of A D Fox to be identified as the author of this work has been
asserted with accordance with the Copyright, Design and Patents Act 1988.

1

www.adfoxfiction.com

❦ Created with Vellum

PROLOGUE

'*Say sorry.*'

'What?' He looked genuinely confused. Like he really had no clue. Like he'd forgotten. And that was just it, really. How little it meant. So very little, it hadn't even lodged in his memory.

'Say sorry for what you did. Write it. Write it down.'

The guy screwed up his handsome face, trying to understand. It was going to be necessary to explain.

Afterwards, he looked even more baffled. 'But... that was seven years ago! I mean... we weren't much more than kids...'

'So... you're not sorry?'

'Yes... yes, of course I'm sorry. I'm really sorry.'

Well, he would be, wouldn't he?

He blinked at the curved edges, wrote his apology in red ball-point on the soft, pristine white, and then he seemed to think that was it. All sorted. Like writing sorry was going to make it all right. He realised that sorry wasn't enough as soon as he saw the gun. That was the most satisfying moment - the dawning real-isation.

Even so, he tried to talk his way out of it, as they walked towards the steamy spot beneath the palm trees. He talked and talked and talked, right up to the point when the blade cut through his voice box and he literally couldn't talk any more.

'ALLIGATORS!' screamed Ellie.

There was instant squealing and shouting. Ellie took a deep breath. Nearly thirty kids were running towards her, arms flailing wildly through the air, eyes wide, hair streaming.

It was going to be carnage.

'ALLIGATORS — MARCH!' she yelled. 'ALLIGATORS — SNAP! ALLIGATORS LIFT YOUR HANDS AND CLAP!'

The kids got into an unruly line as she marched them around the ballroom floor, snapping and clapping for a couple of minutes until all the stragglers had caught up and joined on the end. Settling back with their drinks and watching with indulgent smiles, the grown-ups started to clap along to the 'Time For Bed Song' in the happy knowledge that soon all the little rugrats would have buggered off to go by-byes, and they'd finally be allowed to say the F-word without fear of censure.

'EACH AND EVERY ALLIGATOR — EVERYONE SAYS SEEYA LATER!' sang out Ellie — along with a good number of cheerfully pissed adults — as the house band took up the tune on the stage behind her. Nettie, her fellow Buntin's Children's Aunty, skipped down to bring up the rear of the alligator line, singing heartily along with the kids now as they replied: 'WE HAVE HAD A LOVELY DAY, NOW IT'S TIME TO HIT THE HAY!'

The lyrics were somewhat confusing. *Alligators didn't tend to hit the hay*, thought Ellie, not for the first time. Crash in the swamp, yes... but that didn't really rhyme, and she guessed it wasn't Sir Tim Rice who'd been hired to write the Buntin's Alligator Club 'Time For Bed Song'.

'SNAP! SNAP! SNAP-SNAP-SNAP! ALLIGATORS MARCH! ALLIGATORS SING! ALLIGATORS SNAP AT EVERYTHING!' Ellie warbled on. Jesus. It was probably the twenty-fifth time she'd sung the bedtime song and it was still just as crap as it had been on the day she'd learned it. Happily, the kids didn't seem to care. The more ADHD ones were trying to snap the heads off the kids in front of them, encouraged by this nightly exhortation to pretend their arms were crocodilian jaws.

'AUNTY ALLIGATOR SAID,' Ellie and Nettie sang out, with feeling. 'ALLIGATORS OFF TO BED!'

A roar of approval, accompanied by cheers and applause, followed the kids through the Embassy Ballroom doors — held open by a couple of fellow Bluecoats — and out into the carpeted foyer. The children never seemed offended by their rapturous nine o'clock send-off. Once in the foyer, the mums (and occasionally the dads) would come out too, waiting for the last loop of the Alligator March. This last loop went once around the flower beds and then through the top end of Buntin's Jungle Water World — in one door, past the pool, and out through the other door, while everyone waved goodnight to Martin, the Bluecoat lifeguard.

Jungle Water World was emptied of kids at seven and closed to all punters by eight-thirty. So by nine, with its Rapid River now just rippling gently beneath the fake palm trees, and the main pool azure and mirror-still, it was all rather calm and serene. Ellie and Nettie had discovered that this atmosphere settled their troupe of overtired under-tens down quite nicely as they marched through it. By the time the line came to a final halt, back in the foyer, their charges were usually yawning and resigned to being taken off to their chalets for the night.

As they stomped through the outer doors and headed for the pool complex, Ellie wished she could hit the hay herself. She would love to go back to the chalet and crawl into bed. She was absolutely knackered. But her shift ran from ten in the morning to ten at night. Her last hour, after the children had gone, was to be spent trying to chat to holidaymakers at their tables. 'Mix and Mingle' was what Gary, the Entertainments Manager, called it. Well, actually, he called it *Mix an' Fuckin' Mingle*, in a gravelly voice — like Ray Winstone warning off a fellow gangland boss. Any Bluecoat caught out just standing by the bar or chatting to a fellow Blue, would soon experience Gary creeping up behind and growling, 'Oi! Mix an' fuckin' mingle!' in their ear.

So, mandatory jollity with the Buntin's holidaymakers until ten... and after that she was expected to party with all the other Blues until midnight. She didn't know how they did it. She was nineteen and ought to be able to keep up, but she really wasn't cut out for all the drinking and smoking and shagging that was just normal after-hours life for most of her workmates.

'SNAP! SNAP! CLAP-CLAP-CLAP!' sang out Ellie and Nettie as they approached Jungle Water World. Not long now and Ellie could get down to the last hour of mixing and mingling. She and Nettie would be vying to hang out with little Tyler's hot dad for a bit, while Tyler's mum tucked him into bed.

Ellie had to shove the pool door open. Martin must have forgotten to wedge it like he usually did. He normally liked to get up on his high lifeguard chair in time to wave the kids through, but the chair was empty tonight.

'ALLIGATORS, NOT SO LEAPY! ALLIGATORS, GETTING SLEEPY!' Ellie and Nettie heavily implied in song, Ellie walking backwards and waving her charges in.

There was some extra squeaking from two little girls nearest to her. Rosie-Mae and Blossom were shouting, 'LOOK! IT'S ALL PINK!'

Others were joining in, too, thrilled at the sudden change of water colour, as if it had been magicked up just for them. Ellie blinked and felt something thud in her throat. The water wasn't meant to be pink. It wasn't meant to be red, either, but it looked red, up in the corner where the main pool flowed across a waterfall of tiles and into the Rapid River. The red faded to fuchsia, and the fuchsia to pale rose.

Shit, thought Ellie. She started leaping up and down, waving her arms madly. 'HEY!' she shrieked. 'WATCH THIS! Let's see if I can clap my hands over my head and walk out of the other door BACKWARDS!'

Some of the kids looked at her, but most were still staring at the pink pool.

'WATCH MEEEE!' Ellie heard the desperation in her own voice. In the corner of her eye she could see a trousered leg floating amid that reddest part of the pool, just protruding from the corner, beneath a palm tree which overhung the Rapid River run-off. Her need to keep the children's eyes away from it was battling with her own instinct to stare — to work out if it was real. Suddenly, she stopped, just as Nettie arrived in the doorway at the end of the Alligator March. 'AND ALLIGATORS — TURN AROUND!' Ellie yelled, gesturing wildly at a puzzled Nettie. 'BACK THE WAY WE CAME!'

At this point, there was a loud bubbling sound and the Rapid River suddenly started to gush. It shouldn't have happened — the rapids machinery ran on a timer every ten minutes and by now it was meant to be switched off. The trousered leg and its black-shoed foot began to bob up and down and move across the pink pool. Ellie felt the thudding in her throat increase in frequency.

'EVERYONE! TICKLE NETTIE!' she shrieked, going for cheeky and landing on terrified. Still, she nearly did it. She nearly pulled it off as two dozen kids turned to mob poor, baffled Nettie. But Rosie-Mae and Blossom could not be distracted for quite long enough.

They turned back to look again, just as Martin, glassy-eyed and leaking a crimson ribbon from his slit throat, floated across the pool.

When the screaming started, Ellie couldn't even tell whether or not she was joining in.

2

Her head was abruptly jerked back.

Then she was violently propelled forward, the belt cutting into her skin.

She thought maybe she was going to die. Here, in this metal coffin which smelt of 1979.

'Jeeezuz! Francis, can you stop stamping on the bloody brake at the last minute? You need to brake way earlier than that!'

Her brother huffed and rolled his eyes, but he had *asked* for this, so he couldn't really give her a hard time. 'I *am* braking early,' he said. 'It's just that it takes a while for anything to happen.'

Kate Sparrow gripped the seatbelt a little tighter and watched the car ahead pull away into the distance, wisely shaking off Francis's unintended tailgating. 'Well, maybe that's because instead of buying a new Nissan or VW, you irrationally went out and snapped up a piece of retro junk. '

The gunshot blast scared rooks out of nearby trees. Kate jolted in her seat and caught her breath, and Francis pulled the Ford over to the side of the road and killed the engine, looking stricken. 'Sorry, sis,' he muttered. 'It does that some-times. Really didn't mean to trip your PTSD.'

'No... no it's fine,' muttered Kate, through gritted teeth. 'I mean... it's a good six months now since I got shot; why would your backfiring 1970s shitwagon be a problem?'

'Look - it's got a few issues, but it's a collector's item,' he said, patting the wheel as if defending its feelings. 'These babies really hold their value — getting it for ten grand was an absolute steal.'

Kate opened the passenger door and ducked awkwardly out of her brother's bargain buy. It was mercifully cooler out here. Another charming original feature of the Ford Capri was its total lack of air conditioning. She closed her eyes and breathed in the scent of rapeseed blossom and nettles. The long, flat road they were travelling stretched away between fields of almost neon yellow, hemmed with green, under a bright blue sky. Apart from the offensive mustard hue of the Capri at its centre, the rest of the scene could have been painted on a plate by Clarice Cliff. Kate took long, slow inhalations of the warm May air and reminded herself that everything was fine. Nobody was shooting anyone. Nobody was suffocating anyone. Nobody was drugging or starving anyone. It was all fine. Just fine. It had to be. She had just been promoted to detective inspector with Wiltshire Police; a little PTSD was *not* going to hobble her career.

Francis arrived next to her, carrying two magnetic L plates. 'You want to drive the rest of the way?' he asked.

She let out a long sigh. 'No... no, it's OK, Fran. I said I would help you learn and that's what I'm going to do. You're doing fine, apart from the braking thing. You should be good for your test.'

Her brother raked his fingers through scruffy blond hair and looked less than confident. He'd been taking driving lessons for a year now, embarrassed to still be learning at twenty-four. Kate had passed her test ten years ago, when she was still seventeen. She had agreed to let him get some more practice on their journey to Suffolk. She shouldn't have given in about the car, though. She should have stuck to her guns and made him drive her Honda.

'How's the shoulder?' asked Francis, and she realised she had been rubbing it, distractedly, again.

'It's fine,' she said. 'We should get going. Put the learner plates back on. We're only half an hour away, you might as well keep driving.' She tried to think of something nice to say about his choice of car as he reattached the magnetic L plates front and back. 'The wheels are cool,' she said, eventually.

'They're original thirteen-inch alloys,' he enthused, grinning. 'And the engine is a two-litre which could do nought to sixty in 10.4 seconds back in 1979. That was world-rocking stuff back then.'

'Right...' She smiled, shrugged, and got back in. She really needed to be a bit more upbeat. This whole trip was meant to be fun. She'd invited him along because he spent too much time cooped up in his room, online. It was his job — he was some kind of IT guru, working from home — but it was also all his downtime and it wasn't healthy, given that her brother wasn't a vampire. If he didn't get some daylight and Vitamin D soon, he was going to turn from pasty-pale to see-through. He needed to get out and meet other people, too, in the flesh.

When Talia had got in touch a few weeks back about the *Magnificent Seven After Seven* plan, Kate had initially thought she might give it a miss, but Talia insisted, 'You *have* to come, or it'll only be the *Sorry Six*. That's no good. Kate — I *demand* that you come!'

Talia had always got what she wanted seven years ago when they were working as Bluecoats at Buntin's Holiday Village, and it appeared nothing much had changed. And Kate knew it would be fun, meeting up seven years on from that first summer, when she had just turned twenty and was earning a little money before starting her last year at uni. A *very* little money, it turned out. The pay at Buntin's was piss-poor because so many excited young luvvies applied, hoping the weekly Bluecoat cabaret shows might earn them an Equity card. They were wrong about that, it turned out, but by the time they realised it they were usually fully on board for fourteen weeks of entertaining holidaymakers for little more than their keep. It was hard work but a lot of fun, and a total shagathon from start to finish. Nobody but Kate had gone to uni, so this was their Freshers' Week equivalent and it had lasted for an entire summer.

Kate had only gone for the job because Talia had. Bruised by constant drama school rejections, her Salisbury College friend had opted for Buntin's, hoping for that elusive Equity card. After all, an assortment of comedians and telly presenters had started out as Buntin's Bluecoats, so why not try that route? It had to be worth a shot.

Kate could still vividly remember the day she'd first arrived at the site, perched on the chilly Suffolk coast. Talia had booked a later train, having stopped off in London to see some theatrical friends en route, so after a rail journey through the flatlands of East Anglia, followed by a bus ride through the Fens, Kate had found herself standing alone at the bus stop opposite the entrance to Buntin's Lakefield Holiday Village.

And wondering what the hell she was doing there.

Dragging her wheelie case down the long drive, between neatly tended flower beds, she had reached an empty car

park and a whitewashed pavilion with WELCOME TO
BUNTIN'S emblazoned on a rainbow hoarding over its
three sets of glass double doors. Inside, on a carpet of
violently red and orange swirls, Gary, the Entertainments
Manager, had welcomed her with a pack of forms and
badges, a ticket to collect her Buntin's Bluecoat uniforms,
and a key to the chalet she would be sharing with Talia.

Seven years later, Kate smiled to herself as Francis drove
sedately along the straight Suffolk B- road, pointing out
windmills on the horizon. She was glad she'd been able to
bring him. It was her condition in agreeing to come, which
Talia had readily agreed to. Seven years ago, Kate had
written old-fashioned letters to a teenage Francis and posted
them home with a different piece of Buntin's gift shop tat
every week. She was pleased to be able, finally, to show him
the strange world she'd inhabited that summer.

It would be fun to see everyone again and find out what
had happened to them since they'd last met. She might edit
her own life experiences slightly; it wouldn't add much to
the party spirit to tell them her mum had died a couple of
years after she'd departed Buntin's — and that she herself
had nearly died twice in the past six months. Although they
would be fascinated with *those* stories, she didn't doubt, the
truth was she was still getting over the trauma and this daft
holiday reunion was part of that process.

It would be lovely to just get silly and forget about her
work for Salisbury CID — forget about murderers and
kidnappers and victims... and dowsers. Yes. She was going
to forget about dowsers too...

'So... tell me again who I'm going to meet,' said Francis.
'Give them a rating — Snog, Marry or Avoid.'

She laughed. 'That's a very wise idea! Well, OK. Number

one is Talia, who I think you met a few times when we were at college together.'

'Oh — the hot black chick,' said Francis.

'I think you'll find we say "woman of colour" these days,' Kate said, primly. 'But yeah — she's the hot black chick and I think she'd prefer that title. She always wanted to be an actress and she almost made it. Now she's doing teacher training in Bristol.'

'Boyfriend?' he asked. 'Or... girlfriend?'

'Between men at the moment,' said Kate. 'Possibly quite literally if I know Talia. You must DEFINITELY AVOID. OK. Number two - that'll be Craig. He's camp as a row of tents and working for British Airways as a steward. Also wanted to be an actor.'

'OK... avoid too?'

'That's *your* call,' she said. 'He was always mad as a jar of gerbils, but under it he's a sweetie.'

'Noted,' said Francis, changing gear with a struggle. Kate winced but resisted making another disparaging comment on his baffling vehicle choice, grateful that there was no car in front for the Capri to snuggle up to.

'Then there's Martin,' went on Kate. 'He stayed on at Buntin's when we all went at the end of the summer season and he's never left. The pool is open to locals in the off-season months, so he's always had work. He's kind of half-Bluecoat, half-lifeguard, really. Big, manly, sporty — not too bright.'

'Snobby graduate elitist,' accused Francis. He hadn't bothered with uni himself and was now earning a shedload of money, without forty thousand in student debt hanging over him. He liked to rub it in from time to time.

'You can't avoid him — he's too big,' Kate said, ignoring

the dig. 'You probably won't want to marry him but who knows? A snog might not be out of the question.'

Francis grinned and shook his head.

'Then there's Handy Bendy Julie,' she continued. 'She ran all the fitness sessions. Body to die for — double-jointed. Can literally bite her own buttocks.'

Francis gaped through the windscreen, clearly picturing this. 'Marrying her — definitely,' he said.

'Think she's a PE teacher now... Number five is Bill — works in finance these days, but back then he was a singer and he always fancied himself as Idris Elba with vocals. Massive ego, shagged anything with a pulse.'

'You included?' Francis shot her a worried glance.

'Shit, no! I mean, god, I'd do *real* Idris on the bonnet of my car... in Sainsbury's car park on a Saturday morning,' she said. 'But Bill? *Avoid, avoid!* Was always way too in love with himself for me. But not for most. Which brings me to Nikki — number six.'

'Oh yeah?'

'Sharp, funny, Welsh,' she said. 'Kind of Rizzo in *Grease* with a Cardiff twang. But she fell hard for Bill and he took full advantage, and then dumped her mid-season.'

'And they're *both* coming along on the *Magnificent Seven After Seven*?' he marvelled.

'Yup! Apparently it's water under the bridge,' said Kate. 'If you can believe that. Nikki runs a nursery school now, apparently. Snog at your own risk, I'd say. Anyway, number seven is me, who you can't avoid or snog *or* marry.'

'Don't be so sure. We're in darkest Suffolk now.'

She chortled and rolled her eyes. 'I think Norfolk has the edge on that,' she quipped. 'Every other baby grows an extra finger up there... here it's only one in four. Oh my god - this is it!'

The gateway to Buntin's Lakefield Holiday Village suddenly loomed up on the left, so incredibly familiar to Kate, and yet so strange. Seven years had seen the trees along its perimeter grow to almost twice the height she remembered, and there was now an electronic car barrier and a guy sitting in a little hut next to it. He got out as they arrived, smiling in his Buntin's blazer, and asked for their booking number and their names. 'Cool car,' he said to Francis. *He's just young enough to think that*, thought Kate. He hadn't been here seven years ago; he was probably still in school back then.

As Car Park Youth checked down his clipboard of incoming guests and car registration numbers, pen poised to tick them off, Kate saw something shift in his expression. 'Oh,' he said, a flush creeping up his face. 'You're in the Talia Kingston party.'

'We are,' said Francis, a querying note in his voice.

But the guard just nodded, avoiding eye contact, coughed and then said, 'Go right on in, sir. Park up and take your bags into reception. Have a... a nice stay.'

Francis said thanks and drove carefully along the tarmac drive. Kate turned around in her seat to peer back at Car Park Youth and saw him scurry into his little wooden hut and pick up a landline phone. She didn't get a chance to see much more, but still caught the agitation in his movements. What the hell..? Suddenly, goosebumps rose across her skin. She reached into her jacket pocket and mashed up a lump of plasticine she liked to keep there. Her panicky episodes had been receding for some time now, but she was glad to be able to squeeze the modelling clay whenever she got a fizz of anxiety. Joanna, her therapist, had recommended the plasticine-squishing approach as a distraction and it worked very well. In fact, it had been an absolute lifesaver.

It worked again now. By the time they'd parked up and got out of the Capri, hauling their holdalls out of the boot, she'd dismissed her goosebumps and was allowing the pleasant ghosts of the past to drift across her mind. As they walked up the steps to the pavilion she noted that it had been repainted not long ago, but the hideous swirly carpet was still in place. Above all, as she pushed open the heavy glass door, it *smelt* exactly the same. It made her want to laugh... and sort of cry, too. Nostalgia was a bitch. She was remembering what a fun time she'd had... and a moment later she was remembering that when she'd come home at the end of that summer, Mum had been tired and a bit fluey. She was still under the weather when, two weeks later, Kate returned to uni in Bristol for her final year.

It wasn't until she came back for Christmas that Kate had begun to understand what was really going on with Mum. By then it was too late.

Anyway. She shook her head, determined to put all that stuff back in its box. It was Friday and a weekend of Buntin's regression beckoned. Why the hell not? She'd had enough fear and misery to last a lifetime. She deserved a break. So did Francis.

'Kate!' called out a gravelly Essex voice and Gary stepped towards her, arms wide, skin leathery, hair improbably highlighted. The snarky old bugger looked just the same and she gave him a hug, grinning.

'Still mixing and fuckin' mingling?' she asked.

He pushed her away and looked her in the eyes, and that's when she saw there were tears in his.

3

'Oi! Look! It's one of those fuckin' twig-wavin' weirdos!'

Lucas Henry sighed. It was hard to concentrate now the local Thick Short Plank Brigade had turned up. He'd been aware of the gang of teenagers for the last half hour, well before he laid eyes on them. You didn't need to be a dowser to pick up the miasma of Lynx body spray, roll-ups and sexual desperation, even at twenty metres. He had hoped they would bugger off to nick beers from the local Co-op before he reached the end of the field, but they had not.

It was a warm Friday afternoon in late May, and he guessed they'd come over here right after school. There were five of them, hanging around a fallen tree close to the perimeter of the Stokeley Lodge Estate. If the gamekeeper found them, there would be shouting and rifle waving. It was private land.

'What you lookin' for?' shouted another one of them.

He decided to pretend he was deaf. He really wasn't in the mood for this. Taking the job had been a mistake. He should be working on his next art collection back in Wiltshire instead of mapping the subterranean levels of Lord and Lady Botwright's extensive grounds in Norfolk. With the amount of rain they'd had over the past week, there was a short answer to how much water lay beneath their grassy acres. A *fuckload*, was the correct term, he believed. They would need to site their new guest lodges pretty carefully to avoid the structures sinking into ground. Creating decent foundations in the Fens was a nightmare and the astute project manager of their new venture had advised some extra help in locating the driest ground for building. Her ladyship had heard about Lucas Henry's talent from a mutual friend, and had offered him stupid money. Stupid to turn it down, at any rate, even though he'd sworn off dowsing last November. It was too dangerous. And he'd more or less kept to his pledge. Trouble was, money was running out, and...

'Oi! You deaf or summint?'

Lucas finally had to look up and let out another sigh as three of the group started capering around in front of him, holding out their hands in a mockery of his dowsing pose. Two of them had even been clever enough to pick up some twigs, which they were waving towards the shallow basin of turf they were dancing on. He slotted the long ends of his steel rods into his jeans pockets and let his hands drop to his sides. He normally used Sid, his blue glass pendulum, for dowsing, but there was a lot of ground to cover and he wasn't being paid by the hour. Pausing every few steps to still Sid on his chain and take a fresh reading would have taken two or three times as long; rods were a quicker option. Sid still sat against his chest, though, directing from above like a bottle-stopper general.

'I'd get off that patch if I were you,' said Lucas.

The youths looked at each other, full of grins and uncertain swagger. They were bored and itching for a dust-up of some kind. The shortest one, with thick spiky brown hair and a stud in his eyebrow, waved his twigs aggressively. 'If you can do it, we can do it. We can wave twigs as good as you. We might even find water! That what you're after? You lookin' for water?'

'You might very well find water,' said Lucas, mildly, pushing the straggly dark hair off his brow and fixing the youths with a sad smile. 'If you don't move across from where you're standing.'

'This is — what — dossing?' sniggered Stud Brow. 'Or tossing? Are you out here tossing?'

'It's called dowsing,' said Lucas, feeling a vibration through the glass stopper. 'Really... you need to move.'

'Or what?' said another youth, stepping in to join the other three. The vibration in Sid went up a pitch.

'You're in danger,' said Lucas. 'Seriously — move back towards the log if you don't want to—'

'We're in danger? What? Are you gonna take us *all* on, bro?' The second boy, his hoodie drawn in tight around his pale, acne-speckled forehead, started leaping about, making stabby hand movements towards the earth, as if he was a performing hip hop artist. Looking more like Scooby-Doo than Snoop Dog, he didn't quite pull it off.

'I'm not going to take any of you on,' sighed Lucas, beginning to feel really quite gloomy. He might be calling 999 shortly and he honestly didn't want to do that.

'Because, like, you can TRY it, man!' went on Scooby. 'You know what, though?'

Lucas shook his head and stepped back a bit. He never found out what. A second later the bottom fell out of Scooby and Stud Boy's world as the thin layer of turf and soil they'd been stamping on collapsed into a sinkhole the size of a small truck. Three out of the five of them vanished underground in less than a second.

The two left behind scrambled backwards in astonishment as the grinding and snapping of earth, stone and roots filled the air. Lucas dropped to his hands and knees and, taking care to spread his weight, crawled to the edge of the sinkhole. 'Call 999!' he yelled across to the stunned boys left topside. 'Get an ambulance on its way!'

Peering over the torn turf into the new-born crater he was relieved to see that it was only about four metres deep. The three boys lay wallowing in a small underground lake, shocked and whimpering. 'It's OK,' he called down. 'You'll be all right. It's not going to drop any further. You're on bedrock.'

'Get us out of here!' whimpered Scooby, scrambling to his hands and knees, mud smeared across his face. He suddenly looked about ten years old and Lucas felt a twinge of pity for him.

'Take it easy,' he said. 'Get up if you can, but go slowly. You won't drop any further down, but there could be a further cave-in at the edges and I don't want you under that, OK? All of you, sit up and sit still. We're getting help.'

He got his mobile out, switching it on to call Grant, the project manager, who was based in a portable cabin up by the big house. 'We've had a collapse,' he said, 'A big sinkhole down in the south-east corner of the lower field. Some local lads have fallen in. We need sacks, ropes and ladders.'

It took twenty minutes to get them out, by which time the ambulance had arrived in the lane on the far side of the perimeter, and a couple of paramedics had wormed their way through the gap in the hedging that the boys had used to gain entry an hour before.

'They're OK,' said Lucas, as the three twig wavers, soaked in mud, confusion and embarrassment, were checked over. He guessed he should get back to the house and file his first report of the day, fine-tuning the sketched map and notes which described the underground courses and their levels, as reported back to him though the rods, Sid and his own instincts.

'It's hazel twigs, by the way,' he said, picking up one of the ladders to carry back, alongside Grant and a couple of his labourers who'd come to the rescue. Stud Brow looked up at him, still dazed and confused as his wrist was bandaged up. 'If you want to learn to dowse,' Lucas added, with a lopsided grin. 'Hazel seems to work best. But hey — you found *masses* of water with those sticks of oak. Really impressive for your first go. So who am I to tell *you* what to do?'

He left them staring after him wordlessly and joined Grant and his two guys on the long walk back.

'Little shits got what they had coming to them,' said Grant. 'They've been pissing us off, trespassing, for weeks. They're lucky they didn't break their necks.'

'Yeah, nice one, Lucas,' said Jim, one of the labourers. 'That's a bloody superpower, that is — when people who piss you off get dropped into the bowels of the earth.'

'I *wish*,' Lucas said, laughing. 'It was just about to go. Our little venture scouts just hurried it along. Could be worse — a sinkhole in Norwich swallowed a double-decker bus back in the eighties. There was a medieval chalk mine underneath the road. And two houses fell into a sinkhole in this area back in 1936... a couple of residents were killed.'

'I heard about that,' said Grant, waving the labourers on to dump their ladders beside the cabin. 'It was up Kett's Hill. Eighty foot deep, it was. Oh no. Poor Jessie.'

This last comment was directed at the figure of a young woman who was wandering the formal gardens around the big sandstone lodge, wearing a blue apron and carrying a basket. Although she was, at first glance, serenely gathering long-stemmed roses for the house, at second glance it was evident she was crying.

'What's up with her?' asked Lucas. 'Boyfriend trouble?'

'You could say,' replied Grant, turning away from the garden and carrying his own load of ladder and sacks towards the cabin. 'Her fella offed himself last week.'

'Shit. That's grim,' said Lucas. 'Depressed, was he?'

'She says not, but the facts say otherwise. Poor bugger slit his throat and dropped himself in the pool he was a lifeguard at, after hours. He left a note, they say. Bit of a shocker.'

'It would be,' said Lucas. 'Can't have been a pleasant find, either.'

'No — especially with all those kiddies around,' agreed Grant, stacking his ladder against the cabin and dumping the sacks next to it.

Lucas did the same. 'What kiddies? Was it a leisure centre?'

'Holiday camp. Buntin's, just over the border into Suffolk, down south of Lowestoft. They reckon a couple of kiddies saw him. Nasty. Bet those families will be getting free holidays for life.'

Lucas stretched. 'Well, I think I'm done with the rods for today. I'll go in and work on my map and notes. I'll know more after tomorrow, but I think it's safe to say you should avoid building on the lower field.'

Grant grinned. 'Reckon you're right, there. Maybe put in a swimming pool instead.' He chortled and then stopped, clearly thinking of the dead lifeguard again.

Lucas headed back to his guest room in the manor house, trying to clear his mind of the image of a dead man floating in a cloud of his own blood. He needed to stop dwelling on stuff like this. He needed to move on from that kind of thing. He'd successfully avoided thinking about death, murder, bodies and blood for at least a week. He'd almost not even thought about Kate Sparrow. Almost.

But now something was making Sid charge up under his shirt.

'Give it a rest, you buzzy little bastard,' Lucas told it, as if it was the old blue bottle-stopper that was actually causing the problem, rather than his own messed up psyche.

As he reached his room — a pleasant wood-panelled chamber with a high Georgian window overlooking the extensive manicured lawns of Stokeley Lodge — his eye was drawn beyond a row of stately cedars to the far south-eastern horizon. The Suffolk border lay in that direction, just a ten-minute walk from here. This holiday camp with the dead lifeguard was off in that direction too.

It had absolutely *nothing* to do with him. *Nothing.*

'I told you, Sid,' he said, slamming his bag and his rods onto the antique side table. 'Shut *up.*'

4

'It's much better than I expected.' Francis dumped his holdall on the sofa and turned around to take in the cream walls, wood-effect floor and pleasant pine furniture. 'You always made out it was a total dive!'

'Well, *our* chalets *were,*' Kate said, dumping her own bag and feeling a little spaced out as she made for the kitchenette area and the kettle. Tea. She needed tea. 'They put us in the run-down, mildew-infested sheds down the end by the bins,' she went on, opening the fridge to find a welcome pack of milk, butter and two strawberry yoghurts. There were teabags and instant coffee too, in paper packets by the kettle, and a loaf of sliced white bread. She made tea on autopilot, still trying to process what Gary had told her.

Shit. Martin. She couldn't believe it.

'You OK?' asked Francis, pausing on the way to check out his room. 'You've looked a bit freaked out ever since we got here.'

She pushed her hair — the same colour as his, but a little less messy — off her face, and shook her head. 'Gary - that's the Ents Manager guy back in reception — he just told me some really sad, awful news. The whole gang's going to be shocked.'

'What?' prompted her brother, leaning in his bedroom doorway, his face creasing with concern.

'Martin — the big, sporty guy I told you about? He... he killed himself last week.'

'*Fuck!*' Francis came back and sank onto the sofa. 'What the hell happened there?'

'I don't know,' she said, turning back to the tea, needing the ritual. 'They found him in the pool. He'd cut his throat.'

Francis shook his head. 'Did he leave a note or something?'

'Yeah, apparently so,' she said, squeezing the tea bags and then firing them into the bin under the sink. 'It just said "I'm sorry", according to Gary. He said he'd thought about phoning us all before we arrived today, but then decided he wanted to tell us in person.'

'God, that's going to put a serious damper on everything,' said Francis. He blinked and shrugged guiltily. 'Sorry — I mean—'

'No — you're right. It is,' she agreed. 'Although if I know Talia, she'll turn this whole weekend into a party in Martin's honour. I guess that's the only thing to do... get pissed and stupid in his memory.'

'Did you know him well?'

'Not really,' she said. 'He was one of the gang, of course, but he and I didn't spend much time together — he always worked in the pool complex and outside, running the sports sessions. He only put his Bluecoat uniform on in the evenings and then he'd hang out with all of us for the last hour or two. I was looking after the kids all day, in the Buntin's Children's Theatre with Talia and Uncle Bobby, so I didn't see him that much. I do know Craig had a massive crush on him, though... unrequited... God, he's going to be really upset.'

Her phone buzzed in her pocket and she picked up a text from Talia: **Should be there in an hour! We're all meeting in the Embassy Ballroom at seven! Magnificent Seven After Seven meeting at seven! Geddit?**

Kate sighed. She couldn't bear to ruin the last hour of Talia's journey. It would be better to talk about Martin when they could give each other a hug. Gary had said he was telling everyone as they got there, so she guessed Julie, Bill, Nikki and Craig might already know. She didn't have their phone numbers, so there had been no texts. She guessed she could have been in contact with them all on social media, but she didn't really do much of that. Talia was the link between her and the rest of the Magnificent Seven. *Six* now. Six.

'Come on,' said Francis. 'Drink up your tea and then take me down to the crap chalets at the end. I want to see the seamy side!'

It was a good plan. Sitting here drinking tea and brooding wasn't helping anyone. She drained her mug while Francis checked her room, making sure it wasn't better than his, and briefly toured the bathroom. It wasn't five-star luxury, but it was a great deal prettier at this end of the site, where it was being paid for.

'It'll do,' he said. 'Now... the grotty hut exposé!'

She laughed and they headed out, locking the single-storey chalet — one in a row of six opposite another row of six, with a wide stretch of grass between them. The smell of the sea on the air instantly took her back to sunny days on the steep, stony shore with Talia, a bunch of kids in their care. And rainy days, too — plenty of those. There was no sea view from their chalet, but a walk along the broad tarmac path towards the lower end of the site revealed glimpses of cornflower-blue English Channel. The site had wisely been built a good half kilometre away from the crumbling low cliffs that overlooked the beach. The east coast was eroding at a rate of at least a metre a year, so there was only a stretch of molehill-dotted field between them and the sea, a straight gravel path across it to access the shore. Buntin's hadn't even bothered to buy the land and put a crazy golf course on it. The grassy buffer was pretty much as it had been when she'd last been here... but there had to be at least seven metres less of it by now.

It took five minutes to get from their chalet to the sheds of shame at the arse end of the site. Past the ballroom, the pool complex and the adventure playground, then down the side of the indoor games centre and amusement arcade, along a narrow passage bordering the launderette and groundsman's hut. And... there it was. A row of twelve chalets which looked like they'd been left exactly as they were when the place was first built back in the 1970s. Pebble-dashed and squat, with fraying felt on their flat roofs, accessed by a walkway of concrete slabs along the front. A washing line stretched between two poles along the length of the terrace, with swimsuits, towels and underwear pegged on sections of it. Further down from this outlying block was an area of scrubby land with a Land Rover and a caravan parked on it, along with piles of sandbags, some old guttering and a couple of upturned wheelbarrows. Kate remembered that the travelling acts who performed in the Embassy Ballroom sometimes preferred to stay in their own mobile homes, rather than pay the discounted fee for a chalet. So this area was made available for caravans and camper vans, with electricity hook-ups and a standpipe for fresh water. She wondered if Backflip Barney still called in each week.

In spite of the awful news she'd been landed with on their arrival she felt her mood lift and a smile weave across her face. 'It looks exactly the same,' she said, walking past at enough of a distance to avoid looking actively nosy, but unable to resist squinting through the Bluecoat block's windows.

A young woman suddenly stepped out of the chalet on the end, her brown hair in a ponytail, wearing the Buntin's blue and yellow tracksuit combo that Kate remembered so well. The girl glanced up at them with the ever-ready Bluecoat smile that was a non-negotiable legal requirement between 10am and 10pm. 'Are you lost?' she said. 'This is the staff end of the site — nothing exciting down here.'

'No, we're not,' said Kate, smiling back. 'We were just being nosy. I was a Bluecoat here seven years ago. I was in the chalet next to yours.'

'Oh!' The girl laughed. 'So you know all about the luxury, then?!'

'Oh yeah,' Kate said. 'Does the shower still suddenly stop and then gush freezing cold water down your back?'

The girl rolled her eyes. 'It bloody does!' She turned to lock the door behind her. 'Sorry — I have to head up to the pool now. I've got to start a shift there.'

'Oh,' said Kate as she and Francis fell into step with the girl. 'Um... Ellie, is it?' she queried, peering at the name badge on the tracksuit top.

'That's me!'

'I'm Kate — and this is my brother, Francis. We heard about the... about Martin,' she said.

The girl glanced at her, shocked. 'Did you?'

'Martin was here seven years ago,' explained Kate. 'We

were expecting to meet up with him. Gary told us right away, when we arrived in reception today.'

'I'm really sorry,' said Ellie. She looked sorry, too. In fact she looked suddenly pale and shaky.

'Woah,' said Francis, taking her arm as she swayed. 'Hey... I think you need to sit down.' He led her to a wooden bench at the edge of the path and she slumped onto it, holding her head in her hands.

'God, I'm so sorry,' she said. 'It's just that...' A sob escaped her. 'I keep seeing him.'

Kate sat down next to her. 'Were you there?' she asked. 'Did you find him?'

'It was awful.' Ellie sniffed, lifting her head and wiping her eyes. 'He'd cut his throat. The water was pink with his blood... a couple of the little girls saw him. I tried to get them back out of there, but I was too late.'

'Wait... you mean it happened while the pool was still open?' asked Kate. She felt a rush of baffled horror.

'Not exactly,' said Ellie. 'It was after hours but we always take the Alligators through at nine, when it's bedtime. The kids, I mean. I'm one of the children's aunties... we run the Alligator Club. It's—'

'It's OK, I was an aunty too,' said Kate. 'We ran the Alligator Club back then, too. But go on...'

'We do the Alligators' song and get them marching around the ballroom before bedtime — you remember, I expect. Well, we've always marched them outside for the last couple of minutes and then, a couple of weeks ago, we started going through the pool complex every night, just for fun. It's closed to swimmers by then, but Martin would leave the door wedged open for us and get up on his high life-guard seat, and wave. He used to leave the low lights on and it was all calm and peaceful... it sort of settled the kids down.'

'But this time..?' prompted Kate.

Ellie gulped and dug out a tissue, blowing her nose. 'He was in the water, in his Bluecoat uniform.' She suddenly shook her head. 'I shouldn't be telling you this,' she said. 'You're guests. You really shouldn't be hearing all the horrible details.'

'No, it's OK,' said Kate. 'We're not just guests. I'm an ex-Blue so I'm not the same as a normal guest. Also, for the record, I'm a detective inspector. On holiday — off duty — but you know, this kind of stuff happens a lot in my line of work.'

This seemed to reassure Ellie, who sat up straighter and nodded, looking from Francis to Kate and regaining some colour. 'It's just *mad*,' she said, shaking her head. 'I mean... I know people kill themselves and everyone says they never knew how depressed they were... or they would have done something. And, like, I didn't know Martin that well. We work in different areas. But I knew him well *enough*. He loved kids. He *knew* the kids came through every night. I can't believe he didn't think about that before he killed himself in the pool.'

Kate felt chilled. She looked at Francis, who shrugged at her, his mouth a flat line of concern. 'So... how certain are they that it was suicide?' she asked. 'The police, I mean.'

'They found the note,' Ellie said. 'And... he had some problems, apparently.'

Kate stood up. 'Ellie — are you going to the pool now? Can we come with you?'

'Sure,' Ellie said. 'It's open until eight. You can swim if you like. I mean... they closed it for a couple of days but it's all clean and fine now.'

'I'd just like to see the area it happened in,' said Kate. 'Is that OK?'

'I can show you,' said Ellie. 'But we'll have to be, you know…'

'Discreet. Of course,' said Kate. 'We won't be saying anything.'

'OK, then,' said Ellie, getting up and picking up the pace. 'I'm going to be late, so can we go quickly?'

'Kate,' hissed Francis, as they hurried along behind the young woman. 'What are you doing? This isn't your investigation!'

She shot him a dark look. 'I *know!* I just… I just want to see it.'

He rolled his eyes. 'The police already did… whatever police do.'

'Yes,' she said. 'I'm sure they did. But… I just want to see it for myself, OK? It's not a crime scene; everyone's allowed in. I just want to know *where* it happened.'

'The point being?' he said, raising his eyebrows at her and looking, for an instant, exactly like their mum.

She slapped his shoulder. 'Shut up,' she said; always a sign she was losing an argument.

He was right, of course. She had no business switching into CID mode. Even as an old friend of Martin's, she really couldn't claim to be close enough to involve herself in this. Still, as they reached the pool complex, she didn't see the harm in it. It might even help Ellie to get her head around it; having the chance to talk about it.

The steamy warmth of Buntin's Jungle Water World enveloped them the moment they pushed open the glass door. It looked much the same as it had seven years ago, except there was now a jacuzzi area off to one side, where an overweight pink-faced man sat, his eyes closed, amid the bubbles. The palm trees seemed to have had a bit of an upgrade too.

Ellie walked along the side of the pool, past the run-off into the Rapid River, which was slewing along gently at the moment, awaiting the next surge of power which would speed the water up. Above them, a see-through flume curled from one side of the structure to another, ending in a plunge pool behind the jacuzzi. Nobody was using it and there were only two swimmers in the main pool, doing lengths. Kate remembered that arrival day could often be quite peaceful around the site, as guests settled into their chalets and went to find food. Tomorrow morning this complex would be seething with kids and the pool would look like bubbling child soup.

Ellie walked to a cluster of three fake palm trees over-hanging a small tiled lagoon. Here there were shallow steps into the water for those who preferred taking it gently to dive-bombing in at the deep end. She pretended to check a stack of floats shaped like the Buntin's Bear — a favourite furry souvenir in the gift shop. 'It was here,' she muttered quietly, while Kate and Francis attempted to look like ordinary punters checking out the facilities. 'He must have killed himself on the steps and then fallen in. The water kind of eddies in right here and doesn't travel so fast, so I guess he just floated for a while... and then... just as we came in, he floated out.'

Kate looked around the pool house for lenses. 'Were there any cameras running?' she asked.

'There were,' said Ellie. 'But they're not very good. They steam up all the time. I don't think the police could see anything.'

'Did they find the blade he used?'

Ellie nodded. 'It was a kitchen knife,' she said. 'They found it at the bottom of the pool.'

'And the note? Where was it?'

'In his chalet,' Ellie said. 'The police found it there.'

'So... he went back to his chalet,' said Kate, trying to get her head around Martin's final hour. 'He got changed into his Bluecoat uniform, wrote a suicide note, and then he came up to the pool with a kitchen knife... and cut his own throat?'

Ellie shrugged and looked miserable. 'It's horrible isn't it?'

'It's baffling,' said Kate.

'Ellie!' called a young red-haired guy, from the far side of the pool. 'Are you taking over now?'

'I've got to go,' said Ellie. 'We're all filling in with extra shifts in the pool until head office sends another lifeguard.'

'Thank you for telling us,' said Kate. 'I hope it's not too hard for you, being in here.'

Ellie shrugged again. 'The new guy arrives on Monday. It's not for long.' She headed away around the pool, pasting on her mandatory smile as she passed the guy in the jacuzzi.

'Satisfied?' asked Francis, leading Kate back outside into the fresh air of early evening.

'Not even slightly.' She got out her mobile.

'Who are you calling?' he asked, raising his palms.

'Suffolk Constabulary,' she said.

'Oh Jeezuz,' groaned Francis.

5

'You know what will happen next, don't you?'

Lucas glanced across his casserole at Lady Grace Botwright and raised an eyebrow.

'They'll be getting in touch with threats to sue me,' said her ladyship, raising an eyebrow back at him. In her forties, she was well preserved and attractive, with a regal nose and jawline, and a haughty mouth. She tended to dress in pastels and pearls and was almost a dead ringer for Lady Penelope from *Thunderbirds*, give or take a few lines around the eyes.

'Sue you?' He shook his head. 'They were trespassing on *your* land!'

'Doesn't make a jot of difference,' she said, cradling a glass of Merlot in her fingers and rolling her eyes. 'It'll be my fault for not securing the boundary and stopping them coming in — you'll see. It's happened before. A farmer around here got sued to fuck by a burglar after his dog bit the bastard in the balls.'

Lucas laughed. He loved the way posh folk swore with such refined alacrity. Grace had the knack of enunciating 'fuck' so properly, it sounded like Latin. He had dined with her for the past two evenings, much to his initial surprise. When he had been invited to the Stokeley Lodge estate by Grant, he'd been told his bed and board would be provided, but he hadn't expected a room in the stately home itself. It turned out that the place was all faded elegance and the current Lord and Lady Botwright were taking desperate steps to raise funds to stop the roof falling in. This meant playing host to paying guests in the east wing for the past three years and the plan for twelve holiday cottages in the grounds, to be built as soon as Lucas had advised on the water table.

The River Waveney passed along the boundary of the 2,000-acre estate and the hope was that the holiday lets could be built close to its banks, for the view. Lucas had ruled out part of it already but was sensing that a good half-kilometre along the more easterly stretch would prove to be suitable. He hadn't told Lady Botwright yet. He wanted to be sure before getting her hopes up. Not that she hadn't asked — daily. She was agog at his dowsing talents and he knew she was only just restraining herself from asking for party pieces.

'So... we can rule out the lower field,' said Grace — who had instructed that he call her Grace when she first insisted he join her for dinner earlier that week. Her husband was away in France and she was desperate for intelligent company, she said. 'Maybe we should just dig it up and plant watercress!' she sighed. 'I swear half the country estates in Norfolk and Suffolk will end up as water sports resorts one day.'

'Probably not in our lifetimes,' said Lucas.

'So... Lucas... you know I am not the type to pry,' she said, taking a sip of wine and twinkling at him over the fine crystal goblet. 'But I feel as if we know each other well enough now...'

'Oh my,' he said. 'Where is *this* leading?'

She put down the glass and leant forward, forearms resting on the damask table cloth, affording him a pleasant view of nicely presented décolletage. 'Mariam told me not to ask you... and I absolutely won't if you don't want to talk about it.'

Lucas sighed. Mariam, his friend and mentor back in Salisbury, had helped him out a lot over the past year — first by commissioning an exhibition of his abstract art for her gallery, then by selling his works at a very good price. She'd also once distracted the police from hunting him down in her roof space... More recently, she'd put Lady Grace in touch with him, realising that despite his burst of artistic success, he was running low on funds again and so a week of East Anglian water divining for a good fee was worth pursuing. Lucas hadn't been keen. He told her he'd sworn off dowsing of any kind for the foreseeable future, but Mariam had worn him down by pointing out that there were openings for customer service assistants in the NatWest call centre and if he wasn't going to dowse, he might as well fill out the online form. He thought he would probably make some more money from his next collection, but it was coming on slowly and not slated for the gallery until September. The electricity bill would need to be settled in a fortnight and at present he had no income.

So he had sighed, got Sid a brand new steel chain, and ridden up to the Fens two weeks later on his Triumph Bonneville, recently restored and running nicely.

In checking out his credentials on Google, Lady Grace would certainly have found some interesting reading matter, so in many ways he was impressed that she had managed to hold off asking this long.

'Your crime solving!' said Lady Grace, a little breathlessly. 'Is it true you hunted down the Wiltshire Runner Grabber last year?'

'I helped,' he said. 'The DS on the case found her first.'

'You mean she got herself kidnapped and nearly killed first,' pointed out her ladyship. 'I read all the coverage, you know. If you hadn't dowsed her location she'd be a piece of desiccated art by now, along with plenty more lost lady runners, I don't doubt.'

He shrugged. 'Maybe. She was doing a good job of escaping when I found her.'

'And then the Gaffer Tape Killers!' went on Lady Grace, adopting the tabloid title with enthusiasm. 'That was just extraordinary. Did you really hunt them down with a tin of flapjacks?'

Lucas laughed and shook his head again. 'It was a bit more involved than that. The killer had touched the tin. I just picked up on that when I saw it. It was useful in helping us find him... and his partner.'

'You're being annoyingly modest,' she scolded. 'You and your detective friend saved that poor young man from being electrocuted — and you got knocked out with a spade and stamped on the head for your trouble.'

'Yeah, well... Kate got shot for *her* trouble,' he said, picking up his own glass now and staring into the ruby depths.

'Are you still in touch with her?' she asked, tilting her head. 'I saw her photo in the paper — she's quite lovely.'

He sensed her quickening interest and smiled tightly. 'No, we're not in touch. Not since the court case back in

March. Whenever we meet there seems to be death and mayhem. I think she'd rather not invite any more in.'

'Ah, but you wish she would, don't you?'

'Have you been discussing me with Mariam?' he accused.

She bit her lip. 'Guilty,' she said. 'But you can't blame me. I've had nothing but builders and very dull paying guests to talk to for the past three months, since Roger's been abroad. I'm dying of boredom and your backstory is delicious.' She leaned back, scooping her wine up again and biting her lip theatrically. 'I'm *sorry*. I'm sure it's all been very traumatic for you and here's me treating it like first class entertainment. Which it *is*, of course. I know... I'm very shallow.'

Lucas chuckled, shaking his head. There weren't many people who could persuade him to talk about his recent experiences with Kate Sparrow, but Grace might be one of them. 'I would like to see Kate again,' he admitted. 'But I think there's just too much trauma going on there. She doesn't want to hear from me, and I don't blame her.'

'She doesn't want to hear from you?' Grace rested her chin on her manicured hand and narrowed her eyes at him. 'Darling boy — I find that *very* hard to believe.

6

It was clear from the start that DS Helen Stuart did not want to hear from her.

Kate took a deep breath. 'I'm DI Kate Sparrow, from Wiltshire Police,' she said.

'Yes,' came back a cool voice. 'So they tell me. You're about two hundred miles off your patch, aren't you?'

'True,' said Kate, sitting on the edge of the sofa and waving Francis away into his room. Having her younger brother balefully staring at her really wasn't helping. This was sensitive stuff; she could imagine how *she* would feel if some copper from another county phoned up out of the blue and questioned her policing. 'Helen, I'll level with you — I'm up at the Buntin's Holiday Village for a long weekend with some friends. Martin Riley was one of them. I just heard this afternoon that he was found dead in the pool complex here, last week.'

'I'm sorry for your loss,' said DS Stuart, not thawing one iota.

'Thank you. Um... I wondered if I could just... run something past you?' said Kate.

There was silence at the other end of the call, but she could make out the tapping of a keyboard and got the distinct impression her cross-boundary colleague was multitasking. She bit down on her annoyance. Getting snippy would not help.

'I gather Martin was found, with his throat cut, in the pool — fully clothed. And that he'd left a suicide note in his chalet — is that correct?'

'That's correct,' said the DS. 'What's your point, DI Sparrow? I've got a lot of work to get on with here.'

'I'm just finding it a little hard to understand,' said Kate, carefully swerving the word 'believe'.

'Oh?' The DS couldn't have sounded less interested. The keys rattled on and she called out a muffled thank you to a colleague before returning her scant attention to Kate. 'Why's that then?'

'I suppose I'm struggling with why a man who wanted to end his life would write his suicide note, dress up for the evening, and then go and slit his throat in a pool, where he knew a party of kids would be trooping through less than an hour later.'

'Depressed people do mad things,' said DS Stuart.

'What did the suicide note say?' asked Kate — a pretty hopeless shot.

'I'll tell you exactly what it said,' said DS Stuart.

'You will?'

'Sure. Just turn up at Beccles Coroner's Court in two weeks. You can hear it from the public gallery.'

Kate took in a steadying breath. 'DS Stuart,' she said. 'I'm not trying to tell you your job, but—'

'Oh, aren't you?' came the reply. 'Because it sounds very much like that's where you're heading, *Inspector*. Suicide. That's what it was. The graphologist has confirmed the handwriting was Riley's and his prints and DNA were all over it. The knife had his traces on it, too. The angle of the wound was consistent with self-harm. No sign of a struggle. No shadowy murderer captured on CCTV. I know it's hard to accept when it's someone you know, but ninety-nine times out of a hundred, a suicide is just a suicide. As I said, I'm sorry for your loss.'

The line went dead.

'That went well then,' said Francis, back in the room, arms folded and face full of *I told you so.*

'Snarky cow,' muttered Kate.

'You think she didn't do her job?' he asked.

Kate considered. 'I think she did as little of her job as was strictly necessary.'

'But... could she be right?'

Kate realised he'd been listening in. The DS's voice had carried sharply out of her iPhone.

Kate shrugged. 'Yes, of course she could be right. It's just that...'

'People never see it coming,' said Francis. 'And like you said, you didn't know him that well. All kinds of stuff could have been going on in his life. Stuff he couldn't cope with.'

Kate took a long breath. She knew Francis was right. She was seeing murder everywhere these days. In her line of work there was a tendency towards this anyway, but after the last six months, when she'd been involved way too up close and personal with some nasty killers, it was probably not surprising. She let the breath out and nodded. 'You're right. I'm obsessing.' She checked her watch. 'We need to get ready to meet the Magnificent Sev... I mean... my old mates. I'm going to have a shower, OK?'

'Good', said Francis, brightly. 'We came up here to have some fun. Let's see if we can do that, eh?'

In the shower, she washed away some of the tension, although her mind still flickered around the situation. She wished she could see that suicide note. Wished she could sneakily locate it and make a copy. At the thought of locating things, her mind slid, not for the first time that week, or even that day, towards Lucas Henry. Goosebumps rose across her skin even under the hot jet of the water. She had last seen him outside the court, shortly after Donna Wilson's sentence had been delayed, awaiting psychiatric reports.

The woman who had very nearly killed them both in a remote farm shed probably was a psychopath and therefore belonged in a secure unit. Still, Kate had left the court hoping the bitch didn't get some cushy number in a mental hospital. Lucas, who'd given his testimony a couple of days earlier, had been up in the public gallery while she gave hers. She had made out his dark hair and stubbly beard as he rested his arms on the brass rail of the old balcony. She'd tried not to think about those moss green eyes staring down at her as she spoke to the judge and jury. At the end of the day, after sentencing had been set for another date, she had found her hapless partner in crime-solving sitting on the low yellow brick wall outside Salisbury Crown Court.

He'd got up as she passed, and turned to look at her. After a few seconds of silence, during which the same old attraction–repulsion fight got going somewhere in her belly, she'd looked away.

'You OK?' he'd asked.

'I will be once she gets life,' Kate had replied.

'Ah. Yes. Me too,' he'd said. 'But... are you *OK*? You know... in yourself?'

'Well, my shoulder's still pretty sore,' she'd said. 'How's your knee?'

'Mending.' He'd lifted an NHS issue walking stick. 'Doc says I'll be good as new in a month or two. It'll take longer to fix my bike.'

'Well... good luck with that,' she'd said, trying to walk away.

Here in the Buntin's chalet shower, she could hear his next words as if they were being piped in through the tiles.

'Kate — when we were in that shed...'

She had frozen. 'Yes?'

'I think we were both rambling a bit. I know *I* was. I said some stuff. Do you remember?'

'No.' She had studied her feet. 'I don't really remember anything we said. It's all a blur.'

'Oh,' he'd replied.

'I don't think anything either of us said would be reliable,' she'd continued, giving him a tight smile. 'I wouldn't give it any thought. Take care, Lucas.' And she'd walked away, fast.

The bitch got Broadmoor, as it turned out.

Kate shook her head under the jet of water, getting shampoo in her eyes and grabbing for the towel before the stinging could really set in. Dammit — the shower was meant to be relaxing! She made up her mind to focus on the evening ahead and not give a further thought to Lucas Henry or anything he'd once said... or not said... in a shed.

7

Barney Bagnall - AKA Backflip Barney - locked up the caravan and headed out for dinner. Most days he cooked up something on his stove inside the Sprite but tonight he actually felt like stepping out and dining with company.

Whether 300 holidaymakers from across the UK, including overtired kids, sulky teens and snappy, road-weary parents, really qualified as *company* was up for debate. Half of them would be crushing into the massive Buntin's Family Restaurant now, creating a dull, hangry roar around the tables, the self-service counters, the cutlery bars and the pump dispensers of ketchup. It was hardly a dining experience at all — more a feeding frenzy free-for-all.

But there might be a chance of meeting Kate Sparrow as he queued for a burger. It had been seven years since he last saw her, but she was seared into his memory. She had shaken him up. Changed him. That wasn't something that slipped your mind.

Barney was casually dressed and had not yet performed

for the Buntin's audience; his first booking was in the children's theatre the following afternoon. So nobody knew who he was yet. This meant that any attention he might get from the female guests was entirely down to how he looked and nothing to do with wowing them all with his circus skills. In his tight-fitting jeans, fashionable trainers and the kind of thin sweatshirt that hugged his iron-hard six-pack, he was used to getting a bit of attention. After all these years he still found it hard to accept the flirty glances as genuine. He still, occasionally, looked over his shoulder in case the girls were in fact eyeing up someone *actually* good looking, just behind him. Emotionally, he was still the weedy teenager, nervous and awkward — a perpetual outsider with no social skills. He'd been told his curly dark hair and brown eyes were gorgeous but that made him feel more like a labradoodle than a stud. Even though he now knew how to dress to enhance his highly toned physique, he still felt like the clothes were wearing *him.*

That was down to her, wasn't it? The one who still weighed on his thoughts every day and ultimately messed with every relationship he ever attempted. As if it wasn't hard enough being a traveller, drifting from venue to venue, never fitting in, never there long enough to find real friends.

'Hi Barney!' One of the Blues went past — Ellie, he thought her name was — wearing the Buntin's tracksuit.

He waved as she headed off towards the staff block with her regulation Bluecoat smile welded to her face. As soon as the punters got here a Bluecoat had to be smiling across every waking hour, like a strychnine victim. He'd heard resting bitch face could get you fired.

'OH MY GOD! BARNEY! BACKFLIP BARNEY!'

He jolted and looked around to see a tall, good-looking

black girl running towards him, her arms wide as she
dumped her case on wheels. He blinked and squinted,
trying to place her.

'It's *me!* TALIA!' she supplied, trotting over and flinging
her arms around him and making his shoulders freeze; he'd
never got into all that hugging. He remembered her though.
Of course he did.

'Oh my god, are you doing your show tonight? Is it the
same? TELL me it's JUST THE SAME!' gushed Talia,
releasing him and going back to grab her case. She seemed
very emotional - actual tears in her eyes. 'We're having a
reunion tonight! We're back after seven years! You do
remember us, don't you? I mean... you can't forget Kate!'

'I haven't forgotten any of you,' he said.

'Loo-kin' goood, Barney-boy!' she went on, eyeing his
jeans, trainers and skinny rib sweatshirt combo with
approval and then checking out the hair, which was probably too long and girlish, even though he got it cut at least
once a month. 'God!' She peered at his face, gnawing on her
plump lower lip. 'I would *kill* for eyelashes like that! Who
knew you'd turn out to be such a hunk! When are you on?
We'll be there.'

'Not until tomorrow,' he said. 'I'm doing the kids' show
at midday in the children's theatre and then I'm doing the
full show at seven in the Embassy Ballroom.'

'Oh — OK. Well, maybe tonight's not the best night
anyway,' she said, her bright smile fading a little and the
teary eyes filling up. 'We're going to be processing things a
bit. You heard about Martin, yeah?'

He nodded. 'Really sad. I never knew he was depressed.'

She shook her head, sniffing. 'Such a shock. We're going
to have to get royally pissed in his honour tonight... so yeah,
much better for us to catch your show tomorrow. I gotta get

to my chalet and then meet up with everyone. See you tomorrow, yeah?' She waved and trotted away at speed.

She hadn't changed much. Still the same Talia. He shrugged and went to the dining room. The roar, as he opened the door, hit him like a tsunami.

He backed away. Maybe not. Maybe just pick up a hotdog in the small café by the gift shop instead. He reckoned Kate would probably do the same. Maybe he would see her. Maybe he would even say hello. Or maybe he would just watch her for a while.

———

ELLIE CHECKED into the entertainments office and scanned the rota pinned to the wall behind Gary's desk. She was relieved to see that she wasn't scheduled for another pool shift until the middle of next week, by which time the new guy should have joined them. She would be happy if she never went into Jungle Water World again. Not that she did very often, anyway. Friday evening and early Saturday morning were the only times it was safe to swim. As soon as she, Uncle Bobby and her fellow children's aunty, Nettie, had met the kids and started building teams in the Alligator Club (she ran the Snappers; Nettie ran the Crackers) they were owned. Totally owned. The kids literally saw them as their own personal Bluecoats, and if they were ever daft enough to get spotted in the pool there would be an almighty crush of Snappers and Crackers attempting to duck them under the water. Martin had needed to blow his whistle more than once over the years to save a naive children's aunty from drowning. Uncle Bobby hadn't been near the pool for at least ten years of repeat summer seasons.

Ellie breathed her sigh of relief and was about to leave

the office to get into her evening uniform when the laptop on Gary's desk pinged and she glanced instinctively at it. Gary was crap at security; there was no screensaver running and his emails were clearly on view. Ellie wasn't the nosy type, though, and she would have done no more than glance and leave if she hadn't seen the title, LIFEGUARD ISSUE — WE WANT DAMAGES on the header.

She went hot and cold. Oh god. The parents of Blossom and Rosie-Mae! They must be considering legal action for the horror that their daughters had witnessed. She felt sick. She could never have known what was waiting in the pool that night, but she still felt horribly responsible for leading all those kids right into a scene out of a Stephen King movie. At the time, both sets of parents, while shocked and horrified, had been more sympathetic to her than she could have expected. Neither had talked about taking legal action. They had seemed genuinely appalled for the family of poor Martin.

In fact they had asked her to pretend it was a big hoax — a trick that Martin had played on her before — purely for their daughters. So they could all make believe it wasn't real and save the girls from long-term trauma counselling. Gary had agreed to the pretence, because it was for the best of reasons, and Ellie and Nettie had both met up with the girls and gone into the performance of their life, pretending that Martin had been *really naughty,* and the camp manager had sent him home for the rest of the week. Gary had even given them a couple of Martin's signed photos to give to each of the girls, with SORRY I SCARED YOU! written on it in marker pen — and a free Buntin's Bear.

But now it looked like it hadn't worked. Maybe the parents had had second thoughts. Maybe they were sending the lawyers after Buntin's... maybe after *her*. She took a long, shaky breath and spooled the text up the screen.

What happened in the pool with my daughter was totally unacceptable, she read.

'Everything OK in here?'

She jolted violently and saw Mike, the security guy, peering around the door.

'Oh — oh, yeah... fine,' she said. 'I was just checking the rota. All done now. Better get changed and head off to mix and mingle!'

Mike nodded, his doughy face impassive. 'OK,' he said. 'I'm going to lock up here now.'

'Sure,' she said, feeling a scarlet flush burning up her throat. She scuttled away, guilty as a cat on a wet carpet with an upturned fishbowl. She really hoped Mike wouldn't say anything to Gary about her snooping around his laptop. Mike seemed OK, though. He probably wouldn't.

'Oh, um, Mike,' she said, pausing outside as he locked up the office. 'Have you had a snorkel handed in? A mum asked me about it at the pool and I said I'd check.'

'I've already got a whole box of stuff,' said Mike, rolling his eyes. 'It's like losing property is some kind of sport. Come by the hub and take a look whenever you want to.'

'Will do,' she said, and ran for her chalet, trying to disregard the email on Gary's laptop. Even if they *were* trying to sue Buntin's, there was surely no way they were going to come after *her*. She was a broke nineteen-year-old. No. Martin's death was nothing to do with her and there was nothing she could have done to prevent the kids from seeing it. They would get over it in time... especially if they believed the lie... and when you were five you were easily convinced.

She just wished someone could come along and lie to her about it too. She would take the lie over the truth any day. Any day at all.

8

'*S*ay sorry.'

She stared up at him. 'What?'

'Say you're sorry for what you did.'

She saw the pan and what was in it and her pretty eyes grew round and scared.

'What did I do?' she whispered.

'You broke something — something very special to me.'

'How? I mean... what did I break?'

She looked exactly like the poolside Adonis had — absolutely baffled.

'Do you even remember me?'

'Um... well, yes... I mean, you used to... you were here back then, weren't you?'

'You're looking very slim.'

That silenced her. She looked down at her flat belly and up again, eyes darting to the pan. 'What have you got in there?' she asked.

'Have you kept that flat belly naturally... or did you get liposuction?'

'Look... I don't know what this is about,' she said, standing up,

glancing towards the door. 'But my friends will be wondering where I've got to.'

'I think you're a little too skinny. You could do with eating a bit more.'

'I EAT PLENTY,' she said, lifting her chin. 'I just keep it low fat, low carb, and do lots of exercise.'

'Fat is underrated,' he said. 'Everyone needs some fat.'

The pan was full to the brim, its contents warm, pale and viscous, slopping gently as it was set down on the chest of drawers. With both hands free it was easy to pin her to the bed. She screamed, of course, but not for long. Once she was quiet and no longer moving, it was quite rewarding, filling her up.

9

It was a warm evening and Lucas didn't feel settled enough to go up to his room. He also didn't want to spend any more time drinking with Lady Grace. He was getting a bit of a vibration there. Grace was bored and lonely. She hadn't said as much, but he was pretty sure hers was a marriage of convenience. The items he had picked up while wandering idly around the elegant drawing room spoke of her husband Roger, quite clearly.

Roger was definitely gay, and Lucas was pretty sure he was spending his time in Italy in order to be with a male lover. He was fairly certain Grace knew about it and that it was an arrangement the couple had come to many years ago. He guessed her end of the deal was to get a title, a couple of children, a grand house to live in — and carte blanche for her own love life, as long as she was discreet.

Lucas was getting the feeling she was going to discreetly proposition him quite soon, and although he did find her attractive, he wasn't sure he wanted this. If he got drunk with her, though, she would seduce him, he had no doubt about that. It had been more than a year since he'd had sex and he doubted he could resist for long, especially if he focused on that blonde hair and slim figure and thought about... but no. That just seemed seedy, whichever way he looked at it.

So he had excused himself from another glass of wine and headed to his room. Once there he settled down and tried to read a Brookmyre thriller. It took some effort to concentrate, even though he liked the writer and usually avidly read his work. He was distracted by the sense that he could hear something... something approaching... the way tracks begin to sing before a train comes into view around a distant bend. A train did not come, but his phone rang.

The number was withheld; something that always made him tense. He hit ACCEPT and heard a hiss and a click, but no voice. *Bloody sales calls.* He was about to cut it off before some chirpy voice asked him about the state of his pension/windows/whiplash from that recent accident, but something made his finger pause over the END CALL button and slowly bring the phone back up to his ear.

Someone was there. Someone he *knew.* He felt his skin prickle as he made out breathing... only just discernible over the hiss of whatever network was connecting them. 'Kate..?' he murmured, at length. The call cut out a second later.

He sat back on his bed, pulse suddenly racing. Had that been Kate? Had he just picked up her patterns through the phone? If so... why had she called him and not spoken to him? That wasn't like her. She was a very straight-shooting kind of person... well... up to a point. There was some straight shooting she hadn't quite got around to yet where he was concerned.

'Oh for fuck's sake, Lucas!' he said, staring at himself in the age-spotted oval mirror above the old oak dressing table.

'You've got to stop obsessing. That was just a sales call which didn't connect.' The face glaring back at him did not look convinced. Trouble was, dowsing was at its least reliable when it involved someone close to you. He couldn't be sure whether it was divination or desire pushing this mental agenda. If he knew anything, though, it was that he should never chase it, either way.

He put down the book and sighed. There was no way he was going to be able to settle down now. He left his room, ran lightly down the sweeping curve of the stairs, and headed outside into the warm evening air. The scent of roses and lavender spread around him as he wandered the gardens. Rooks cawed in nearby woods and squirrels chased up and down the cedars on the expansive lawn.

He found a young woman, wearing an oversized blue and black checked shirt, sitting on a bench near the kitchen garden, staring into the middle distance. He recognised her as Jessie — the girl who'd been tearfully snipping roses earlier that day.

'Was that his?' he asked, sitting down next to her and nodding at the shirt.

She looked up at him in surprise, wiping away a fringe of brown hair and revealing red-rimmed blue eyes.

'I'm sorry,' he said, realising he was being very presumptuous — they hadn't even been introduced. 'I'm Lucas — the dowser..? Grant told me about your boyfriend. I'm really sorry.'

She sniffed and nodded. 'Yeah,' she said. She gathered the thick weave shirt around her. 'And yeah — this was his. It still smells of him.'

'Were you together for long?'

'Just over a year,' she said.

'They say it was suicide,' he went on, aware that he was

prying, but also picking up that she was not averse to talking about it.

'Yeah,' she said. 'That's what they say.'

'What do you say?'

'I say it's bollocks. He wasn't depressed. He was worried, yeah, but not depressed.'

'Oh... what was he worried about?'

'You ask a lot of questions, don't you?' she said, tilting her head and fixing him with a stare.

He shrugged and pulled Sid out of his shirt. 'This pendulum thing... it helps me dowse for water and other lost things. It's telling me you're a bit lost.' He lifted his hands. 'God — that sounds like a cheesy come on — it's really not. I'm just picking up that you might want to talk, that's all — I promise.'

She sighed. 'It's OK.' She peered at the blue bottle stopper. 'Can you really find stuff with that?'

He smiled. 'It's not magic,' he said. 'And it's not really this that does the work — dowsing is something anyone can do, if they work at it. It just helps to have a focal point, like rods, hazel twigs or a Y diviner. Or a pendulum like this — I call this one Sid.'

'So... if I hide something... you can find it?'

'Usually,' he said. He decided to break his rule. If anyone needed a party piece, this young woman did. 'Hide something if you like.'

She gave him a watery grin and pulled a pound coin from her pocket. 'Wait there, then,' she said and slipped away around the far side of a tall yew hedge, completely out of his sight. Two minutes later she jogged back to him. 'Go on then. Show me.'

He smiled and got to his feet, pulling Sid out of his shirt and looping the chain over and off his head. He let the pendulum drop between his fingers and waited for it to show him the way. Sid did his circle, then his figure of eight, and then his back and forth swing, giving Lucas a clear direction. He followed Jessie's route around the yew and then did a sharp turn to the left, down a stony path and some steps to a sunken garden. Jessie followed, saying nothing, but looking fascinated and distracted, for now, from her grief.

He reached a formal flower bed with a statue in the centre of several blooming, highly scented rose bushes. The carved stone ornament depicted a woman in Roman–style robes, holding aloft a pitcher. Lucas stepped towards it, almost reaching for the pitcher before turning abruptly to the right and taking a few steps to the edge of the rose bed. He dropped to one knee and lifted a nondescript lump of brick. Beneath it, shone the coin.

'Oh my god, you *can* do it,' breathed Jessie, her reddened eyes now wide with wonder. He handed the coin back to her, nodding.

'And you promise you didn't follow me? Because I did go right up to that statue! I *was* going to leave the coin in that stone jug.'

'I didn't follow you, cross my heart and...' he petered out fast.

Her face fell, and she sat down on a low brick wall and let out a long sigh. 'I *am* lost,' she said. 'Confused. They say Martin left a note, but I haven't seen it yet. Apparently it just said, "I'm sorry". What the hell kind of note is *that?* I mean — it didn't even mention me! Or his mum or dad. If he was writing a suicide note, he would have put our names on it, surely?'

Lucas nodded and sat down beside her. 'It does seem odd. You said he was worried... what about?'

'He was having some problems with money,' she said. 'Credit cards maxed out, I think, and his pay wasn't great... and other stuff going on at work that he didn't tell me about. Some guys aren't so good at sharing... but, you know, *normal* stuff. Not *do yourself in* kind of stuff.' She paused for a moment and then added, 'And who slits their own throat?! I mean... wrists, yeah... but your own throat?'

'So... you think someone killed him?'

She shrugged and stared down at the shirt. 'My mum thinks I should let it go. That it's just one of those things... she thinks I'd rather believe he was murdered than admit he'd kill himself without saying anything to me or even leaving me a proper note.'

'It's a very hard thing to accept,' said Lucas.

'You think I'm stupid,' she stated.

'I really don't.' Lucas tucked Sid away. 'Remind me where he worked... a holiday camp, was it?'

'Buntin's down in Lakefield,' she said. 'It's just over the border into Suffolk.'

'OK,' he said, getting up.

'OK, what?' She raised her palms.

'OK... I get why you're suspicious. I understand. I would be, too.'

'Oh. Well... thanks,' she said.

'I'll see you around. Try to do something nice for yourself, eh?' he said. 'Treat yourself like you're your best friend. Kindly.'

'OK,' she said, in a small voice, with a face like a schoolgirl. He felt his heart wrench for her; she was way too young to be dealing with a grief like this. But then, as he'd learned many years ago, being young didn't stop death taking a swipe at your happiness.

He went back in for his helmet and leathers, and was on

the bike and heading out into the last blush of sunset five minutes later, Sid giving him the occasional punch, like a satnav, taking him south east. He'd glanced at the maps app on his phone and seen that Lakefield was only twenty minutes away, a short ride down the coast from Lowestoft. What he would do when he got there he wasn't sure. In fact, he had no idea why he was doing this at all. What was he thinking? Hadn't he got involved with enough death and misery over the past year?

Yet, Sid seemed to think he *should* get out to this Buntin's place. He could ignore the vibrations from his little glass partner, but he had learned that doing so rarely went well. One way or another, the patterns would find him and pull him into their eddies and whirls until he paid attention and went where he was commanded.

This was why he had sworn off all this stuff and shoved Sid in a balled-up sock. If it wasn't for Mariam and his severe lack of funds, he'd have been snug in his bungalow in Wiltshire, working on his next art collection. Probably. If he was honest, it hadn't been going well anyway. He seemed to have lost his mojo in recent weeks; too distracted by recent events and the awareness of one Kate Sparrow being somewhere in the city he called home, but never where he was. Never in touch.

The dreams weren't helping, either. Dreams of the Quarry Girls. Of Zoe who had been murdered... of Mabel, vanished and presumed murdered. Sixteen years ago Lucas had found Zoe's body, but he'd never led anyone to Mabel. He'd found something else though — the start of a nightmare that had yet to end. He wondered if anyone accused of murder ever got over it; the suspicion, the gossip. He and his mum — who had provided a somewhat shaky alibi for him — were both hounded out of their home as the case drew national attention and his involvement in it came to the surface.

After all this time it should be firmly in his past, but his past had a way of popping up like an unwanted Facebook memory. *Hey — we thought you might like to look back on that time when you were staring into the cold dead eyes of your friend, buried under a pile of stones! Here's a video we made for you...*

Only the video took the form of endless, haunting dreams. He'd even had one here, while staying at Stokeley Lodge. Lucas turned left onto the A-road towards the coast and shook his head, banishing an image of Mabel's face, soft in the late summer sun, her fair hair hanging around her chin; her mouth in that teasing pout she liked to try out on him. *Stop it. Focus.*

It was probably good that he was getting out for a ride — distracting himself. Even if he wasn't entirely sure where he was going or why. What did he hope to achieve by visiting the site of a suicide? Because if the police had looked into it and concluded that Jessie's boyfriend had taken his own life, it was highly likely that Jessie's boyfriend *had* taken his own life. Police usually knew what they were looking at. Maybe he would pick something up, though, that might put the girl's mind at rest; give her some closure.

He would take a look, as far as he could, and then turn around, ride back to the lodge and get to bed, carefully avoiding Grace and her Lady Penelope charms.

The holiday village was a flat few acres of chalets with central, low-level buildings housing restaurants, cafes, bars, adventure playgrounds and the pool complex where Martin had ended his life. It was like many such places he'd seen before: unpretentious, low-rent versions of Butlin's. Plenty for the kids to do, nightclub entertainment on hand for the parents, a beach within walking distance.

He was stopped at the entrance by an earnest young man in a Buntin's blazer, carrying a clipboard and a two-way radio. 'Are you a guest here, sir?' he was asked.

'Ah — no,' said Lucas. 'I was just hoping to stop in for a quick drink... maybe catch one of the acts.'

'Well, you need to sign in and buy a day visit ticket,' said Earnest Boy. 'You can go straight into reception and buy it there. Get your ticket and a visitor badge for your bike, and then park it in the main area beside the pool complex.'

'OK, I'll do that,' said Lucas. 'Thanks.'

'Have fun at Buntin's,' said the young man, with a weak smile, perhaps realising belatedly that Lucas wasn't nine.

He paid a tenner for a day visit ticket, which wasn't great value given that it was now nine-fifteen and it expired at midnight. He parked the bike where he'd been advised, close enough to the pool complex to see the soft after-hours lighting through its steamed-up windows. There was a CLOSED UNTIL 7AM sign on the door.

He climbed the few steps up to the entrance and found that it wasn't locked. There was a CAUTION — WET FLOOR notice standing on the tiles inside and he guessed a cleaner might be finishing up in there. He took a look around and then stepped in, pulling the door quietly closed behind him. A warm fug of chlorinated air enveloped him at once. He allowed Sid to guide him around the mirror-still main pool, along the stretch beneath the see-through flume, past a drum-shaped jacuzzi, empty and silent, and finally to a shallow set of steps into the aquamarine splash pool, beneath a clump of full-sized fake palm trees.

Here. This was it. The area where Martin had breathed his last. Here was where he had taken a knife from his pocket and slit his own throat. There were dark twists of residual energy still vibrating through the stone of the tiles and the high-pitched frequency of the glass in the atrium overhead.

But *not* the vibrations he would associate with a desperate, hopeless soul, seeking an escape into oblivion.

'She was right, Sid,' he said. 'He didn't kill himself.' He sighed. Now what? What was he meant to do with all this certainty and not a shred of evidence to back it up? Damn. He should never have come here. Why the hell couldn't he be content with a quiet life?

A scream rang out across the water.

10

'Oh shhhh-sugar — I'm sorry!' Ellie was consumed with embarrassment. 'I just didn't expect anyone to be in here. It's shut for the night, you know…?'

The good-looking guy in a black bike leathers smiled and raised his hands. 'No really — *I'm* sorry. Lurking around here like this after hours. I'm not surprised you were scared. I was just having a quick look at the facilities — the door wasn't locked.'

'You can come in for a swim from seven in the morning,' she said, holding a stack of three Buntin's Bear floats across her chest like a shield, although it was clear the guy was perfectly nice.

'I might do that,' he said, and for the first time since last Tuesday evening, she thought there might be *some* reason to want to come back into the pool complex. He looked pretty fit. What the hell was he doing at *Buntin's*?

'I'm off to meet my friend in the bar,' he said. 'I'm just dropping in; not staying on site.'

'OK — good — well, have a great time,' she said.

'Um...' he paused by the door. 'Were you here when that guy... that guy killed himself last week?'

She felt a surge of adrenaline. 'Are you a reporter?' she said, dropping the sweetness. Gary had warned her about this.

'No, I just heard about it... wondered...' he said, staring at her very intently.

'I'm sorry, but I have to close up now,' she said, putting on her best brisk, no-nonsense voice. 'You need to go and find your friend in the bar.' She gave him a tight, end-of-conversation smile and he, thank god, took the cue and buggered off.

As soon as he'd descended the steps outside the side door and vanished from sight, she locked up. She really could have done without this. The Alligators March this evening had not taken in the pool complex, and never would again while she was on staff. She was planning never to come in here again, but another Blue had gone off sick, so she'd been abruptly put back on the rota to double-check the pool and lock up, as soon as she'd sent the kids off to bed. It was a bit bloody much, really, considering. She would have to talk to Gary and get taken off this duty. The new lifeguard was arriving on Monday, but she honestly couldn't do this again tomorrow night. It wasn't fair.

She tidied the floats and checked everything that needed to be switched off *was* switched off. Then, keeping her eyes firmly away from the spot where Martin's body had floated out, she walked back to the main door facing the pavilion, then stepped outside and locked that too, with a shiver.

She dropped the key back to Mike in the security hub. As soon as he saw her, Mike rolled his chair away from the bank of screens in the darkened room and waved a snorkel at her.

'Excellent,' she said. 'I'll tell the mum to drop in for it tomorrow.'

'Huh. She's probably still up, partying,' said Mike, rolling his eyes. 'You could give it to her in the bar.'

She grinned and folded her arms, leaning in the doorway. 'You don't really approve, do you?'

'Of what?'

'All these mums letting their hair down while their kids are asleep in the chalets.'

He shrugged. 'It's up to them,' he said. 'The kids are safe enough with me and the Sleep Tight Team on the case.'

'It's a pretty good system,' said Ellie. 'No kidnaps yet, anyway.'

It *was* a pretty good system. For parents who signed up, Buntin's offered the Sleep Tight service — which gave the Sleep Tight Team visual access to the chalets via outside security cameras, trained on the doors and windows, and inside cameras in the living areas. Once triggered by a call from the chalet from a parent, the Sleep Tight team switched on and monitored all the visual feeds, as well as a baby monitor audio feed direct from the children's bedrooms. If any infants cried or started wandering around looking lost, the parent would be immediately contacted via their mobile phone. Or via the PA system in the bars if they didn't answer. They could be back at their chalet within five minutes.

This part of Mike's job, along with four night security staff who patrolled the avenues of chalets in pairs from nine-thirty until midnight when the bars shut, was basically a massive babysit.

A whimpering sound issued from one of the feeds, a red

light flickering under CHALET 49. 'Uh-oh,' said Mike. 'Mummy might have to stop necking vodka and Coke.'

She laughed and went on her way, checking her watch. It was 9.30pm and she would dearly have loved to go to bed, but her contractual mixing and mingling continued for another half hour and Gary wouldn't miss that she hadn't shown up. She headed for the Embassy Ballroom, giving Backflip Barney a wave as he wandered down the lamplit main walkway towards his caravan.

'You bringing out the World's Smallest Bicycle tomorrow?' she called.

'Of course,' he called, thumbs up. She smiled and did a thumbs-up back at him. Barney pedalling around the children's theatre on a teeny-tiny bike was the bit the kids always loved the most.

'Get a move on!' growled Gary from the side door to the ballroom. 'Mix 'n' mingle! Mix 'n' fuckin' mingle!'

11

'*DOES HE LOVE ME? I CAN'T GUESS...*'

Kate grabbed the microphone from Talia and bellowed, 'HOW WILL I TELL IF IT'S NO OR YES?'

In the mirror tiles at the back of STIRRERS Cocktail Bar, she could see herself and Talia in their little glittery dresses — Talia's electric blue, and her own a vibrant red — shimmying across the stage and giving it the full, pissed-up karaoke blast. The on-screen lyrics were fuzzy and they were both mostly making it up as they went along.

As they vocally slaughtered the old soul hit, cheered on by Nikki, Bill, Craig and Francis, it occurred to her that they were all having way too much fun for a bunch of friends who'd discovered only hours ago that one of their number had topped himself. In fact, within thirty minutes of meeting up in the Embassy Ballroom, after their initial huddle of shock and tears, they had moved into *celebrate Martin's life* mode with great alacrity. It was a bit fast and unseemly, really.

'*IS IT IN HIS VOICE?*' sang out Talia, giving it the full

Cher as she bestrode the small stage in front of a backdrop curtain of gold streamers right out of the seventies.

As she stomped her high-heeled black boots along in rhythm, Kate wondered how well they really knew each other at all. One summer season, from May to September, full of intense ups and downs, sharing chalets, sharing beds, sharing crises and celebrations. But she didn't really know Martin that well and, in truth, it was probably only Talia that she could claim to know at all. She'd *liked* them all, yes, and she thought they liked her, although she was pretty sure they were a bit put off by her undergrad vocabulary.

From the stage, even with the lights in their eyes, Kate could see Nikki flirting madly with Francis, flinging her arms around his neck. It was a pretty blatant attempt to provoke Bill, she was sure about that. Although Francis was cute — as far as a big sister could ever judge — he was really not Nikki's type. She was a beefcake kind of girl, and Bill was probably even brawnier now than he had been seven years ago. Nikki herself had filled out a little and probably gone up a dress size, but she was still pretty and vivacious, and Francis wasn't exactly repelling her.

Craig was very easy to like — an instant gay best friend who styled himself on eighties pop stars (he had once been told he had a resemblance to a-ha's Morten Harket). He was always great company, but he hadn't stayed in touch for even a week after the season ended. Handy Bendy Julie had also vanished into grownupland without so much as a backward glance, so it would be interesting to see what she looked like now. When she showed up. She was late. *Very* late. Talia had texted her twice and got no response. Maybe she had decided not to come after all. Maybe they were down to just five, if you didn't include Francis, of the original Magnificent Seven. They would have to be the Fabulous Five.

Kate knew she was drunk. It didn't feel too bad. It blurred her concerns about Martin's suicide and that incredibly irritating phone call with DS Stuart. She should lighten up, really. Have some fun. Bill launched himself up onto the stage just as they got to '*HOLD HIM... YEAH, HOLD HIM TIGHT*', lifting his arms and inviting them to enact the lyrics, which they did. Bill's taut, muscled upper body was emanating heat beneath his shiny grey shirt, and he smelt of quality aftershave. His hand slid around her waist, warm fingers pressing into her rib cage through the red silk of her dress, and she felt a little stab of desire. Not for Bill, especially. Even when she was drunk, his attractiveness could never compensate for the arrogant vanity which had always turned her off. But desire for *some* man. *A* man. Someone to be with. Some uncomplicated sex. That was what she needed. A face flickered into her thoughts and she shoved it quickly away until a better choice of face could be found. Ah yes. Conrad Temple would do nicely. The criminal psychologist she'd worked with a few times now back in Salisbury — boyish good looks, wide brown eyes and floppy dark fringe. Preppy, with a cute Boston accent. She reckoned he fancied her a bit, too, and thought maybe a date might be in the offing sometime soon.

As she continued the three-way karaoke she imagined being watched from the audience. Wearing her sexy red dress, hair in a wild blonde mane, eyes made up with smoky glitter shadow, lips glossed. Her work colleagues *never* saw this version of Kate Sparrow; she spent much of her time playing down her looks. Pretty blondes tended to get patronised and sidelined in the police and she did not intend to be one of them.

But sometimes it was nice to let the inner vamp out. Too bad she hadn't thought to invite Conrad up here this weekend instead of Francis. But that wouldn't have been uncomplicated sex, would it? A guy she sometimes had to work with. That other face reasserted itself in her mind's eye just as she found the mic back in her sweaty palm and was singing, *'OH NO! HE'S NOT THE ONE!'*

And *that* was the truth. The very LAST person she should be picturing at this quasi-horny moment was Lucas bloody Henry.

Which was when she glanced to the end of the bar and saw Lucas bloody Henry.

She didn't *actually* drop the mic, but near as dammit. Bill was pulling her and Talia into a spin with him as the number rolled towards its finish, and Talia grabbed the mic and carried on singing. When Kate looked back at the bar there was no sign of Lucas. Christ, how drunk *was* she, conjuring *that* up out of nowhere? Must have been someone who just looked like him. She was relieved to get off the stage and leave it to Bill and Talia, who were now segueing into *I Got You Babe*.

She wiped her hair off her face and walked, a little unsteadily in those high heels that she wasn't used to, back to Francis, Craig and Nikki. She drained her gin and tonic and considered getting a pint of soda water. She probably shouldn't get much drunker. She was already getting mirages of Lucas Henry at the bar. What would her sozzled brain conjure up next? No. Time to sober up a bit. She swiped up her shoulder bag, rolled over to the bar and ordered the water, resting her forehead briefly on her folded arms.

Nikki joined her. 'Your brother's been telling me all about his sexy new car.'

'Oh god, just humour him,' said Kate. 'It'll make him very happy.'

'He's lush, your little bro. Have you got change of a fiver? I fancy another go on the karaoke.'

'No... I'm all out. Sorry. Nearly done for the night,' said Kate, picking up her pint glass.

Craig arrived between them. 'You're never calling it a night now!' he protested. 'It's not even ten! What are you — a pensioner?'

Kate laughed. 'Yeah — I hit middle age last autumn and I'm just sliding into my dotage this spring. That's what happens in the police!'

'You were just the same seven years ago,' scoffed Craig. 'Couldn't take the pace. Way too soft.'

'I just need my sleep!' she said, and took a long gulp of water. 'And I could only stand so many hours a day of you bunch of pissheads.'

'You were just as bad as us,' said Nikki. 'God, remember the things we did?! Remember throwing up in the kids' play area and covering it with sandcastles, Craig? And the time when you got up on the pavilion roof and drew a massive dick and balls with white chalk, for passing aircraft to spot?'

They fell about, clutching at each other.

'It washed away in the morning rain,' mourned Craig, wiping his eyes. 'What about those days off on the beach, trying to get a tan and then giving up and doing graffiti in the old concrete World War Two bunkers? I bet the cliffs have fallen on them and buried them by now. Entombing all our empty cans of Stella and Dry Blackthorn.'

'It all sounds very *Famous Five*,' said Francis, drily.

'It *was*,' said Craig. 'All we needed was a dog and a missing scientist.'

Bill and Talia left the stage, handing the microphone over to someone with an urge to perform *My Way,* and joined in the reminiscing. 'Oh god — remember that ginger girl who got fixated on you, Craig?' said Bill, with a snort of laughter. 'The fat one with the nylon trousers from the special needs group?'

Craig choked on his rum and Coke and wafted his hands frantically, calling attention as he got his voice back. 'Red Ruthie! She used to sniff my hair!' he squeaked. 'Actually creep up and *sniff me* like a dog.'

Everyone just about lost bladder control at this, remembering the pink-faced girl who'd imagined Craig was her prince charming because he'd done a duty dance around the ballroom with her. It would have been one of many duty dances every Bluecoat undertook in the low season weeks when the old and the vulnerable came to holiday.

Kate felt a familiar wince. This was something she'd struggled with seven years ago. There was something about having to be professionally nice to people, for twelve hours straight, six and a half days a week, that would sort of tip them all over at the end of their shifts, into something quite horrible. The things that came out of their mouths; the horrendous, bitchy, shallow, insensitive things. She couldn't claim to have never joined in. Maybe not as much as the rest, and she had definitely always been the first to try to reign it in, earning herself a five-star goody two-shoes rating, but she was guilty of it, too.

She had since met all kinds of wonderful people who worked like heroes, supporting down and outs, addicts, rape victims and abused children. One or two of them had admitted to her how they sometimes went off on a rant with a trusted colleague or friend, making the most appalling jokes about the very worst things imaginable and howling with laughter. Afterwards they felt both ashamed and tremendously relieved, as if they just had to puke up all that vileness to stay sane. She knew this was a normal coping mechanism... and she knew the Blues had needed some of that, too, on a much lesser scale, of course... but it was still uncomfortable.

'Little Mickey,' choked Bill, fighting for breath through gales of laughter. 'And the Six-Fingered Sister!'

Talia screamed and bit on her knuckle, weeping with mirth. 'God... all the east coast inbreds we had to entertain. Martin was always trying to stop them pissing in the pool... Didn't one of them start following us around when we were doing the bunkers on our days off? When she wasn't stalking poor Martin in the pool. I think Handy Bendy Julie had to give her a talking-to in the end. Where the hell *is* Handy Bendy?' Talia reached for her mobile to find out if Julie had been in touch.

'She should be here any minute,' said Craig. 'Kate — you *have* to stay up for that. I want to find out if she can still bite her own buttocks!'

Kate felt her own phone burr in her bag. She picked it up and saw a message from Death.

'Hang on — just got to take this,' Kate said, moving away into a dark corner. A message from Death should never be ignored. She glanced across at Francis, who'd gone back to the flirtathon with Nikki, and was glad he wasn't watching her. She hadn't admitted to him earlier that she'd sent a message to Bryan De'ath, the police pathologist back at Salisbury — whom every copper predictably called Death — asking him for a favour. She'd asked if he could find out anything about Martin Riley's suicide from any contacts in Suffolk. And now, some hours later, he'd responded.

Sorry for your loss, he'd texted. **It's an odd one. People do slit their throats from time to time — and usually make a pretty poor job of it, which is a ghastly way to go.**

This one did it right, apparently. Sad but could have been worse. Suicide note very strange, though.

Kate thumbed back: **Wait — calling you.**

She moved quickly into the carpeted lobby outside the club, the sound of more god-awful karaoke caterwauling muffled as soon as the heavy double doors swung shut. Death picked up at once. 'It's not the message that's odd,' he said, in his clipped way. 'That's just the standard "I'm sorry", and you'd be surprised at how many are just that. The serious ones don't stop to write much, if anything. No — it's his choice of stationery that was odd.'

'What was it?' Kate pictured a banknote or a pillow case.

'It was a sanitary towel.'

ate staggered slightly in her high heels and leaned up against a Buntin's cork board of posters for events and shows.

'A *what*?'

'A sanitary towel. Ultra-thin. Adhesive backed.'

'You're joking!'

'I am not.'

'Uuumm.... right... OK. Was it..?'

'Clean? Yes. It was. Apart from his note — in red ball-point. The graphologist matched it to his handwriting and there's no doubt he wrote it.'

'Jeeezuz. What was he trying to say?' she pondered.

'That,' said Death, 'would be the domain of the Suffolk crim psych, if they have one. Now, if you don't mind, I have a late supper to eat.'

She thanked him profusely and then ended the call in a state of shock. Of all the things she had expected to learn, she would never have guessed at *that*. Maybe Martin just couldn't find a bit of paper. But it was hard to imagine him unwrapping a sanitary towel, unfolding it and writing his farewell message on it. Hard to imagine him even *having* such a thing. Was this something she should share with the others? No. Right away it was a no. It wasn't any of their business. Not hers, either. She shouldn't have pried. She shook her head, regretting her actions, and went back into the bar, determined to make her excuses now and get to bed. Her party mood had evaporated.

'Maybe she changed her mind,' Nikki was saying, back at their table. 'Didn't fancy it.'

'No,' said Talia, checking her mobile yet again. 'I bet she's doing fucking yoga in her chalet. Let's go and find her. She's next to yours, isn't she Craig?'

'That's what Gary said when I arrived,' Craig said. 'But I haven't seen her at all. Mind you, I went for a burger at six-thirty and came right up to meet you guys at the ballroom at seven, so she probably got in after I left.'

They set out along the main pathway towards Julie's chalet block but on the way there, Nikki started getting extra giggly and demanding to see this legendary Capri that Francis and Kate had arrived in.

'Come *on*,' she said, throwing her arms around his neck. 'You've got a 1980s hot rod and I have GOT to see it!'

'You've got a Capri?' snorted Bill. 'Seriously?'

'Yep,' said Francis, grinning. 'Collector's item.'

Bill gave a derisive hoot of laughter. 'They're fucking roller-skates! Has it got go-faster stripes and furry dice?'

'Shaddup, you,' said Nikki. 'Just because you're jealous! Come on, Frankie — show me!'

So they all rolled past the pool complex and on to the car park, which was well lit enough to showcase the yellow gleam of Francis's pride and joy. Kate did her best to say nothing as her brother lovingly stroked the bonnet and opened up the driver side door so Nikki could get in.

'Keys!' said Nikki, hand outstretched.

'You're not driving it,' laughed Francis. 'None of us is going for a spin. We're all pissed as farts already.'

'I just want to get a feel for what's under the bonnet, you know?' Nikki winked up at him meaningfully, and couldn't repress a sly glance at Bill, who was kicking the tyres as if he was about to make Francis a low offer. 'Get the motor running, that's all!'

Francis passed the keys and Nikki started the Capri up. At the third attempt. The first two key twists produced only a reluctant whine from the starter motor but then the engine burbled into life. 'See? She's a beauty!' said Nikki, clapping her hands on the steering wheel.

'Did you *really* drive all the way up here in *that?*' giggled Talia in Kate's ear.

'Don't,' she whispered back. 'He's never been so happy! It's opened up a whole new world for him. It drives like a Tesco trolley and stinks like the fag deck of a seventies bus, but he is *so* in love!'

'Oooh, now that's really turning over nicely now,' Nikki was saying. 'Shall I get my revs up, eh, Frankie?'

Francis grinned, and nodded. 'Go for it!'

Keeping the old gear box in neutral, Nikki put her foot down and produced a growl from the engine.

'Jesus — look at the smoke out the back of it,' spluttered Bill. 'You just put back the UK's carbon neutral target by about five years.'

'Jealous!' sang out Nikki, revving again. There was a massive bang. She screamed and let the engine stall.

'Fuckin' hell!' Bill shook his head and clutched at his heart. 'What have you got in that tank? Barbecue briquettes?'

'She just backfires a bit sometimes,' muttered Francis,

helping Nikki out of the driver's seat. 'I haven't had time to
fine-tune the engine yet.'

'Well, you can fine-tune *my* engine anytime, sweetheart,'
said Nikki. Kate wondered if she might actually pull a
feather boa out of her shoulder bag and go into a burlesque
act.

'Come *on* everyone!' protested Craig. 'Let's go and find
Handy Bendy Julie!'

Francis locked up the car and five minutes later they
were all weaving down the grass strip between the chalets,
giggling and singing, and occasionally shushing each other.
Kate, though, was running out of steam. The revelation from
Death was fighting for her attention and all she really
wanted to do was turn in now and mull it over. As soon as
she'd said hi to Julie, she was planning to fake a migraine
and escape. Francis could hang on and party if he wanted to.
Although she hoped he wouldn't end up shagging Nikki...
not when there was so much unfinished business between
her and Bill.

'SHHHHHH! Kiddies will be asleeeeep,' warned Craig in
a stage whisper that could probably be heard back in the car
park. He found chalet 28 at the far end of the line, next to
his own at 27, and rapped on the door. 'Julie! Juuuuuuulie!
Come out and join the Magnificent Six! We're waaaaiiiiting!
Handy Bendy Julie! Juuuuuulieeee!'

There was no reply from Julie's chalet, even though the
lights were on. The curtains were drawn across the patio
doors that served as the entrance but there was no sign of
shadowy movement behind them. Kate felt a prickle of
unease. Then she stamped on it. This suspicion of death
and disaster around every corner really was getting out of
hand. She took a deep breath and shoved her hand into the

front pocket of her handbag to locate her lump of plasticine. She found it and mashed it hard between her fingers.

'I bet she's hanging out with the new Bluecoats or the punters,' said Talia. 'Fickle cow!'

'No — she's gone all New Age these days, hasn't she?' said Nikki. 'All connected with her chakras and whatnot. I reckon she's gone down the beach to do tai chi in the moonlight or something.'

'Well, let's go down and see!' said Craig. 'We used to go down the beach at night all the time. It's the *best* time, when there are no screaming kids and beached whale parents. Come *on!*'

Kate groaned but Francis grabbed her by the arm. 'Don't you drop out on me,' he said. 'I'm not missing this!'

'But I'm really tired,' she whimpered. *Really spooked, too,* she wanted to add, glancing at Julie's unanswered door.

'Look, you're always telling me I should get out more,' said Francis, propelling her along behind the others, who were skipping drunkenly towards the coastal path. 'And now here I am... getting out right now! You can stay awake long enough for this! You can always lie in tomorrow.'

She knew he was right. It was a warm night in early summer. A crescent moon was hanging like a jewel in the sky amid a scattering of stars. It was beautiful and inviting and, despite the tragedy they'd encountered on their arrival, she owed it to Francis — and herself — to unwind a little and have some fun. She bent down and unzipped the high-heeled boots and took them off, depositing them in her capacious satchel bag — glad she hadn't opted for some glittery clutch with only a lipstick, tissues and mobile in it. Then she grabbed his arm and they both ran along in the wake of Craig, Bill, Talia and Nikki. She could already hear the sea and smell the salt in the night air. She let out a long exhalation and made the decision to chill the hell out.

She was on holiday and yet she had been so tightly wound, so obsessed by recent events in her life, that her subconscious had even conjured up the ghost of Lucas Henry in the bar. This kind of thing had to stop.

'Wait for meeeeeee!' she sang out, letting go of Francis and breaking into a barefoot run with her arms in the air as if she was literally fleeing from her wild imaginings.

13

'Seriously?! I mean... what the *actual fuck?*' Lucas was so freaked out he was berating Sid at full volume as he got back to the Triumph.

He had been so shocked at what he'd just seen, he'd seriously doubted his own faculties for a moment there. After all, he'd had a bit of concussion a few months back and they did say there could be long-term effects. Maybe this was one of them. *Hallucinations.*

That was all blather though. He knew he *had* actually seen Kate Sparrow — Detective *Inspector* Kate Sparrow now, he'd recently learned — singing karaoke in a sexy red dress and high-heeled, black patent leather boots. Her ensemble could have been something he'd concocted via an online menu for his own furtive entertainment. For a second, as he'd stood there — waiting to catch the bartender's attention and get himself a Coke while he pondered on his findings in that pool house — seeing Kate reflected in the mirror tiles beneath the gin optics had seemed perfectly natural. After all, Sid had been buzzing like a demon all evening and had dragged him out here, across the county border, on the flimsiest of pretexts. Why should he care so much about some stranger's boyfriend topping himself? People died every day. He must have encountered newly bereaved people all the time and not felt the urge to investigate the circumstances of their loved ones' deaths.

No. This whole thing had a Kate Sparrow flavour to it.

All of this passed through his mind in a matter of two, maybe three seconds as he leaned on the bar, squinting at that reflection, before the reality of this freakish coincidence hit home and he began to question his sanity, slowly turning around for a better look. And at that very moment, Kate, giving it her best Cher, had swung in his direction, her golden hair loose and wild, and the stage lights picking out the intense silver-blue of her eyes and the sheen of red gloss on her lips. She had looked right at him while her own jaw had dropped in tandem with his.

And then she was whirled around by the handsome black dude on stage with her and Lucas had taken the only sensible course of action. He'd fucked right off out of there. At speed. He just hoped he'd done it fast enough to deny her the chance of a second look. With any luck she would think she was mistaken; that she'd only seen some guy who looked a bit like him. His long, straggly dark hair and short beard combo... kind of hipster meets biker... was quite in vogue at the moment. Loads of guys probably looked like him. In fact, even as he'd pushed out of the double doors of the lobby, he'd nearly barged right into another guy who looked quite like him - dark curly hair, jeans and T-shirt, designer stubble. Very fit. Fitter than he was, probably.

He stopped himself checking the guy out before he could get caught erroneously on gaydar and all but ran back to Hugh (as he liked to call the Triumph Bonneville). Because he *must not be here* a moment longer. Kate must

NEVER know he had dropped in and seen her. He guessed she was here on holiday, although he would never have pegged her for a Buntin's Holiday Village punter. Still... with a bunch of friends he guessed it was a fun, cheap weekend away. And it had looked like she was there with a bunch of friends. She clearly knew the man and the woman on stage with her, and there were others, whooping and cheering them along. It seemed odd to think of Kate with normal, party-animal mates.

It seemed odder still that he had, once again, inadvertently dowsed his way back into her world. Still, at least it wasn't a crime scene this time. But as he unchained his helmet from the rear wheel and dug his gloves out of his backpack, a tide of goosebumps was washing over him. Because this *was* a crime scene, wasn't it? That guy — Martin — had not killed himself. Someone else had.

There was some commotion across the well-lit car park and he realised, with a belt of shock, that Kate had come after him. For a few seconds he froze, his mind in free fall. He couldn't see her amid the tangle of pissed-up mates threading their way through the cars, but he sensed her with too much intensity to be mistaken. He could make out the handsome black dude too, among the knot of six or seven people.

Then he realised, with relief, that they were not coming his way. They stopped at an old, mustard yellow... what..? Was that a Ford Capri? Yes. Someone had actually *paid* for a Ford Capri and driven it off on holiday. They were all crowding around it and he wondered if he should just walk over, introduce himself, and inform Kate that they were doing it again: meeting under the shadow of death.

The Capri started up reluctantly and then backfired, causing some shrieks and shouts of hilarity. No. He and his gothic warnings did not belong here, regardless of what Sid was trying to get him into. This wasn't even her patch — it was a couple of hundred miles away from Wiltshire. She really didn't need some dark sentinel looming up like something out of *Buffy the Vampire Slayer* and suggesting there was another unsolved murder case they needed to see to. He could already hear her response. Words of only one syllable. Or maybe a high kick to the solar plexus. Which, in those high-heeled boots, was going to hurt.

'Oh no, Sid' he said, pulling on his helmet as the party of friends locked up the car and wandered off towards the rows of whitewashed chalets. 'Oh no no no. We are leaving right now.'

———

BARNEY HAD ALWAYS FELT like this. Forever on the outside. Going to the bar had been a bad move. He had watched the friends from the shadows, nursing a vodka and Coke and trying not to look weird. Even after all this time, he still couldn't locate *normal*.

He remembered the black guy well... Bill, his name was. Tall and loud and a good singer, he and Talia were belting out a Stevie Wonder track up on the small stage and Bill was strutting around, getting a lot of attention from everyone in the room, of course. He'd been just the same seven years ago. Back then, Bill had been the one who'd called him a *pikey*. Right to his face with a grin, like it was a joke they were *both* sharing. Barney had smiled back and not responded. That was the way he'd been taught. *She* had insisted on that. 'Never rise to it, Barney — never give them the satisfaction.'

'Bill, you bloody bigot!' That was the girl called Nikki,

her shrill Welsh voice rising through his memory. 'You're in the bloody 21st century - not the 1970s! Apologise right now!'

'Ah, Barney don't mind, do ya, pal?' Bill had said, smacking him hard on the shoulder.

He hadn't said anything. He wasn't a pikey, anyway. He'd spent a fair bit of time with travellers — proper travellers like the Jericho fair that he'd toured with for a couple of years when he was in his late teens. He should have felt more comfortable with them, but as his mother had gone to brick before he was born, they really regarded him more as a joskin. They were nice enough — and none of *them* ever called him a pikey — but he still didn't fit in. It had occurred to him that if there was ever a club exclusively for people who didn't fit in, he would have to join it. Except that by the very nature of its membership, such a club could literally not exist, because as soon as its members started to fit in by not fitting in, they would have fitted in... and instantly no longer qualify for membership.

He spent far too much time on stupid thoughts like this. And stupid, unhelpful plans that had now led him to the corner of a shuttered ice cream kiosk, trailing Kate and her friends and spying on them from the shadows. What he should be doing was just sauntering over to the small group, and saying hi. They would probably remember him because Talia had. They bloody well should remember, with all the fun they'd had out of him.

He should have taken the chance to go after Kate, back in the bar, when she'd walked past at speed, tapping urgently into her mobile phone. He could have followed her outside and got her alone... but instead he'd waited a bit longer by the bar until she came back in. He'd just stood there, brooding over his glass, as the karaoke ended, and they all gathered together and then left.... shadowed by the awkward outsider from seven years past.

The yellow car — it looked like an old Capri — started up and then backfired. Then they got bored and wandered off again, towards the chalets. He followed them. At a distance. He didn't need to try too hard; they were clearly drunk and probably wouldn't notice him if he ran past in his boxers, blowing a trumpet. So... whose chalet were they heading for? And what would happen when they got there?

He felt a surge of anxiety. It was too soon. All of this was too soon. It should be tomorrow. He needed more time. But he loitered anyway, by a clump of lilac trees at the corner of the short avenue of chalets, watching them knocking on the patio doors.

He held his breath as they all waited for a response. Nobody opened the chalet door. And after a little more discussion, they all headed off again, towards the beach.

So... should he go back to the Sprite? Or should he follow..?

14

It was incredible how quickly they all regressed. Bill had stopped by his chalet, en route to the beach, and grabbed a bottle of Jack Daniels, which he now offered up for everyone to swig from.

'It's cheap shit,' he said, settling back into the shingle on one elbow. 'I normally only drink fifteen-year-old single malt these days... but I thought we should do some more JD for old time's sake.'

Nikki took an enthusiastic slurp before passing the bottle to Francis. 'Hope you don't mind that I've had my tongue around that,' she said, giving him a broad wink.

Francis laughed, shaking his head, while Bill rolled his eyes. Water under the bridge, *like hell*. This whole thing was descending into pantomime. Kate was tempted to shout at Nikki: 'Leave your sticky past BEHIND YOUUUU!' This whole performance was nothing more than a massive ego boost for Bill — whose ego was quite boosted enough.

'It doesn't feel like seven years, does it?' said Talia, sitting close to Kate and leaning in. 'Feels like seven *minutes* where

Nikki and Bill are concerned. God, she doesn't learn, does she?'

Francis passed the bottle along and Talia took a swig before handing it to Kate.

'I'll pass,' said Kate.

Talia shook her head. 'Nothing's changed with you, either,' she snorted. 'You always were soooooo fucking sensible! No surprise you've ended up as a copper.'

Kate felt stung. Some of the decisions she'd made in recent months had been far from sensible... although they'd been right on the money. She remembered how often she had felt this sense of defensiveness around Talia, who was such an instinctive party animal.

'So... it's about time we got the inside story on the Runner Grabber,' said Talia, loud enough for everyone to prick up their ears. 'And the Gaffer Tape Killers!' Everyone's head swivelled towards her and Kate realised her friends must have been talking about it when she wasn't around. Maybe they had even planned to be sensitive and discreet... but it didn't take much alcohol to erode that kind of thinking.

'Look... it's all been out there in the press... you probably know everything already,' she said.

'Oh come *on!*' Craig threw up his hands. 'This is *us!* The Magnificent... Six.' He gave a forlorn hiccup. 'I mean, girl... details! Like... did that BBC guy really die dangling from the top of his own radio car mast? And were you really surrounded by naked Barbies in the Runner Grabber's basement?'

Kate felt a wave of nausea and took a long slow breath, while Francis reached out and squeezed her shoulder.

'Most of all,' said Nikki, grabbing the JD bottle from Craig and taking another swig. 'How *hot* was that dowser guy? I mean... he runs in and saves you with his little swingy pendulum... and then he's back again to save the day with the Gaffer Tape Killers and... I'll tell you what, he can use his dowsing rod on me *any time...*'

'Fucking nonsense,' said Bill, picking up a stone and skimming it expertly across the breakers and over the surface of the moonlit sea for three skips. 'Waving crystals and hazel twigs about, making out they've got some magic path to all the answers.'

'But he did!' protested Nikki. 'He bloody did. He dowsed exactly where she was and got there just in time to stop her being strung up naked and killed for the benefit of an *art* installation!'

Kate felt Francis getting tense. She didn't blame him. 'You know... this is what I've missed most about you lot,' she said, breezily. 'Your *diver's boot in the bollocks* approach to sensitivity!' She got up, stretching. 'Look — Julie's not here. You guys can hang on and get pissed for old time's sake... I'll go to bed like a boring old goody two-shoes for old time's sake.'

She stalked away along the beach, rattled and angry... but at the same time, kind of sad for them all. None of them seemed to have matured a week since the last time they'd met, not even Talia. Although she and Talia had met up a few times since, and Talia had seemed to be getting her adult life on track, all it took was a few drinks and the company of the other ex-Blues, and she'd instantly become puddle-deep.

She could hear Francis making his excuses with the others as she walked away, and felt grateful for his support but also a little guilty to drag him from the party. She reached the sandy walk up between the sea grass and hedges of gorse and sedge, bent into humps by the prevailing North Sea breeze. And for a second she froze, thinking she saw someone move at the top of the path. A tall, lean, dark figure.

Her heart skipped a beat and by then the figure was gone. She took a deep breath. It was night. The lights from the holiday village cast long shadows across the field, easy to mistake in the moonlight.

But what if Lucas really *had* been there tonight? What if she *hadn't* just had some kind of over-wrought brain fart? By the time Francis caught up with her she was already dismissing that thought. It was too bizarre and thinking about it any more was just feeding her PTSD.

'They're all coming,' warned Francis. 'They're sorry for being so insensitive.'

Kate groaned. 'Oh god... I just want to go to bed. They're great, you know? In their own way. But not when they're pissed and I'm tired. Let's go.'

They hurried away up the path, where there was no evidence of any shadowy Lucas-alike, and headed off towards their chalet, which was at the top end of the site. Unfortunately, the others had made it their mission to catch up, and so in a couple of minutes they were all together again.

'I'm sorry, lovey,' said Talia, grabbing her arm. 'You should arrest me for being a nasty drunken tart with no filter!'

Kate laughed. Talia was always a highly entertaining drunk, too.

'Come on,' said Craig. 'One last try at Handy Bendy Julie's door! She's got to have come to bed by now so we can bloody wake her up again!'

And they veered off back to the block where Craig and

Julie's chalets were located. Kate sighed and shook her head at Francis. 'One quick hello, and I'm going. No argument.'

The chalet looked the same as before; lights on, curtains drawn. Craig knocked loudly and called, 'Juuulieeeee! Handy Bendy Julieeeeee!'

'Sshhhh!' said Nikki. 'Children asleep!'

So Craig staggered against the door and whispered at the keyhole. Kate glanced down at the foot of the sliding patio door. That prickle of unease was suddenly back. Something was wrong here. She stepped up to the door and pulled it. As Craig had already demonstrated, it was clearly locked. Kate frowned, trying to think clearly. Most likely Julie had set out to find them a couple of hours ago; she'd probably met up with Gary in the main ballroom or maybe some of the guys from the house band. She'd always got on well with Gary and had been on friendly terms with the girl singer who was still fronting the band. It was after midnight now, though and the ballroom would have shut. Even the bars would be closed now, so where would Julie be? And why hadn't she just dropped Talia a text?

Kate looked at the bit of orange striped curtain caught in the locked patio door. It chilled her. Why? Because of Julie. Everyone knew that Julie was borderline OCD. Incredibly neat and organised. The idea of her slamming that sliding door shut and locking it, when a bit of curtain was stuck in it, just seemed utterly impossible.

Or was she just imagining things because of too much time spent in the company of Lucas Henry and his unhappy knack for picking up *very bad things* through his dowsing instinct? He was always going on about how everyone had the capacity to dowse. Was *she* dowsing now? Was she picking up something? Or was she just so shit-faced that she was imagining it? She'd imagined *him* after all, back in that bar.

No. That bit of curtain. It was wrong.

'She's probably still up in the ballroom,' said Bill. 'We should go and find her. She'll be wondering where the hell we are.'

'Well, all she's got to do is bloody answer my texts!' grumbled Talia.

'Wait,' said Kate, rummaging in her bag. She extracted a skinny piece of metal. She glanced left and right and then inserted it into the lock on the chalet's patio door.

'What you doing?' hissed Nikki. 'I thought you were a copper an' all — not a bloody burglar!'

Kate didn't answer; she just concentrated. She'd got into a property more than once this way; it was preferable to smashing glass when you couldn't get an answer. It wasn't strictly legal, but it did no harm and it was always possible to claim the door hadn't been completely closed. The lock gave without much manoeuvring, and Kate pulled the door aside.

'Phew!' Craig wafted the air in front of his face. 'She's gone insane and had fish and chips!'

The stink of chip fat *was* strong; it looked like Craig might be right. Maybe Julie wasn't handy and bendy any more. Maybe she'd abandoned her healthy lifestyle and put on five stone since they'd last seen her. That might explain her reluctance to show up tonight.

The curtain in the door. No. No, there was a very strong sense of wrongness about this.

'Julie?' called Kate, tugging the curtain back. Some inner voice told her to pause and turn back to her fellow ex-Blues and her brother. 'All of you — stay there,' she said. 'Don't come in unless I say so. OK?'

Everyone seemed to sober up at once. They looked at each other and then back at her, nodding. Francis was narrowing his eyes, folding his arms and looking disapproving. Not because she'd just broken into Julie's chalet but because he could see Holiday Kate withdrawing and DI Kate Sparrow stepping up. It was written across his face.

Kate turned back to the half-open door, and the curtain, and the smell of old, cold chips. She stepped around the curtain, pulling it closed behind her out of pure instinct. Instinct which was, as it turned out, bang on. She took a sudden, hitching breath and put her hands over her mouth. Then she turned and pulled the patio door completely shut, before letting the breath out again, slow and steady, between her fingers, marshalling her heartbeat and focusing her attention on the details.

Julie lay on the sofa, staring at the ceiling. The chip fat smell made absolute sense as Kate stared into the greasy face of her former colleague. Her legs — still gym bunny lithe and slim in running shorts — were sprawled halfway off the sofa, her arms flung up as if waving. There were spatter stains on her tight grey T-shirt. Her long dark hair hung in oily strings across her brow and cheeks. Her mouth was gaping wide and completely filled with solid white matter. It seeped from her nostrils too and slowly dripped, like candle wax, across her bruised purple throat.

At this distance, Kate could see she had probably been killed by strangulation.

But there was an outside chance Handy Bendy Julie had been choked to death with lard.

15

Holiday Kate had vanished. Detective Inspector Kate Sparrow had shoved her aside and taken over — and both Kates were glad of it. The first thing she did was step carefully across the wood-effect flooring and, grabbing a latex glove from her oh-so-useful bag, double-check that Julie *was* actually dead. It seemed like a foregone conclusion given her colour — pasty grey-white — and the lack of movement. Oh — and the fact that all her airways were jammed with solid white fat.

As expected, there was no pulse. The body was cool and unyielding, the eyes still fixed and staring waxily at the ceiling. Julie looked like an exhibit from the True Crime section at Madame Tussauds. Kate took a long, steadying breath as, outside, Craig called out: 'Juuuuuuulieeeeee.'

Oh god. She had somehow imagined her horror had transmitted through curtain and glass, and instantly sobered up everyone waiting outside — but of course they had no clue what was going on. Why would they? *Their* lives weren't dominated by murder.

Speaking of which, whoever had done this to Julie could

still be in here. Her instinct was that the chalet was empty, but she carefully checked the bedroom, opening the wardrobe and looking beneath the bed, and then the bathroom, pulling the window over the bath shut as she did so. She knew she must secure the scene. Checking her watch, she went back to the curtain, and pulled it closed behind her before sliding the door open and rejoining her friends. She quickly brought the glass panel shut and barred the way in case any of her drunken pals decided to run inside and verify what she was about to say to them.

She glanced around and fixed on her brother, arms still folded, expression shifting from annoyance to concern. 'Francis — I need you to go to the main office, opposite the pavilion, and find the security guy. You have to bring him right here.'

'What the fuck?' said Bill. 'What's going on?'

'I need you all to stay calm,' she said, hoping for the best. 'You might want to sit down on the grass here. You need to stay quiet, too... we don't want to wake any children.'

'*What?!*' insisted Bill, and Nikki and Craig came in on the chorus.

She took a deep breath. 'Julie's in there,' she said. 'But something bad has happened to her. No!' She raised her palm with authority and stopped Craig in his tracks. 'There is nothing you can do for her. It's too late.'

'What happened to her?' gasped Nikki, eyes welling up, sinking onto the grass.

'Francis? Now would be good,' she said. Her brother nodded and hared away.

'Has she killed herself too?' whispered Craig, his angular face stricken.

'No,' said Kate, getting her mobile out and thumbing 999.

Emergency services picked up fast. 'My name is Detective Inspector Kate Sparrow,' she said and reeled off her collar number. 'I'm with Wiltshire Police but I have just secured a crime scene at the Buntin's Holiday Village in Lakefield, south of Lowestoft, in Suffolk. You need to get an SIO out here right away. There is a deceased female who I can identify as Julie Everall and it's clearly a homicide. No sign of a suspect at the scene.'

She rattled off more information, turning away from the appalled faces of her friends while the call handler demanded more and more detail. They had indeed sunk onto the grass, holding on to each other and murmuring in shock. After a couple of minutes on the line, she was relieved to spot Francis returning with a guy in a Buntin's uniform, carrying a two-way radio and wearing a peaked cap with SECURITY on it.

The first thing he wanted to do, of course, was enter the chalet. Kate, ending her call with a promise to stay on site and welcome the SIO, knew she needed to handle this carefully. 'Um — Mike..?' she hazarded, remembering his face vaguely from seven years ago. He nodded, perplexed and wary. 'Can you hang on a moment?' Still barring his way, she rummaged in her bag and produced her ID. He raised his eyebrows at it. 'I've called in the Suffolk Police. There's a dead woman in this chalet and she didn't die of natural causes - or by her own hand.'

Mike's jaw dropped and he instinctively rested his hand on his radio. 'Before we speak further,' Kate went on. 'I think we need to get my friends to go back to their chalets. I really can't chance them getting overwrought and running in here. She was a friend, you see? And we don't want to attract too much attention if we can help it.'

He nodded and radioed for a couple of other staff,

usually only required to handle the Sleep Tight patrol, while Kate tried to persuade Talia to take Nikki, Bill and Craig back to her chalet and keep them all together. She did not want Craig to go into his own chalet, just next door, and overhear the crime scene investigation.

They all resisted, as she had expected them to, desperate to know what had happened to Julie. Then Francis surprised her by stepping over to them and saying: 'Kate's got to do this, OK? She's a police officer. It's her duty to secure the scene.' He looked at Talia, his young face serious. 'I think she's depending on you.'

'OK,' sniffed Talia, pulling Nikki, weeping, up from the grass. 'All of you,' she said, hanging on to Nikki and looking around at Bill and Craig. 'Come back to mine. Right now. Kate will come and see us and let us know everything as soon as she can... right Kate?'

Kate nodded at her friend gratefully. 'I promise,' she said. They walked away, supporting each other, slumped and shocked. Kate turned to Mike. 'I think you need to call Gary over too,' she suggested.

'I need to see what's in there first,' he stated, 'before I go waking the boss.'

Kate weighed this up. She was quite capable of keeping him out and it was her first instinct to do just that - but this was his patch and she wasn't on duty. Also, she would prefer to keep him on her side while she waited for backup.

'OK, you can take a quick look,' she said, pulling the sliding door along. 'But you cannot touch *anything*, OK? You know the deal?'

'I know the deal,' he said, raising his hand in an authoritative wave as two of his staff arrived on the scene, heading down the grassy walkway. 'Hold on there, Stu, Janine,' he said in a quiet, measured tone. 'We've got a situation.'

His staff did as they were told, glancing at each other with excited fascination. Kate guessed the Sleep Tight patrol didn't usually get much action beyond asking drunken punters to keep it down a bit.

She went back into the room, almost gagging at the smell of lard, which seemed even heavier now than the first time she'd inhaled it. Mike followed and gave a good impression of a man just about holding it together.

'Shit,' he said, gulping. 'What the hell is *that* in her mouth?'

'I think it's lard — or fat of some kind,' she said. She felt suddenly very tired and sad. What a way to end your days... alone in a cheap holiday camp chalet, filled up with stinking grease, like a foie gras goose.

Outside she heard Gary's voice, talking to the Sleep Tight crew in hushed, stressed tones. Word had obviously already reached him. 'Come on,' she said to Mike. 'We need to go and break it gently to him.'

She was glad to have the backup when they stepped outside. She really could not allow Gary inside the chalet — two of them possibly contaminating a crime scene was bad enough — and it was going to be difficult to persuade him of that. Mike could at least verify what she was telling him.

'I just met Talia and the others,' said Gary, his features strained with disbelief in the dim light. 'I can't take in what they just told me.'

'I'm sorry, Gary,' said Kate. 'It's true. The local police are on the way.'

'I want to see her,' said Gary, in a strangled voice.

She grabbed his arm before he could move closer to the chalet, and then pulled him into a hug. 'You can't go in there, Gary. It's a crime scene. You need to try to take a few deep breaths... maybe sit down on the grass.' She was painfully aware that the chalets around them were full of families, mostly asleep. She knew the double glazing was pretty soundproof, but it was a warm night and windows would be open.

Gary sank onto the grass, shaking his head. 'First Martin... now Julie... what the hell is going on here?'

'We don't know,' said Kate, kneeling down next to him. 'We'll find out more when the police arrive. Gary — when did you last see Julie?'

He sniffed and rubbed his face. 'I didn't see her. I was hoping to catch her in reception, like the rest of you, but she came through when I was dealing with an urgent staffing issue and I missed her.' He blinked and shook his head. Then realisation dawned over his features and he stared up at her, his jaw dropping. 'What... wait a minute. Are you asking me this because—'

'Gary, I'm not asking you *anything*,' said Kate, hurriedly. 'I am not on duty — I'm just a friend. But the local coppers are going to ask you the same thing because they ask *everyone* that, OK? Don't take it the wrong way.'

She was deeply relieved to pick up the distinctive static of a police radio. The local guys were here, and she would be so, *so* glad to hand over to them. No copper should have to guard a crime scene with their own friend lying dead in it.

Two uniforms and a plain clothes arrived. The detective was a severe-looking middle-aged woman with scraped back hair and a grey suit. 'DS Stuart,' she said. 'Suffolk Constabulary. I assume you're DI Sparrow?' She gave Kate a hard stare. 'DI Sparrow, I was surprised to hear you'd been trampling through a crime scene.'

'Well, I didn't know it *was* a crime scene until I'd entered it,' said Kate, keeping her voice even. 'I checked her pulse with sterile gloves on. Other than that, nothing has been touched. Mike here is Head of Security and needed to verify what he was being told, so he has stepped in and seen the body — then come straight back out again.'

Stuart pursed her lips and, pausing to put fabric slippers over her sensible black shoes, pulled the door open with gloved hands and entered the scene. As the constables began to gather notes from Mike and Gary, Kate followed the DS to the door, peering past the opened curtain.

'I hope you weren't planning to go home tomorrow,' said Stuart, scanning the murder scene with the impassive expression of someone who'd seen it all before, and worse. 'I had a feeling from your phone call this afternoon that my weekend was going to be wrecked.'

'They're connected,' said Kate, keeping her voice low and directed away from Gary and Mike outside. 'Martin Riley, who supposedly killed himself, was one of our party. There were seven of us here for a reunion weekend... and now there are five.'

Stuart fixed her with a jaded expression. 'So you think there's a connection, do you? Nice of you to help me out there.'

Kate gritted her teeth. 'You have to admit it's one big coincidence.'

'I admit nothing,' said Stuart, edging around the far side of the sofa to take in the full grimness of Julie's death.

'I'm sorry... but a suicide note on a *sanitary towel?*'

The DS jerked her head up. 'How did you come by that information?' she snapped.

Kate folded her arms and tilted her head. 'Same way you would, in my position.'

The pair of them locked eyes for a moment and then the faintest twist of acknowledgement travelled across Stuart's face. 'Wait outside, please, DI Sparrow. We've got much to talk about.'

Outside, Gary was going into a low-volume meltdown and Kate couldn't blame him. He was faced with a horrible situation. Happy holidaymakers were snoozing within *metres* of a murder scene. As soon as the full investigative team — complete with lights, tape and forensics boiler suits — showed up, a lot of families were going to be freaking out.

'I think you'd better get the guests out now,' said Kate. 'Before it gets any later and before the full CSI team shows up. It's only going to get worse.' She glanced at the male and female uniformed officers. 'Don't you think? Shouldn't they be getting the families moved away from here?'

'What really happened to her?' said Gary, in a choked voice, as DS Stuart emerged from the chalet to consult with the PCs. 'Mike says someone smothered her in fat? Is that true?'

'You're going to need to get these other chalets emptied,' said DS Stuart, echoing Kate. 'As soon as my officers have questioned the occupants.'

Gary put his face in his hands.

'Gary — listen — get your Bluecoats together,' said Kate. She glanced at her watch. 'They'll probably all still be up, and hopefully not too plastered yet. They can help the police and make the whole thing less scary.' She glanced up at Stuart, raising her eyebrows.

'That sounds like a good plan,' said Stuart.

Gary nodded. And then shook his head, looking wretched as the enormity of his task hit him.

'*Use* your Blues,' Kate urged again, squeezing his arm. 'They'll be really helpful in keeping the lid on all of this. And remember — everyone gets a free upgrade to the deluxe chalets, yes? You've got some spare? Made up and

ready to go for drop-ins, yeah?' She remembered that
Buntin's usually kept chalets ready to let out to last minute
drop-ins, particularly on weekends.

'Yeah,' he nodded. 'Yeah — that's a good idea. OK. I'm
on it.'

Francis arrived back on the scene as Stuart was quietly
briefing her officers to work with the manager and his Bluecoats. He wandered up to her, looking tousled and tired and
freaked out. 'Jesus — this is your day job?'

'Yup,' she nodded, sighing and resting her forehead on
his shoulder. 'A dead body. The very thing we came here to
get away from.'

'Bloody hell,' he said. 'The next thing we know, Lucas
Henry's going to show up with his magic pendulum and find
another one for you.'

'He can't be *that* unlucky,' said Kate.

16

I t was very hard for Lucas Henry to get to sleep that night. Largely because he was utterly spun out by seeing Kate.

But, at least partly, because Lady Grace Botwright was straddling him.

She had been waiting in the leather armchair in the corner of the galleried landing outside his room, wrapped in an oriental silk robe, her hair loose and her eyes dancing with promise. 'I want to be clear, Lucas,' she'd said, as he crept up the stairs. 'I'm too old to bugger about. I find you divinely attractive and I simply want to shag you senseless at least once while you're staying here. Is that wrong of me?'

He hadn't known what to say to that, so he just chuckled, shaking his head at the freakish day he was having. 'It's not wrong, *as such*,' he said. 'Not sure Lord Botwright would agree, though.'

'Lord Botwright is perfectly happy with it,' Grace had said. 'As long as he gets to bang Giuliano in Rome for most of the summer.' She smiled and winked. 'We have an arrangement. I don't take advantage of it very often, but this time...' She stepped across to him and stroked his stubbly chin. 'Unless you don't want to, of course. In which case, I will vanish like the ghost of Lady Macbeth and we shall never speak of this again.'

Two minutes later they were on his bed and she was flinging her silk robe away, revealing a very pleasing naked physique, along with some very persuasive naked desire. He wasn't particularly into the whole dominatrix thing but he very much enjoyed confidence and enthusiasm — which Lady Grace had plenty of, along with some very adroit technique.

As she bent over him, her long fair hair brushing his throat and chest, he closed his eyes and gave himself up to her exploratory kiss and confident touch, sliding his fingers down the smooth skin of her back. Her mouth tasted of wine and her scent was unmistakably Grace. She had a good decade on him but she was super fit — and everything any man could want. He was responding entirely as he should, provoking a small 'Wow!' from her as she kissed her way down his belly.

But his imagination was playing with him just as expertly as her ladyship, as she wrangled a condom like a professional. The silky slide of her fair hair across his chest flashed an image of the tousled mane of Kate Sparrow, up on stage, through his mind, twisting a double-edged blade of desire and guilt through him. *Stop it.* But it was too late. He couldn't. He pulled Sid and the chain off over his head and dropped it on the floor, as if his little glass stopper friend was watching and judging. *Kate... in a short red dress and high-heeled glossy black boots... oh god.*

Stop it now.

In the end, it wouldn't matter, would it? Grace might be thinking of someone else herself, for all he knew. She'd never know that another woman was sharing this coupling, like a wanton ghost. And it wasn't as if he didn't find the flesh and blood woman on top of him very attractive too...

Just stop mixing it up. No good will come of this. Don't go there. Not now. Not next week, not ever.

Oh god.

Afterwards he decided he had nothing to feel bad about. His furtive imaginings hadn't damaged his performance — far from it. Grace, sprawling elegantly across the bed with a drowsy smile of satisfaction, said, 'Best... shag... ever.'

'Will you post a review?' he chortled. 'I'm on Check-a-lay.'

'Yes,' she said. 'Lucas Henry was proficient, passionate and very expert. He arrived promptly and didn't stop halfway through to ask for tea. He got the job done beautifully and was very polite throughout. Clean and tidy. Five stars.'

'You should have your own entry, too,' he pointed out.

'Oh no, darling,' she said. 'We don't do *trade* at Stokeley Lodge Estate.' She gurgled with laughter and got up on one elbow. 'Don't you tell Mariam about this. She'll never speak to me again! She already thinks I'm an unconscionable old slapper.'

'Your secret's safe with me,' he promised.

'Lucas... I have to ask... why are you here? I mean... why are you even available to an old biddy like me? You're hot stuff — you must be fighting the girls off with brickbats!'

'Not so's you'd notice,' he said. 'And you're no old biddy, Grace. Sheesh — the energy of you!'

'So... no girlfriend. No *boyfriend*, either, I'm guessing, given the last forty-five minutes. Unless you're one of these pansexual, get-it-up-for-any-gender types.'

'Is *that* what that means?' he said, rolling onto his back. 'I thought it was people who got horny for Le Creuset.'

She snorted at his terrible gag.

'Nope, I'm straight,' he said. 'Well, sexually, anyway. Pretty twisted up in other ways.'

'So... it's the lady detective,' Grace went on, circling one finger around his belly button. 'Don't start denying it; it's obvious. Every time I mention her your eyes do this flickery thing. What are you going to do about Kate Sparrow?'

He covered his face and let out a long sigh. 'Stay away from her,' he groaned through his fingers.

'Really? You can do that?'

'Apparently not,' he confessed, and then told her of the events of that evening.

Afterwards, she slid across his chest and scooped Sid up off the floor. 'So this little stopper keeps dragging you off to cross her path. That is *spooky*. Are you *sure* you didn't know she was there?'

'I had no idea,' he said. 'Like I said, I haven't been in touch with her since March. How could I have any clue where she was?'

'And yet you find yourself here... just minutes up the road from Buntin's,' mused Grace, swinging Sid between her elegant fingers. 'And then you find a reason to go there... and then you walk right into a bar and there she is.'

'It's weird, I know,' he said.

'So... that's it? You're not going to go back?'

'No!' He sat up and collected Sid from her, dropping the stopper and chain into his bedside drawer and closing it with what he hoped was finality. 'Honestly — what would she think? That I'm some kind of stalker, that's what. There's just a chance I got away with it. She only clocked me for a second and then I got the hell out of there, so she could believe she was mistaken — that she just saw someone who looked a bit like me. In fact, there was a guy walking in just as I left, who looked a bit like me. Hopefully she saw him later on and decided that's who she'd seen at the bar. So... I'm safe. I just have to keep it that way.'

'Even though fate is steering you relentlessly into her path, time and again,' said Grace. 'Don't you think you should just go with your destiny here?'

Lucas shook his head. 'With all due respect, your ladyship, fuck destiny. Destiny is not my friend. Destiny tricks me, trips me up, punches me in the face, throws me off my bike, ties me up, drugs me, chases me, Tasers me, arrests me and then dumps me back where I started when it's done having its fun.'

'Yes... but what about the downsides..?'

He chucked a pillow at her. 'It's no good, Lucas,' she spluttered, fending it off and then sitting up and reaching for her silk robe. 'You can't fight it. Sooner or later, you're going to have to deal with whatever it is that connects you and Kate Sparrow.'

Lucas sagged back onto the bed and stared at the ceiling. This was only what his own psyche had been telling him for the past six months. Except... dealing with it was going to open up a whole new, nasty can of worms. He could picture Kate's face all too well as he finally told her everything... confessed the truth about those last few days of summer nearly seventeen years ago.

Imagining her expression for real made his insides set like concrete.

17

'So... we can't leave the site?' Francis sat Kate down at the table in the kitchen-diner area and placed a cup of hot chocolate in her hands.

'Nope,' she said, taking a grateful sip. It was nearly 2.30am and she was still in her sparkly red dress, but as far from Holiday Kate now as it was possible to be. Here in Talia's chalet, her brother and her four remaining friends were in a state of shock. Each of them had by now been interviewed by one of the Suffolk officers, in an unbooked chalet requisitioned as an incident room, and each one had said the same thing — they hadn't seen Julie for seven years. Not one of them had clapped eyes on her that evening. Julie may have got herself to Buntin's Lakefield Holiday Village on the planned date, but she hadn't met up with any of them.

The only person to see her had been the young man — Tyler — on the entrance gate, but his memory of her was fleeting. As Gary had missed her when she'd checked in to reception, Julie had probably had no knowledge of Martin's death the week before.

The Suffolk coppers had accompanied the Bluecoats as they knocked on all the doors of the neighbouring chalets, asking everyone to pack up and move to another, deluxe upgrade further along the village site. There was much grumbling, but the presence of the officers got people moving. Before any of them could depart, though, the police had asked if they'd seen or heard anything in or near chalet 28. Only one person thought they might have seen Julie letting herself into her accommodation, but it was just a brief sighting as they headed off to the restaurant. They remembered little more than a dark-haired, slim young woman, hauling her holdall over the threshold and vanishing.

'This just doesn't make sense,' said Craig, looking pale as he slumped onto the sofa next to Talia. 'Why would anyone want to kill Julie?' He gulped and wiped his eyes.

None of them were aware of the details of Julie's death; Kate knew better than to divulge them and Mike, the head of security, had also been cautioned to say nothing of what he'd seen in the chalet.

'Can't you *tell* us what you saw?' pressed Talia, giving Craig's shoulders a squeeze as she stared at Kate. 'I mean... was she strangled, stabbed, shot... what?'

Kate shook her head. 'I'm sorry. I literally cannot tell you,' she said. 'I'd be revealing details that could compromise the investigation.'

'Some pretty freaky shit, going by the look on your face,' pointed out Bill, who was sitting up on the breakfast bar, his feet on one of the high stools, drinking a glass of Talia's Merlot. 'Was she into some kind of kinky sex game stuff? Did it go wrong? You never know, do you? All the yoga and clean livin'... it's got to give sometime.'

'That is SO bloody inappropriate, Bill!' snapped Nikki,

from her seat at the table next to Francis. 'Christ — you don't change, do you?'

'Nobody ever changes,' grunted Bill. 'Not really. I'm just the same as I ever was, but with better clothes and a better motor.'

Kate had noticed the way he'd ostentatiously swung his Audi key fob around earlier that evening. *Tosser,* she couldn't help thinking.

'Still shagging everything with a pulse, then?' Nikki bit back.

He grinned down at her. 'You after another one, for old time's sake?'

'You are fucking unbelievable,' she muttered.

'That's what they tell me.' He lifted his arms in a shrug of faux modesty. 'Chalet number 158 if you want a little refresher, Welsh Rarebit!'

'I didn't bring enough protection,' she bit back. 'You must be packing fifty shades of clap by now.'

'Stop it, will you?' said Craig, glaring from one to the other. 'Just leave it alone. I can't believe you're bickering like a pair of teenagers after everything that's happened. I mean... haven't you taken it in? Julie... is DEAD!' He stared at Kate, biting his trembling lip, welling up. 'Can you at least tell us she didn't suffer?'

Kate stood up, wiping her hands over her face. 'Look... the best thing now is for us all to try to get some sleep. I think we'll probably be allowed to go home at the end of tomorrow, if you're thinking of going early, but the SIO will be wanting to talk to us again before we go anywhere.'

'Shit,' said Bill. 'So much for a fun weekend away from work. Two dead mates and house arrest in a fucking Buntin's chalet.'

'We don't have to stay in our chalets,' said Kate, wearily.

'We just can't go off-site until they've spoken to us again tomorrow.'

'Well, I hope they've said the same to every other fucker here this weekend,' said Bill. 'It could be anyone, couldn't it? Why pick on us?'

'Come on,' said Francis, getting up and coming around to Kate's side of the table. He took her arm and steered her to the door. Looking back at the others, he filled her with sisterly pride as he said, 'Do as she says. Get some sleep. And Bill... don't be a tosser.'

She grinned up at him as they walked the lamplit alley down to their chalet, which was, happily, situated far from the crime scene. 'You took the words right out of my mouth.'

'Will you be able to sleep?' he asked, knowing her way too well. Insomnia was a regular visitor to the Sparrow household, especially when she was on a murder case.

'I've got my plasticine,' she said. 'I might make a few things. Settle my mind down.'

Back in their chalet she took a shower, washing away the make-up and the hairspray, but not the image of poor Julie, filled up with lard, which repeatedly flared across her mind's eye like the persistent memory of a camera flash. She was really tempted to talk to Francis about it, and she knew she could trust him to keep it to himself, but honestly, why wreck his sleep too?

When she emerged, wrapped in her robe, hair twisted into a towel, Francis had gone to bed, leaving her latest packet of plasticine on the table with a note: *'Make a cat.'* He knew she liked a challenge. She smiled and sank into a chair, reaching for the packet. Twenty minutes later she had made one cat and three kittens, snuggled up against their mother's belly. The adrenaline pounding through her veins for the past three hours had finally settled down and sleep began to beckon.

She hit her pillow with damp hair, uncaring. What a night. She'd had some shockers, recently, but this was uniquely disturbing. She couldn't make sense of what had happened to Julie. Who would do that to her? And why? She had never seen anything like it.

Stop thinking about it now. Sleep.

Who would go to so much trouble to create that horrifying scene? They must have poured the fat in as liquid, knowing it would set hard and white.

Think about something ELSE.

Lucas Henry flashed through her mind right away.

No... not HIM.

She was conjuring him up way too often. Usually in her sleep, though. Often along with Mabel and Zoe, both in varying degrees of life, death and decay. Tonight she'd outdone herself, though, seeing that vision of him in the bar.

Wait.

She sat up abruptly. The look on the Lucas-alike's face... it had been... *shock.* The jaw was dropped, just like hers, as if he was amazed to see her. If she had been merely conjuring him up — or mistaking someone else for him — why would that face have been mirroring her own? Unless...

'Shit! No!'

She flung herself out of bed and threw on some running joggers, her sports bra and a sweatshirt. She rummaged into her holdall and found her Nikes, slipping them onto her bare feet. Letting herself carefully out of the chalet, she locked up as quietly as she could, keen to leave her brother undisturbed, and tucked the single key and its wooden fob into the sports bra. Then, with her slim leather wallet in one hand, she broke into a run along the grassy path towards the main pavilion and the car park beyond.

She reached the car park in four or five minutes. Dawn was lightening the eastern sky and she could hear the sea hissing and sighing in the distance. A security guard was in the little hut by the car park. She ran up to it and rapped on the glass window. He looked up; an older guy than the one who'd ushered them in yesterday — grey-haired and careworn.

He slid the glass across. 'Can I help you?'

'I'm DI Kate Sparrow,' she said, flashing her ID. 'Looking into the investigation that's ongoing here tonight.' She didn't mention that she was, to all intents and purposes, just a punter here. 'Just a quick question — can you check the vehicle log for me? I'm looking for a motorbike that may have come in yesterday evening.'

He pulled a foolscap book open and ran a thick finger down its handwritten entries. 'Um... yes... a biker came in last night. Bought a day pass for the evening's entertainment.'

'The number plate?' queried Kate, a rush of goosebumps already hitting her shoulders.

He reeled it off. Every letter and every number sliding into place with a precise, chilling clunk of validation.

Kate drew a long breath and let it out slowly, resting one palm on the side of the hut. She had memorised that registration months ago, and not forgotten it. She knew she wasn't mistaken. Unless he'd recently sold his Triumph Bonneville to a new owner, who had randomly decided to drop by a holiday village in Suffolk yesterday evening, Lucas Henry had not been a mirage in the bar last night.

Lucas Henry had been standing there, watching her, in the flesh.

18

'Are you awake?'

Ellie turned over and stared across the narrow strip of carpet to the single bed opposite, where Nettie was gnawing on her lip, the duvet pulled tight around her neck.

'Yeah. It's hard to sleep, isn't it?' Ellie prodded her bedside clock. It was just after three-thirty and they would need to be getting up in four hours — five, maybe, at a push.

'I can't believe it,' said Nettie. 'Two people dead within a week. What the hell is going on around here?'

Ellie sighed and sat up. Outside, the eastern sky was growing paler; dawn wasn't far away. She felt dog-tired but her brain wouldn't shut down. Not long after midnight, she and the other Blues had been rounded up by a strained-looking Gary and informed that their help was needed to guide eight families out of their chalets and along to the deluxe lodges at the other end of the site. Ellie had already tumbled into bed and fallen asleep, and had to be woken by Nettie, but most of the others were still up and dressed. She had flung on her tracksuit in a daze to join them.

At first, Gary had said only that there had been an 'incident' in chalet 28 but, faced with eleven agog and slightly pissed Bluecoats and their incessant questioning, he had confessed that someone was dead. That was all he knew, he said. He didn't know if foul play was involved, but the police were already on site, and after speaking to all the families in nearby chalets they wanted everyone moved out, away from the cordoned-off area.

It was a bloody nightmare. Getting those families out quietly and discreetly was about as easy as herding cattle through a glassware factory. Still, they had done it, within an hour. After that the police had wanted to talk to each of the Bluecoats, too, but not one of them had a clue who was dead or who had been in that chalet when they were alive.

'We don't usually come anywhere near here,' Ellie had told them, when it was her turn to talk to the stern-looking woman in a grey suit, who'd introduced herself as DS Stuart, and her uniformed constable who was taking notes. 'The Bluecoat chalets are right down the end of the site.'

'Have you seen anyone on site who you thought was suspicious?' DS Stuart asked her.

Ellie shrugged and shook her head. 'There are about three hundred guests here,' she said. 'It's Friday — well, Saturday now — so they've all just arrived. We've mixed with them in the big ballroom, but we haven't really had time to get to know anyone yet.'

Shortly after that, realising she knew sweet bugger all, they had let her go. Some of the Blues had congregated in the lamplit adventure playground for a while, speculating in hushed voices about what the hell was happening, but eventually Gary had come along and ushered them all off to bed. 'I'm expecting you all to rise an' fuckin' shine as usual,' he'd growled at them, with his usual show of affection and respect. 'Go get your ugly sleep!'

But there didn't seem to be any ugly sleep to be had. 'Cup of tea?' suggested Ellie, and Nettie nodded, sitting up. Ellie filled the small kettle and dropped teabags in mugs. Through the nets across the patio door she could make out soft lighting inside the single caravan parked close by. 'Looks like Barney's up, too,' she said. 'He might have heard about it. Shall we invite him over?'

Nettie rolled her eyes. 'For god's sake, Ellie! We hardly know him and you want to ask him in for tea, while we're in bed?'

'He seems nice,' said Ellie.

'He seems weird,' said Nettie. 'I mean... he's nice-looking and all that, and pretty fit... but he's a gypo, isn't he?'

'Seriously?' said Ellie, getting milk out of the tiny fridge. 'Gypo? What the hell is *that*?'

'Well, all right then... *traveller*,' said Nettie, making apostrophes with her fingers. 'He's, I dunno, different.'

'Yeah, god save us from the *different* people,' snorted Ellie, handing over a mug.

They drank their tea in silence for a while and then Nettie said, 'Maybe it's connected... you know... to Martin.'

'But they said Martin killed himself,' said Ellie, suppressing a shiver as a memory of pink water rose in her mind again.

'So... maybe it's a suicide cult,' breathed Nettie. 'You hear about these cults, don't you? They get people all brainwashed so they top themselves.'

'I still can't believe he killed himself,' said Ellie. 'Why would he? He seemed fine and even if he wasn't, why would he do that to you and me and the kids..? You know what?'

She drew her quilt around her shoulders and shivered. 'I think the parents might be planning to sue us.'

'You what?' said Nettie. 'But they seemed lovely about it... after we'd lied to their kids, of course.'

'I know but...' Ellie took a sip of tea and shook her head. 'I wasn't snooping or anything, but while I was checking my shifts on the wall in Gary's office, I knocked his mouse or something and the screen lit up... and there was this email saying LIFEGUARD ISSUE — WE WANT DAMAGES.'

'Oh holy fuck!' breathed Nettie. And then she wrinkled her face and added, 'No! *No*... I know what that was about! That's not about the kids. That's about some stupid teenager saying Martin groped her in the pool.'

'What..?'

'Yeah, I heard it from Jenny, who heard it from Martin before he died. Some girl was screaming, saying she had cramp or something and Martin had to go in and get her. Then she goes and says he felt her up.'

Ellie shook her head. 'I can't believe he'd do that, either.'

'Of course he didn't bloody do it!' said Nettie. 'Those girls were always giving him the come-on and pretending to get cramp so he'd carry them out. I saw them do it. She probably got pissed off because he wouldn't pay attention to her. Anyway, silly bitch will have to shut up about it now he's dead. That'll give her a bit of fuckin' perspective.'

'So... would Martin kill himself over something like that?' Ellie wondered.

'No way,' said Nettie, draining her mug, putting it beside her bed and settling back down on her pillow. 'Good-looking lifeguards get that kind of crap all the time. But... if they were pushing for damages it might have got a bit further up the line this time. Maybe Gary was going to have to do an investigation or something... not any more, though.'

Ellie sighed. She settled back down, too. A few minutes later some rhythmic breathing told Ellie her chalet mate was drifting off. It was nearly four in the morning and she really needed to get some shuteye too. She was going to be a zombie — a zombie wearing a Buntin's perma-smile — at breakfast.

As she drifted off she was aware of a flickering of light outside and thought, for a second, she saw a dark figure looming by the window.

'Did you see that?' hissed Nettie, suddenly awake.

But when Ellie sat up, squinting through her tired lids, there was nobody there.

'It was probably one of the other Blues,' she muttered. 'Come on. We *have* to get some sleep!'

———

BARNEY WAS TOO WIRED to sleep. He couldn't even settle inside the Sprite. He had to pace around outside, his belly fizzing. Seeing them all collapse, weeping, onto the grass outside Julie's chalet was something he couldn't get out of his mind. It was bizarrely shocking. They had always seemed so... indestructible.

Apparently not.

The shock at what Kate was telling them was palpable even at a distance. Something very bad had happened to Julie.

Well. Who knew?

He would have liked to watch for longer but the security team was on its way and he didn't want to be caught loitering. He would pick up the rest of the story soon enough. He just hoped they wouldn't all abandon the holiday park right away.

He needed more time...

———

Lucas was woken by the sound of his mobile buzzing on the bedside table. Grace had taken herself off to her own bed a couple of hours ago, leaving him to fall asleep with a weird mixture of sexual satisfaction *and* frustration. Grace "shagging him senseless" as she'd elegantly put it, really had done him the power of good. He didn't get enough physical release these days. But it had also woken up those repressed feelings about someone he really shouldn't be thinking of.

That someone had been stretched out next to him in bed — a sensual phantom — when the buzz of his phone had made her evaporate. He stared blearily at the small, bright screen, trying to work out what it meant, getting a call at 3.55am. It was number withheld.

He sat up, suddenly very awake, and answered. Again there was a click and a hiss and... nothing. He decided to stay silent; just wait. It might yet be one of those automated sales calls. The skin began to prickle on his neck and shoulders as he waited for the caller to speak. He heard a sigh. He *definitely* heard a sigh. He was just about to give in and ask who was there when the call cut off again.

He stared at the screen and then dropped the phone back on his bedside table with a curse. A second later it gave three short burrs and a text arrived. He snatched it up, seeing a number this time, but not one he recognised. Who the hell would be texting him at this hour?

He thumbed it open and then sucked in a sharp breath.
What were you doing at Buntin's?

He thumbed back: **Who is this?**

He'd barely sent it before the call came through, the mobile vibrating in his hand as if it was nervous about what it was channelling. He accepted the call, holding the phone slightly away from him.

'I know you were here. I saw you in the bar,' said Kate Sparrow.

A surge of adrenaline shot though him and he slammed the mobile to his ear.

'Oh god,' he said. 'Not again.'

'What do you *mean,* not again? I'm not the one stalking *you!*'

'Nobody's stalking anybody,' he said, affronted. 'Seeing you there was just a weird, freaky, fucking annoying coincidence.'

'Oh really? I'm meant to believe that?'

'Believe what you like,' he said. 'I had no idea you would be there. I was checking something out for a friend, that's all.'

'Lucas... here's the thing... whenever you show up in my life, someone ends up dead.'

'I think you've got that wrong,' he said, grabbing a fistful of quilt in a bid to get a grip on his surging pulse. 'Whenever *you* show up in *my* life, someone ends up dead! Do I need to remind you that *you* were the one who came to *me* last year? I didn't ask for any of it. I never applied for a season ticket to Sparrow World!'

There were a few beats of silence, as if she was acknowledging this. 'Tell me why you were here,' she said, at length, in a more reasonable tone.

'I'm working up the road, at the Stokeley Lodge Estate, just over the border into Norfolk,' he said, settling back against the bedstead and realising, perversely, that he was glad to be talking to her; glad to hear her voice. 'I've been dowsing for the water table so they can decide where best to build some holiday lodges.'

'OK,' she said. 'And..?'

'There's a girl who works here — her boyfriend killed himself, or so they say, over at the Buntin's Holiday Village. He was the lifeguard, apparently. He was found dead in the pool last week, with his throat cut.'

There was a moment of silence at the end of the phone, but he felt a pulse of connection. *Oh here we go again*, some part of him groaned.

'Go on,' said Kate.

'Anyway, she was very upset about it... said she didn't believe he'd killed himself. She was wearing his shirt and his patterns were still in it. I picked them up. They were telling me she was right to be suspicious... so I got on my bike and let Sid guide me to the spot where this Martin guy had died. I got there, told the guy on the gate I was dropping in to meet a friend, because, seriously, dropping in to check out a suicide location is a bit too Goth for me to carry off at my age.'

She snorted with dry amusement and he felt a wave of warmth; it was back. Their connection was fully back, as if he'd floated through space in a shuttle and just completed a successful dock at the Henry & Sparrow ISS.

'So... did you pick anything up?' she asked.

'I did. I got into the pool complex just before it was locked up for the night. I found the spot, under some fake palm trees, in the shallow bit. I picked up his... his final moments.'

'And?' she said, and there was a strangled sound to her voice. He realised at once that she had known the dead man.

'They weren't desperation... hopelessness... resignation;

the emotions you would expect from someone who wanted to end it all.'

'What were they?' she asked, quietly.

'Agitation... fear... and then shock.'

'Are you saying he was murdered?'

'I'm sorry, Kate... I'm getting that he was your friend. But yes... he didn't end his own life — someone else did.'

She took a long breath. 'There's been another murder,' she said. 'Another one of our party. Martin was one of seven of us who worked here as Bluecoats seven years ago. We came up to meet him for a reunion weekend... and now there are only five of us left.'

'Shit,' murmured Lucas, fear creeping through him. 'You think someone's targeting you all?'

'I don't know... but... maybe,' she said.

'How did your other friend die?'

'I can't tell you that,' she said. 'At least... not now. Not on the phone. I think... I think we should meet. Can you come over around lunchtime?'

He paused. 'You're sure you want that?'

She sighed. 'I know it always ends badly,' she said. 'But, yes. If you can. I will understand if you don't want to, though.'

'What's the Taser risk, would you say?'

She gave a dry laugh. 'Not too high. The Suffolk constabulary is all over this — I'm just on the sidelines, off-duty. The DS in charge is a cold fish and she does not want me on her turf, so I have to respect that. I'm just a witness. And nobody here knows who you are. We can do some snooping without worrying about whether I'm going to get suspended.'

'Or shot?' he ventured. 'Or drugged? Or smacked in the face with a spade..? Oh no — that was me.'

She laughed again and then snatched a breath, before saying in a low voice: "Lucas — we need to talk about things anyway.'

He took his own breath before replying, 'Yeah. We do.'

'So... one o'clock at the pavilion?'

'No problem,' he said. 'I'll see you there.'

'Bring Sid,' she said.

'**S**ay sorry.'

 He was still drunk, scrabbling at his bedclothes, baffled and annoyed.

 'How the fuck did you get in here?' he said. 'And what the fuck is THAT?'

 The bucket was heavy and surprisingly lively. Putting it down made it easier to lift the gun and watch his face as it scanned the contents, first baffled and disbelieving, and then — as he clocked the weapon — staggered and scared.

 'What? What do you want me to say sorry for? What did I do?'

 'Write it down.'

 'On that?'

 'Yes. On that.'

 His hand shook as he did as he was told. 'Look... is this about ... I mean, I know I'm no angel when it comes to the girls... I... I'm a bit of a shit. I know. Even my mates say I'd shag anything with a pulse... Did I screw things up with you and some—?'

 'You don't even remember me, do you?'

'I'm sorry... I don't. Just... tell me what I can do to make it better.'

'Show me your feet.'

'What?'

'I want to check your toes.'

'OK, but... why?'

'To see how much they have in common with what's in my bucket.'

It was always that moment when realisation dawned that really felt the best. That and the deep, satisfying silence that would soon follow. The sense of peace while the scene was set.

'Oh,' was the last thing he said.

20

'Jesus Christ, you didn't!'

Talia sat at the breakfast table, Craig on her left, and Nikki and Kate facing her. Her large brown eyes were like saucers as she shook her head at her old friend.

'What?' asked Kate, breaking her croissant. She was befuddled and tired. After speaking to Lucas, there had been another hour of angsting about what she'd just invited him into before she finally got to sleep. She reckoned she'd had three or four hours, tops. She was only here, attempting to eat breakfast in the massive Buntin's restaurant amid the roar of a hundred families doing battle with fry-ups and Rice Krispies, because Talia had phoned her and insisted she get up and meet them all at nine. Francis had waved away the offer of joining them, remaining buried, snoring, in his duvet when she'd left the chalet. She hadn't yet told him about inviting Lucas to Buntin's that day.

'You *did*, didn't you? You bloody did!' said Talia, rolling her eyes and licking the lid of her yoghurt pot.

Nikki raised her palms over her half-eaten croissant. 'What are you talkin' about?'

'I can see it written all over your face,' went on Talia. 'You went back to Bill's chalet last night and shagged him, didn't you?'

'Talia — children nearby,' said Craig, primly. He looked pale and peaky, and Kate guessed she wasn't the only one short on sleep.

Talia whispered, 'Look into my eyes and deny it, Nicola Whitlock!'

Nikki did neither. 'Fuck's sake,' she muttered. 'Julie's dead. I was freaked out. So was Bill. We needed a bit of... comfort.'

'He cheated on you at least three times in one summer season,' pointed out Talia. 'He made you miserable and then tried to put it all on you when you complained. Don't you remember?'

Nikki shrugged. 'It was a long time ago — water under the bridge. He's grown up a lot. He says he's different now.'

'So... him propositioning *me* at the bar, while you were in the ladies — that's his new grown-up thing, is it?'

Nikki gaped and then buried her face in her hands with a sob. 'Oh god. I'm such a loser.'

Kate put her arm around Nikki's shaking shoulders and glared at Talia. 'Nice one, Tally,' she said. 'Haven't we got enough trauma going on?'

Talia sighed and looked guilty. 'Sorry, Nikki... I should have warned you last night. I could see how it might go with you two. He's like catnip to you, isn't he?'

'He's a shit,' sniffed Nikki. 'And it wasn't even that good. He was too drunk.'

'Well, I guess he'll be sleeping it off all morning, so at least you can stay away from him for a bit,' said Talia. 'Let's all go down the beach again, yeah? Get some sea air. We might as well try to have a tiny bit of fun. Or is that wrong?' She looked at Kate.

Kate shook her head. 'No. You're right. I'd like to get some fresh air, too.'

'We need to stick together,' said Craig, pouring cornflakes into his bowl from a mini cardboard box. 'I mean... first Martin, then Julie... who's next, eh?'

Everyone looked at Kate.

'Should we be afraid?' asked Talia. 'I mean... I get that you can't tell us what you saw, but... you can tell us this much. Is someone coming after all of us?'

Kate shook her head. 'I don't know,' she said, although she'd be lying if she said that very thought hadn't occurred to her more than once in the past few hours. 'I mean... if Martin killed himself—'

'Ah!' said Craig, waving his milk-dipped spoon at her. 'You're saying "if", so that must mean you don't believe it was suicide!'

Kate shook her head. 'I didn't say that. But... I don't know. Yesterday, me and Francis got talking to this girl, one of the Bluecoats — Ellie, her name is. She was the one who found his body. She was marching the kids out, singing that alligator bedtime song like they did last night — and she marched them all into the pool complex, and that's when he was found. She was telling us she couldn't believe Martin would kill himself in the pool, knowing she'd be leading kids right past his body a short while later. And look — I don't claim to have known him that well, but it's hard to imagine anyone knowingly staging their death where kids could see it. So... you're right, Craig. I suppose I don't completely buy it.' She didn't mention the note on the sanitary towel. That had been a professional disclosure and wasn't something she felt she could — or should — share.

'So... we have to stay together,' said Craig. 'Until we can get the hell out of here, that is. I'm going to find that copper and tell her I'm heading home as soon as they'll let me. I don't want to stay another night.' He shivered. 'I'm sorry, but when I thought we'd be meeting up and getting slaughtered together, I didn't think it would be *literally*.'

'OK,' said Kate. 'Let me go and speak to the SIO and find out when they'll let us go. They said they'd want to speak to each of us again this morning — now that we're all fully sober. After that, you'll probably be OK to leave.'

'What's to say whoever's done in Martin and Julie isn't going to come after us anyway... in our own homes?' said Nikki, with a visible shiver.

'Look — there's still a chance the two deaths aren't related,' said Kate, somewhat clutching at straws when it came to finding words of comfort. 'It's still quite possible that Martin's *was* a suicide and Julie was just... in the wrong place at the wrong time. But... I agree... for now we stay together to stay safe. Nobody goes off alone. Except I'm going back to chalet 28 to speak to the officers there and find out what's happening... which ought to be pretty safe in broad daylight.'

She drained her coffee and got up, flicking an awkward glance at Nikki. 'And I guess someone should check on Bill, and get him to come and have breakfast and stay with the group.'

'Not me,' grunted Nikki, into her tea.

'We'll all go,' said Talia. 'We can take him some croissants and coffee.'

Kate left them to their nervous conversation and headed back to the police cordon area. It was fortunate that the block of chalets Julie had died in was set a good distance off the main path through the site. Hopefully, nosy guests would be at a minimum. Already, a barrier of white nylon tarp had been stretched across the path between the two chalet blocks, secured to the corners of each pebble-dashed chalet wall. A uniformed officer guarded the tent-flap door through it. She guessed there would be another tarp and another bobby at the other end, boxing the whole area in. She felt a pang for Gary — what a shitstorm to have to manage, just as the holiday season was kicking off.

Judging from the quiet behind the barrier, it appeared that the crime scene investigators had come and gone. Julie would have been photographed in situ, from every conceivable angle, and the area combed for every trace of evidence. The body was probably in the mortuary by now, being examined by one of Death's East Anglian colleagues. She imagined a criminal psychologist would already be on the clock, too. Killings like this, with such bizarre setups, could hardly be explained as a burglary gone wrong. Leaving lard to set hard in Julie's mouth and throat was a unique message. Kate had never heard of such a scenario, even among the London gangland killings she had helped investigate in her younger days, on secondment to the Met.

'Is DS Stuart around?' she asked, as she approached the officer. She flashed her ID and hoped he wouldn't recognise her from last night as she stepped breezily towards the gap in the tarp.

He didn't and he let her move on through it, although he dutifully noted her name and number in his scene log. 'She's gone back to the station, Inspector,' he said. 'But DS Upton is in there.'

'OK — good,' said Kate. Then, on a sudden instinct from nowhere, she added: 'Did a note show up?'

'Yeah,' said the officer.

'I'm guessing not on standard notepaper,' she hazarded, feeling her pulse pick up.

'Nope. Kerrymaid lard wrapper.'

She nodded. *Bingo.* 'And just *"I'm sorry"*? Nothing else?'

'That's all,' said the constable, shrugging. 'Weird.'

'Thanks,' she said, and went to the chalet door.

'Hi,' she called across the X of tape. 'DS Upton? DI Kate Sparrow.'

The DS was a stocky guy in his fifties with a tired face, standing just inside the opened patio door in a pair of blue cotton slippers, regarding the scene impassively. He glanced across at her with one eyebrow raised. 'Shouldn't be inside the outer cordon, should you, Inspector?'

Damn. He'd been fully briefed, then.

'When do you think you'll be done in here?' she asked, noting that the smell of cold lard was still very much in evidence.

'When we're ready,' he said, ducking under the tape and stepping out beside her.

'Only, my friends aren't so keen to go on with their weekend break now, as you can imagine.'

'I hope you didn't divulge the details of the manner of death,' he said, turning to slide the door shut with latex-gloved hands.

'Of course not,' she said. 'It's not something I really want to share. But I *would* like to know when you plan to interview us all again, so we can make plans to get home. Everyone's a bit spooked. Julie, as you'll know, was the second one of us to die here within a week.'

He sighed, screwing up the slippers and shoving them in his pockets. 'I don't blame you for getting the heebie-jeebies,' he said. 'I would, too. But there's a strong police presence on site now, as well as the Buntin's security team. It's highly unlikely our killer will strike again in broad daylight before you've all gone home.'

'So, when would you like to talk to us again?'

'I was just about to contact you all,' he said. 'DS Stuart wants to see everyone in your party when she gets back from Beccles. It'll be early afternoon, so we expect you all to stay put until then, please. You can save me a job and let your friends know that we will see them at 2pm outside the Entertainments Manager's office. They'll all be getting a text to that effect, too.'

'OK,' she said. 'So... this note on the lard wrapper...'

'How do you know about that?' he snapped, fixing her with a narrow stare.

'Well, I *might* have seen it when I found the body,' she said. He looked at her blankly, so she shook her head and confessed: 'Just a bit of detective work at my end,' she said. 'The note said, *"I'm sorry"*, yes? And it was written on a lard packet?'

'I can't divulge the details,' he said. He didn't say no, though.

'Please tell me you're bringing in the crim psych,' she said, adopting a quieter, more confidential tone.

'Oh yeah,' said Upton. 'Crim psychs get a hard-on for this kind of crime scene, don't they? Some serious sicko at work here last night. Ah... but, sorry for your loss,' he added, remembering belatedly that Kate was a friend of the deceased.

'What do *you* think the killer was trying to say?' she said, turning to fix him with her gaze and biting her lower lip. It was an appalling hand to play, but she was not above trying it. 'With the lard... and with Martin Riley... the sanitary towel? Making them write *"I'm sorry"*..?'

'Well, it looks like they both did something to offend him,' he said, quickly glancing up and down her strappy white sundress.

'Or her,' said Kate.

'Maybe. It's an equal opportunities business, murder.' He emitted a dry chuckle.

She smiled and nodded, knowingly. 'Yep. The female of the species...'

As they reached the tarp, she said, 'Thank you.'

'For what?' He dug his hands into the pockets of his worn-looking jacket.

'For not...'

'...being DS Stuart?' he guessed.

She laughed and shrugged. 'I get that she's guarding her patch,' she said. 'I would probably be the same.'

He snorted. 'She's not so bad. Once you get past that tough outer shell there's a... marginally less tough inner shell. Nah — she just likes things done properly. You should see her when those Norfolk boys cross into our patch. Collaboration between the constabularies? Ha! Anyway. I've got several hours of Buntin's security camera video to sit through, so if you'll excuse me...'

'I'll go and tell the others about the debrief at two,' she said. 'We can at least get a walk on the beach in before then.'

'Mind the crumbling cliffs,' he called after her as she left.

She smiled. There was a lot of coastal erosion around here but the cliffs were only about three metres high, so she was probably safe.

Back outside the restaurant, a glance through the window told her the others had finished breakfast and left, so she followed them to Bill's chalet. She'd noted all their chalet numbers last night, before they'd all gone to bed.

Before she reached Bill's block she met Nikki, Talia and Craig heading towards her. Nikki was looking furious. 'You're never going to fuckin' believe it!' she said, as soon as they were close enough.

'What?' asked Kate.

'Bill's gone. He's bloody upped and *gone!*' said Nikki. 'Without a bloody *word!*'

Kate felt a stab of concern. 'You checked his chalet?'

'All locked up,' said Talia. 'Blinds open — can't see anyone inside. We checked with reception and they said his car's gone from the car park. The little shit.'

'And then there were four,' said Craig, nodding his head ominously.

'I don't blame him for going,' said Nikki. 'But he might at least have said goodbye. Talk about wham, bam, thank you ma'am! What a tosser! What a total and utter tosser! What the fuck is wrong with me?'

'Let it go,' said Kate. 'I just talked to the DS down at the crime scene. They want us all to meet at Gary's office at two for another debriefing, and then they'll let us head home.'

'So what about Bill?' demanded Craig. 'He just buggers off home, does he?'

'No, said Kate. 'I'll let them know he's gone. He'll probably get pulled over by traffic and escorted back here. They'll most likely do him for speeding at the same time,' she added, wryly, remembering last night's key fob flashing 'He won't being doing less than eighty in that Audi.'

'Right then — I say we go back down the beach,' said Talia, clapping her hands commandingly. 'Let's get your brother, Kate, and get down there now, before it's choked with screaming kids and their lard-arsed parents staking out their patches.'

Kate winced at the reference none of them would get.

'Still feeling the love for the punters, after all this time, Tally,' said Craig.

'I don't work here any more,' she said. 'I can be as evil as I like.'

There was a pause at that, as everyone dwelt briefly on what evil had visited Julie last night.

'Let's go get Francis,' said Kate, checking her watch. In a couple of hours Lucas would be here. It would be good to let some sea air clear her mind before the dowser arrived to inevitably fog it up again.

21

The Bluecoats' morning meeting had never been quite like this. For a start, a uniformed police officer was sitting in on it. Gary said good morning to all eleven of them as they settled uneasily on the low seats lining the walls. Then he retreated behind his desk and let the constable stand up and take over.

'First of all, I want to say thank you,' said PC O'Neill. 'You were all a great help last night, evacuating the holiday-makers and seeing to it that nobody got too upset. We really appreciated your professionalism. Couldn't have done it without you.'

He smiled at them all and Ellie felt a sense of unreality, not helped by her lack of sleep.

'Now, I know you've all already given a brief statement to my colleagues — and I know that between you there wasn't much to tell us. I gather none of you knew the victim or had even met her. Is everyone still sure of that? I know that you take it in turns to meet and greet at the reception area in the pavilion... are you sure you didn't see this woman at any point during your shift yesterday?'

He held up an A4-sized print of an attractive, dark-haired woman in her 20s; sporty and fit-looking. Everyone shrugged and shook their heads.

'We say hello to hundreds of people,' said Nettie. 'She might have come in, but we just don't remember her.'

'You should be aware that Julie Everall was herself a Bluecoat here seven years ago,' went on PC O'Neill. 'We don't know if this is relevant to her murder but it's possible that it is. Now... we're not in a situation where we're asking for the closure of an entire holiday village because of this.'

Gary blew his cheeks out and shook his head.

'In all likelihood this is the end of it — until we find the person who did this.'

'How did she die?' asked Ellie.

'I'm not able to share any details with you, I'm afraid. Only that her death was not by natural causes and not by her own hand,' he said.

'So what about Martin?' said Ellie. 'Are you still saying his death *was* by his own hand? Because I don't believe it. I never did believe it.'

'Obviously last night's incident has thrown a different light on Martin Riley's death,' said the PC. 'We're not ruling out a link. Which means that you must all be careful to look out for each other.'

'You mean there's a Bluecoat serial killer?' gasped Jenny, always good for a bit of drama.

'I don't mean that,' he said. 'But to be on the safe side, you all need to stay in pairs and make sure nobody is out wandering on their own after hours, OK? Everyone clear on that?'

'Oh yeah — we're clear!' said Nettie.

'And if you see *anything* suspicious... you need to let us know. Right away. Even if you think it's silly and even if it turns out to be nothing, that doesn't matter. We need to know.'

By the time he'd finished, Ellie and Nettie had already exchanged glances several times. Ellie knew what Nettie was thinking — the lights on in Barney's caravan in the early hours... the shadow passing their chalet window. But on any other night they would have thought nothing of it. Bluecoats kept late hours and guests on the site might wander around in the dark, pissed and giggly, trying to locate their chalet. So did it qualify as something suspicious?

That wasn't the only thing on Ellie's mind, though. What about the allegation against Martin that she'd seen on Gary's laptop? Had Gary told the police about that? She had a feeling he hadn't. She suspected he was the kind who would rather cover up such an unsavoury accusation than take it through all the correct channels and risk a public revelation that might damage the Buntin's brand. Like Nettie had said last night, he didn't have to worry about it now. Having Martin kill himself must have seemed like a bit of a free pass from the legal stuff that the family had been threatening. Going back to them to say the man accused had taken his own life was likely to silence them. You can't sue a dead man, even if you have the stomach for it after news like that. She narrowed her eyes, taking in Gary as he shuffled papers on his desk. Would he bump off his lifeguard to save Buntin's from bad publicity? Surely not...

And what possible reason would he then have to kill this Julie Everall, who he'd employed here seven years ago? No. It made no sense. And anyway, Gary just wasn't the type. Under all that Essex hard man gravel he was as soft as butter.

That still left Barney, up in the wee small hours, maybe looming past their window. Question was... what to do?

Should she speak to the police officer now? He'd said he and the crime scene investigators would be in chalet 24, where they'd set up their incident room, for the next day or two. She and Nettie had twenty minutes before they were due in the children's theatre with Uncle Bobby. There was time...

'I think we should tell them about Barney,' hissed Nettie, as soon as they stepped outside. 'Lurking outside our chalet!'

'But we don't know it *was* Barney by the window,' said Ellie. 'It's not like the shadow was backflipping past, is it? It could have been anyone.'

'The lights were on in his caravan. He was awake,' said Nettie. 'And he's always been a bit... you know... weird.'

'He's OK,' protested Ellie. 'He's just... from a different world to us. He's, you know...'

'A gypo,' said Nettie.

'A traveller!' Ellie rolled her eyes. *Honestly* — was she the only Bluecoat who lived in the 21st century?

'He's been coming here for years,' Nettie went on, as they walked on auto-pilot to the small theatre where kids were already lining up excitedly, ready for games and cartoons. 'I heard he's been a regular Buntin's performer for at least a decade. He was only fifteen when he first started touring the holiday camps. Before that, he was with the Jericho fair, doing sideshow acts when he was a kid.'

'You've been doing some research!' said Ellie, raising an eyebrow. Nettie wasn't usually the type to look up more than her horoscope or her Instagram following.

'It's just so freaky,' said Nettie, with a visible shudder. 'What if there *is* a Bluecoat psycho killer, out to get every one of us..?'

'It's not us,' said Ellie. 'Martin was here seven years ago, when that other one — Julie — was here. It's got to be some-thing to do with them, not us.'

'Yeah... and who else was here seven years ago..?' Nettie's eyebrows and palms raised in tandem. 'Yeah — Backflip Barney.'

'So... are you going to tell that policeman?' Ellie could see the sense in it, but she felt sorry for Barney. There was something rather vulnerable about him; the way he waved and smiled but never joined them unless very specifically invited (by her, every time, because she felt bad for him). A guy that fit and nice-looking, you'd think he'd be confident in himself, but he really wasn't, except for the half hour when he was performing for the kids or for the families, in the evening.

He certainly was a loner and a bit odd. She could see why Nettie was suspicious.

'I think we should,' Nettie went on. 'As soon as the morning ramble is over.'

In the children's theatre they met a fresh crowd of young holidaymakers, ready for fun and games, magic tricks and bingo. Buntin's was surprisingly old-fashioned in what it offered the children, but that was part of its appeal for many parents, sick of seeing their kids glued to screens. There were even old cartoons screened in the theatre, while she and Nettie gave out popcorn and fizzy drinks.

This morning, though, it was all about settling the kids into two teams — the Snappers (her team) and the Crackers (Nettie's team). It was noisy and silly, with run-around games in the auditorium, until everyone had been settled into their team and given the correct badge — the Snappers with a fierce pair of alligator jaws on theirs, and the Crackers with a whip-cracking alligator tail on theirs.

Then, checking that every child was wearing their

microchipped bracelet (also stamped with their team insignia) and could be tracked if they were to get lost, Ellie and Nettie led them all off down to the beach for their first Alligator Ramble.

This was one of Ellie's favourite parts of the week. The chance to sit and gossip with Nettie while the kids went scrambling around the beach in search of lucky stones for their team. Happily there were enough stones with holes right through them to keep the kids engrossed and excited for quite some time.

She and her chalet-mate settled onto the pebbles and kept watch while their charges foraged happily, running up from time to time to show off their lucky stones and drop them in either the Snappers or Crackers bucket.

'No — no Charlie!' yelled Nettie. 'Don't go that way. You have to stay this side of the Buntin's flag!'

Charlie cannoned back along the beach towards them and continued his quest without heading any further along the shoreline. It was one of the main tasks she and Nettie had — to prevent them from drowning, obviously, but also to keep them away from the eroding cliff fall area further along the beach, with its overgrown concrete wartime bunkers and unstable upper paths. There were three bunkers along this stretch of coast and every time she saw them, Ellie suspected they'd slid into the sand just a bit more. Although the beach was mostly stony, there were also many patches of sand, much of it eroded from the short cliffs and swept down in drifts towards the sea. But the Buntin's area was clearly marked with flags and quite safe.

'So... what do you think?' Nettie asked her, in a low voice. 'Are we going to see that good-looking copper?'

'Oh... is *that* it? You've got a thing for uniforms?' Ellie teased.

'Well, yeah — apart from bloody Buntin's Bluecoat uniforms, obviously,' said Nettie. 'But also... he did say, *anything at all*. Even if it doesn't turn out to mean anything.'

Ellie sighed. She hated this. Hated to be judging another person just because they didn't fit the norm... but the truth was, if Nettie had suspicions, she probably *should* report them. After all, two people were dead. It didn't get more serious than that. 'I don't know,' she said, finally. 'If you think you should... do it.'

'Not just *me*,' said Nettie. 'You're coming, too.'

Ellie didn't argue. She didn't agree, either. They tried to change the subject but in the gaps between the kids crunching across the pebbles towards them, puffing, pink-faced and excited, to deposit their lucky stones, the talk inevitably circled back to Martin and this murdered ex-Blue.

'Better give 'em another five,' said Nettie, eventually, checking her watch. 'And get 'em back for the magic show.'

'HEY! SNAPPERS!' yelled Ellie, jumping to her feet. 'Come ON — we've got five minutes left to BEAT THE CRACKERS!'

There were squeals of excited determination as the children scooped pebbles up in a frenzy, seeking their hole-y grail.

'C'MON, CRACKERS!' bawled Nettie, getting to her feet and waving her arms in the air.

'Aunty Ellie...' Ellie looked down to see a small, fair-haired girl at her hip, dimpled face turned up with a concerned expression.

'What is it, sweetheart?' asked Ellie, as the girl's warm, sandy fingers snaked into hers.

'The man's making the cliff fall down,' said the girl — Chloe, according to her SNAPPERS name tag.

'What do you mean, Chloe?' asked Ellie, kneeling down

to get eye to eye. The girl turned and pointed south along the beach, to a point beyond one of the sagging concrete bunkers, where what looked like pale smoke was drifting through the air. As Ellie got up, shielding her eyes and squinting into the distance, there was a sudden rumble and a yellow cloud puffed into the air. A second later a large chunk of the cliff slid towards the beach.

'Wow — look at that!' murmured Nettie. 'CRACKERS! Come over to me NOW. Come and see this!'

Ellie was grateful that Nettie had stayed calm and teacherly. She was feeling quite unsettled herself. Even though the cliff fall was small and a good half a kilometre away from them, it was still startling to see it happen.

'SNAPPERS!' she shouted. 'Everyone to me! Come and see what's happened!'

The kids all mobbed them, agog to see the last bit of the cliff slide.

'Does anyone know what causes the cliffs around here to slide sometimes?' asked Nettie. A sea of hands went up.

'It's coastal erosion,' said a boy in the CRACKERS.

'That's right,' said Nettie. 'The sea keeps pummelling these beaches and over time it makes the cliffs unstable, so sometimes they fall down.'

'Will they fall down on *us?*' asked one worried child, huddling close to Ellie.

'No, we're fine,' said Ellie, giving her a reassuring head pat. 'As long as we stay on the Buntin's part of the beach, between the two Buntin's flags, we're quite safe. And you know — it's quite exciting, isn't it, to see a bit of coastal erosion happening right in front of our eyes!'

The subsidence had ended now, leaving just a drifting cloud of sand dust in the air.

'It's time to count the lucky stones!' called Nettie. 'And see who's won!'

It wasn't until the stones were counted, the CRACKERS were declared winners, and they were all heading back up to the holiday village, that Ellie remembered what little Chloe had said.

'The man's making the cliff fall down.' She peered back along the cliff top but couldn't see any man - or anyone at all. When they reached the Buntin's Children's Theatre and everyone was safely counted back inside, she sought out the little girl.

'Chloe,' she asked, quietly. 'What did you mean when you said the man was making the cliff fall down?'

Chloe was distracted by Uncle Bobby stepping onto the stage with a section of colourful props. 'He was hitting it with a pipe,' she said. 'And he was jumping up and down. He was silly.'

'Did you see who it was?' Ellie asked, feeling a prickling sensation across her shoulders.

Chloe shrugged. 'It was just a man.'

'Was it a Buntin's Bluecoat?'

'I don't know. It was a man,' she said and then ran to join her friends.

It was only when Ellie went back to the chalet to change her T-shirt that she began to make a connection about the identity of the jumping man. She had seen someone jumping by the cliffs before, hadn't she? Backflip Barney, working through his routines in the grassy field above the beach. Often with batons or a unicycle and sometimes a pole, which he used for balance when he rope-walked. She felt a surge of worry. What if he'd fallen down with the land-slip? What if he was lying there now? Oh god... not another death!

But as soon as she'd flung the chalet door open to see if he was around, she spotted him heading off up the path towards the pavilion. She breathed out. He wasn't dead then. She felt the relief pass quickly, though. Right now Nettie was telling the police her suspicions about Barney.

And for all she knew, Nettie was right to do that. She followed Barney at a distance and decided not to talk to him. She wouldn't be able to keep the guilt off her face.

A frog hopped across the path in front of her. She blinked and shook her head. This was such a weird day.

22

'You're good all along the north-eastern stretch of the river,' Lucas said.

'That is *just* what I was hoping you'd tell me,' said Grace, peering at the map he'd marked, and then along the river bank as it meandered in a picturesque fashion between verdant — but, crucially, not soggy — meadows.

'I'm nearly done,' said Lucas. 'I can probably finish mapping the rest before the end of the day... or just stop now if you have all you need to know about siting your lodges.'

'Oh no — I think we should have your *complete* mapping,' said Grace, quickly. Lucas caught the look Grant threw him. The project manager was no fool and hadn't missed the way her ladyship had stroked the dowser's arm. Lucas was careful not to meet his eye.

He was keen to get away, though. As much as he'd enjoyed his time with Grace last night, he didn't want to repeat it. There was something more urgent he needed to do and that was to get back to the holiday village and speak to Kate.

'I am going to need to get away soon,' he said. 'There's someone I have to see in Suffolk around lunch time.'

'Oh,' said Grace, cottoning on immediately. 'You must definitely do that. Just come back afterwards, yes? For an update..?' She winked at him, clearly agog.

'Thanks... I will,' he said, folding his annotated map away and putting it into his backpack along with the rods. He felt a tremble in both the rods and Sid, around his neck, as he did so. It made him freeze for a moment and turn abruptly to the south east.

'What's up?' asked Grace, still eyeing him closely.

'Um... something just... shifted,' he said, frowning as a knot began to tie itself somewhere in his belly.

'Oh lord — don't tell me it's another sinkhole!' groaned Grant. 'There's only so many swimming pools we can put in!'

'No,' Lucas forced a smile across his face as he shook his head. 'No... it's further off than that. I'm just picking up something remote... like an aftershock. It's a good distance away... on the coast, I think.'

'You are sooo spooky,' said Grace, tucking her arm through his. 'Can you read minds too..?

'No,' he laughed. 'Well, not unless you're thinking something *really* obvious.' The look on her face was enough for anyone to read, dowser or not.

'I'll get back to the cabin,' said Grant. He hastened away, calling back over his shoulder, 'Wash up meeting at six o'clock?'

'Yeah — that'll be great,' said Lucas. 'Sorry,' he turned to Grace and squeezed her arm. 'I really have to go.' And he really did. He hadn't been planning to leave for another hour but something in the vibrations emanating from that distant disturbance was making him very uneasy.

'Go on then — get going!' she said, shooing him away. 'Do what you need to do! Say what you need to say! Just promise me you'll come back and tell me all about it afterwards!'

'I promise,' he said, all but running to get into his leathers. Five minutes later he was on the road back to Suffolk, anxiety gnawing at his insides. He had texted Kate on the number she'd called through on last night: **I'm heading out to you now. Will call when I get there. Something's going on. Watch your step.**

Rain was beginning to fall as he shot down the A146, sending an oily sheen across the tarmac and forcing him to slow down. It wasn't a much slower journey than last night, but it seemed to take forever and then, as he passed a golf course and its thin screening of trees, Sid began to vibrate urgently against his skin. He pulled over to a gritty lay-by which led into an uneven track. He shivered, remembering a time not long ago when he'd come to grief along a similar track. He wasn't keen to travel this one as the rain pelted down harder and the clouds seemed to darken even with his thoughts.

He killed the Triumph's engine and set it on its stand, pulling off his helmet and glancing along the track. It didn't go far and there was an overgrown area of scrub and spindly trees leading off it. There was also, tucked away behind a thick clump of blossoming hawthorn, a white car. He stepped closer to it and noted the registration. The Audi was new — one of this year's plates, he was pretty sure. It was a slick, expensive, hybrid model, clearly kept in excellent condition. What the hell was it doing parked here, its wheels deep in muddy ruts? If he'd found a Land Rover or some other four-by-four he wouldn't have given it much thought, but this?

He took off his gloves and traced his fingers along the driver's side. As they met the gleaming metal door handle he felt a stab of shock.

'Oh shit, not another body,' he moaned aloud, glancing around. But there was no body inside the car, which was locked. Nothing nearby that he could see or sense. There wasn't a killer here, either, but this car was connected to death, more than one death... deaths that had occurred somewhere within a five kilometre radius, he was certain.

The next thing he was certain of was that this car was also linked to Martin Riley. The patterns screamed the connection at him. Fresh patterns. Vibrant, intense, *local* patterns. He gulped again, feeling his insides shift and tumble like the landslip he'd sensed less than an hour ago.

He got on the bike, checking his phone for a return text from Kate. There was nothing. Should he text her again? No. He was minutes away from her. It was time to find her. Right now.

———

THE WALK along the beach didn't help their mood much. It was late morning by the time they'd all got themselves together and headed for the sea. Francis had declined to join them, saying he wanted to check out a snooker tournament in the sports hall. 'It's OK,' he'd told Kate, fresh from the shower and towel-drying his hair. 'I'll be with people — not on my own, waiting to be picked off by the Beast of Buntin's. Anyway, I'm not one of the Magnificent Seven. *You're* the one I'm worried about.'

'I'll be fine,' she'd reassured him. 'I'll be with Talia, Craig and Nikki on the beach, getting some air and trying to get our heads around what happened last night. Then we've all got to speak to DS Stuart again at two. You'll have to be there as well, OK?'

'Sure,' he'd said. 'But I'm going off to hustle at the green baize first! There's this hot red-headed Bluecoat running the tournament. Come and find me when you're done on the beach… but don't cramp my style if it looks like I'm getting somewhere.'

She was glad he'd headed off for his own fun. She didn't think he'd get much of it from hanging out with *them*. Four of the seven, trying to act like it was still possible to enjoy themselves after one had upped and left and another two were dead. She still hadn't mentioned Lucas to him, not wanting to share a whole extra layer of tension when he was planning to have some lighthearted fun with a cue and a bit of flirting.

They passed a line of kids marching back up with the two Children's Aunty Bluecoats, all chatting excitedly. Kate smiled at Ellie, the one they'd spoken to yesterday, as she passed, but Ellie literally had her hands full — about two children per hand, in fact. She didn't notice.

'Remember when we all went off together like something out of the *Famous Five*, on our morning off?' Craig said, as they walked down the narrow, silty path towards a short bank of stones, which dropped steeply to the lacy white edge of the North Sea. 'When we took a picnic and explored all the old huts..?'

'I remember they stank of piss and we found a used condom in one of them,' said Nikki. 'It put me off my corned beef sandwich. And didn't someone have a panic attack in one of them? Claustrophobia or something..?'

'It was fun, though, wasn't it?' Craig persisted. 'Like the last few weeks of childhood. Before we had to grow up and get proper jobs out in the big wide world.' He sighed. 'We were like family, weren't we — us lot? The other Blues tried to get in with us, but it was always the Seven. God, do you remember how some of them used to trail us around? That guy Mickey and, who else was it? The girl with the funny leg..? And bloody Backflip Barney too... although he always had a thing for you, Kate.'

Craig was going into motormouth mode now. Kate realised it was his way of coping. She didn't want to shut him down. 'He did *not* have a thing for me,' she said, her arms folded tightly against the stiff offshore breeze that she remembered too well from that summer. It always looked warmer than it ever was. She should have worn another layer over her white cotton dress — what was she thinking? This was the east coast of England in May! Cloud was gathering in the west and she guessed it would rain before lunchtime, which would be a pain because a walk along the beach was what she'd had in mind when Lucas got here. The thought of Lucas, *here*, crashing into her world of seven years ago, made her insides turn over. She was nervous — undeniably nervous — about seeing him. But she also really *needed* to see him. On several complicated levels.

Number one on the list was getting Lucas — and Sid — to help her locate whoever had killed Julie and Martin. That was the most important thing and she felt sure he could do it. Together they'd solved two murder cases now and although it had been far from plain sailing and had cost them both a lot, there was no doubt that they were quite the team once they put their minds to it.

And after that? Assuming they *could* do it again of course... after they'd tied everything up here at Lakefield? What then? He'd said it and she'd said it. They needed to talk. About Mabel. About Zoe. About what had happened in that quarry more than sixteen years ago. A shiver ran through her and she had to admit to herself that she was afraid of what he might tell her. There was no question he was hiding something about that day. Every shred of her copper's instinct told her this. She'd been ducking away from it for months now because... because what? She was attracted to him? She owed him her life? Well... they were pretty even on that score at least.

'Kate! Focus!' Craig was snapping his fingers in front of her face, as they ambled down the pebbles towards the gunmetal grey curls of water lapping along the shoreline. 'Little Backflip Barney. Remember what he used to look like?'

She shrugged. 'He was just a kid. We all were. None of us looked as cool as we liked to think we did. I mean, god, the tracksuits we had to wear! All that nylon and towelling!'

'Yeah, but *we* didn't have a choice,' said Craig. 'The state of Barney, though, in his orange nylon zip-up hoodie and his old man baggy joggers, and the hair.... oh god, the hair... he looked like something out of the Jim Henson creature workshop.'

'Smelt like it too,' said Talia. 'God — he could make your eyes water at twenty paces!'

'You see, this was what I *didn't* want to remember,' said Kate, suddenly stopping. 'We were such shits back then. So judgy.'

'Oh come on... we were only mucking about,' said Talia, sounding defensive. 'And we had to be super nice to everyone, twelve hours a day. We just needed to let off steam. We didn't mean anything by it.'

'Yeah, sure,' said Kate. She felt the mood get colder than the water. Everyone was tense and she wasn't helping.

'Fuck it, I'm going back to my chalet,' said Talia. 'It's too bloody cold and that looks like rain,' she waved towards the gathering cloud in the west.

'We've got to stay together!' said Nikki.

'Fine — come with me,' said Talia, and they both marched off. Craig glanced uneasily between them and Kate, torn.

'You go too,' said Kate. 'I need to check in with the Suffolk police.'

'You're not meant to be alone!' said Craig.

'I won't be — I've got Francis!' she said. 'I'll go and find him. I'm crap company right now... so go on with the girls. Persuade them to go to the bar; you might as well try to have a nice time, eh? Don't get pissed though — you've got to talk to the police again at two, remember?'

He nodded and hared off after them, and she breathed a sigh of relief. Managing these old friends while she was trying to focus on what was happening here was a pain she didn't need. She wondered if she should text Lucas and get him here sooner. She checked her phone but couldn't get a signal down here by the water, the short cliffs probably blocking the patchy local cell coverage.

'Kate.'

She jumped at the closeness of the voice. She spun around, for a moment thinking it was Lucas. Backflip Barney stood close by, his hands pushed into the pockets of a leather jacket and the breeze tugging a lock of dark, twisted hair across his face.

'Barney!' She glanced up the beach, wondering where the others were now and if they'd seen Barney. She hoped not. 'How are you? You look great!'

He stared at her with the same old intensity. There had always been something *other* about him. And even though he now dressed better — and smelled better — that quality was still there.

'You look great too,' he said. 'I wanted to... wanted to say something to you...'

'Um,' she said. 'OK... but can we walk and talk? I need to meet my brother in the pool hall.'

'OK,' he said, falling into step beside her.

For a while he didn't say anything, and she got the uncomfortable suspicion he might have heard Talia talking about him on the beach a few minutes earlier. Eventually, she turned to look at him, eyebrows raised. 'What did you want to say to me?'

He stopped and looked at his feet. 'What you did, seven years ago,' he said. 'I haven't forgotten it.'

'Look...' she said. 'The others... they didn't mean the things they said. They were just being stupid, mucking around.'

'They meant every word of it,' said Barney. 'That day... it changed everything for me.' He stared at her again, a flush rising up his smooth skin.

Kate's phone suddenly went off. It was Francis. She really needed to tell him about Lucas. Fill him in properly.

'Barney... can we maybe chat a bit later on? At the bar, maybe? After your act tonight..?'

He shrugged and nodded. 'Sure. It can wait. I need to get to the kid's theatre now, anyway.'

'Thank you,' she said, patting his arm. 'Sorry... I've really got to go.' She scrambled up the path, picking up Francis's call just too late and trying to return it, suddenly awash with guilt. Her brother was meant to be having a relaxing weekend away and instead he was dealing with his sister stumbling across yet another murder victim.

'Sorry, Fran, I'm on my way,' she said. 'Are you still in the pool tournament?'

'No, I'm playing pinball in the Buntin's Bear Arcade,' he said. The pings and chimes in the background bore this out. 'Just checking nobody else is dead yet,' he added, chirpily.

'No, all still alive when I last saw them,' she said. 'I'm on my way over to you. Stay put.'

She stalked quickly across the grassy stretch, skirting the molehills as rain began to spatter across her face. Glancing back, she could no longer see Barney. She should try to make time for him later; he obviously needed to get something off his chest.

She approached the hedge that bordered the campsite, trying to marshal some kind of plan... see Lucas... share what she knew... see if he could dowse some answers... take their findings to the Suffolk police and help them locate the killer... then maybe have time for a swift drink at the bar and take in the evening's cabaret with Barney before getting around to that proper conversation she was now determined to have with Lucas.

It sounded like a plan of sorts. She'd rather stay here and see it through than drive home right after the second police interview at two. She wasn't surprised Bill had bailed; he was probably regretting getting drunk and taking Nikki to bed. Nikki was great, but very needy around Bill.

A dark figure stepped out of the hedge and grabbed her.

23

I t was a mistake. And he paid for it. One moment he was hunched under the bushes and the next he was flat on his back with her knee on his throat.

'Kate... for fuck's sake!' he gurgled.

Her hard expression melted into eye rolling exasperation and she took her knee off and released his airway. *Note to self, Lucas — Kate Sparrow is a black belt in martial arts and not afraid to use it.*

'What the *hell*, Lucas? Why would you do that?!' She crouched down next to him, looking slightly guilty. 'Have I hurt you?' she said. 'Sorry — but if a guy comes at me and tries to grab me, he gets what's coming to him.'

He got into a sitting position, rubbing his shoulder which had hit the ground the hardest as she'd swept the feet out from under him with some kind of roundhouse kick. 'I wasn't trying to grab you,' he croaked. 'I just wanted to tap your arm and get your attention without anyone else noticing.'

She shrugged. 'Well, you got it.' She glanced around. 'And there's nobody else here.' She looked very un-Kate in her strappy white summer dress and sandals. It was quite discombobulating. He'd seen her entirely unclothed once before, but that really hadn't been the time to marvel at the pearly glow her skin seemed to give off; the warm spicy scent that emanated from it. And now wasn't the time either, he reminded himself.

'It's someone close to you,' he said. 'Whoever's behind the deaths of your two friends. They're close. That's why I wanted to get you on your own if I could.'

Kate helped him up. 'Come on,' she said, and led him deeper into the thicket of hawthorn and crab apple trees which screened them from anyone wandering past on their way to or from the beach. A few steps in, she turned and looked at him. 'Do you know where they are now?'

'I'm not sure of exactly where... or exactly who,' he said. 'But do you know someone who drives a white Audi A6 hybrid?'

'Oh shit — that sounds like Bill's car,' said Kate. 'Why? Where have you seen it?'

'It's parked about a mile down the road, hidden behind some trees on the back road to a golf course.'

Kate blinked, trying to take in the meaning of this. 'How... how did you connect with it? I mean... you've never met Bill, have you?'

'I don't know,' he said. 'I might have seen him in the bar last night. Was he the gay guy or the one up on stage with you?'

'Up on stage,' said Kate, looking bleak. 'Shit... are you saying you think it's Bill?'

'I'm not saying that. I don't know.' Lucas hesitated. His readings were all over the place and he was jangly and anxious. In truth, just being within a few feet of Kate was enough to make him jangly and anxious, which didn't help at all. He took Sid out of his shirt and allowed the pendulum to drop and hang still between his thumb and forefinger. He tried to bring on the dowsing state, but it wasn't easy to summon it with Kate so close by and — wait. He realised, belatedly, that Sid wasn't refusing to co-operate because Kate was here. He was refusing to let Lucas detach from her. Of *course*. On this occasion Kate *was* one of the connections... she was a link.

He reached out his left hand and beckoned to her. She paused, staring at him warily, but then blinked and shook her head, seeming to get it, before reaching out to lace her fingers into his. Instantly he felt a charge travel through him. At any other time, this would be the last thing he needed to find the dowsing state but today it quickly pulled every curl and wave and zig-zag of frequency into a cohesive tapestry of information. Sid began to spin and then to swing in a very specific direction. Lucas moved, still holding Kate's hand, taking them both along a skinny, winding path through the line of stunted coastal trees.

Kate said nothing, but he could sense her mounting dread. She was battling with the suspicion that one of her own group was a murderer... and he could not tell her she was wrong. He led her on, in silence, while the leaves whispered in the breeze. Beyond the tang of the leaves and Kate's own distinct scent, he could smell the sea salt in the air and the mineral perfume of freshly moved sandy earth. 'Was there a landslip here earlier?' he said, as they moved quietly on, past the perimeter and the far end of a series of chalet blocks.

'Um... yes,' she said. 'I heard some kids talking about it as they passed us. Not a big one. It's not uncommon around here. The beach is safe — there are flags and notices to stay away from certain parts. Why? Is that relevant?'

'Don't know. I just sensed a landslip around here earlier today. It's why I decided to come and find you earlier than planned. Shit... mind out.'

He had to step over three or four frogs, scrambling and leaping across the damp path.

'What the hell?' murmured Kate.

Hell. Yes. That was very much what he was picking up now. They were getting closer. He led her out of the trees towards the pebble-dashed end wall of a row of chalets. It was quiet. A family was leaving one of them and heading away towards the pool complex, kids already in swimsuits. He could sense that a couple of the other chalets were occupied, one further along the block of six and another in the block that faced it across the stretch of grass and some neatly planted cherry blossom trees. The chalet Sid wanted was the closest.

'Oh god,' murmured Kate. 'That's Bill's chalet. We thought he'd driven home. Did he just stage that? Did he park up and come back and-?'

'Kate,' said Lucas. 'Can you get me in there?'

Kate pulled a skinny piece of metal from the pocket of her dress. 'I used this on Julie's chalet door last night. Didn't think I'd need it again... but obviously I'm more dowsey than I realise. Seems I brought it with me on more than a whim.'

He turned and looked at her. 'Open the door... and then let me go in, OK?'

'No way,' said Kate. 'I'm not getting you into another crime scene!'

'If that's what you think this is,' he said, 'you shouldn't go in either. We should both go and find the Suffolk coppers and bring them here.'

Kate stood, staring at the patio door, flicking the metal in her fingers. 'You're right,' she said. 'But... I want to know first. We can close the door again, and then go and get them if there's anything suspicious in there.' She stared through the window. 'I mean... look... there's nothing to see. It's probably fine. He probably—'

'You're burbling,' Lucas cut in. 'Open it or don't. Make a decision.'

Kate bit her lips together and glanced left and right, and then worked the skinny pin of metal into the lock and jiggled it until there was a click. She slid the door along and stood for a moment, looking into the sitting-dining room beyond. Lucas stepped up behind her. 'Seriously,' he said. 'Don't go in. Go and get your Suffolk coppers. Do it now.'

Kate gave a short exhalation as something landed on her open-toed sandals. 'Jesus — look at that!' The frog had leapt away into the grass a moment later. There were three more making an ungainly bid for freedom across the wood-effect flooring.

'Kate!' He reached for her, but she'd already gone in. 'Kate...' Dammit. She was right. He had no business entering another crime scene. But he was already getting a vivid sense of what she was about to encounter, and he couldn't let her see that alone. *Shit.* He stepped over the threshold, inhaling a mildewy scent mixed with an acrid, urine-like odour. He caught up with her just as she nudged the bathroom door open with her foot.

Another frog leapt past her and he heard the choking noise and the slap of her hands meeting her mouth. A second later he was inside the bathroom with her, taking in the full picture.

A black man, wearing only red boxer shorts, lay dead in the bath. His face was crumpled against the wall of enamel beneath the taps and the overflow and his feet were propped over the end of the tub. There was a small red wound in the middle of his forehead and a sticky smear of blood and matter on the area of tub behind his skull. Also sharing the bath with him were perhaps thirty frogs — most of them alive but some clearly dead. Especially the ones stuffed into the dead man's mouth, their legs splaying out across his chin. The one filmy eye visible was open as if in shock at such an invasion. It was easy to guess that the source of the mildewy scent was the amphibians, but the more acrid smell was coming from the man's feet.

Lucas narrowed his eyes, trying to work out what he was seeing. 'What's that between his toes?' he whispered, as if he might disturb the slumber of the corpse.

Kate was still holding her mouth, her eyes blinking back tears. She stepped closer and stared at her late friend's feet. 'It's... glue,' she whispered. 'Someone put glue between his toes. What the holy *fuck*?'

'Someone webbed his feet,' said Lucas. 'Like frogs' feet.'

'And someone filled Julie up with lard,' said Kate. 'And made Martin write an apology on a sanitary towel.'

'Um... there's that too,' said Lucas, pointing to a child's blue rubber flipper resting on the bathroom window sill. On it, the words "I'M SORRY" were jaggedly scrawled in red marker pen.

He turned and scrutinised her pale face. 'There's got to be some serious backstory to this,' he said. 'Kate... what the hell did you all *do* seven years ago?'

24

'*Say sorry.*'

'*What? Why? I mean... what for?*'

Once again — no memory. It was staggering and it made the fury rise up another notch. Justified all the effort, the expense, the planning.

'*You don't even remember me, do you? Much less her.*'

'*Look... can we talk about this? Please. Let's just sit down and talk.*'

'*Wouldn't that have been nice? It's a bit too late now, though.*'

There was panic building; darting eyes; wild thoughts of escape. It was laughable. Pitiful. If you had any pity left in you.

'*Look... whatever it was I did, I am sorry.*'

'*Good. Write it down.*'

'*On that?*'

'*Yes. On that.*'

Afterwards there was more confusion... and once again a total lack of recognition.

'*Take your clothes off.*'

'*What?!*'

'*You heard me. Take them off.*'

'Look... you don't want to do this!'

'You have no idea what I want or don't want. Take them off. And then put this on.'

The utter bafflement was entertaining to watch. The yellow dress hung between them, crumpled and snagged. Even in the midst of great fear, there was disdain on her face.

'Is it not fashionable enough for you? Don't you like it?'

'No — no, it's... nice.'

'You didn't think so before. I think you said... "It looks like a half-chewed lemon bonbon". Put it on. Let's see how it looks on you. Give me a twirl.'

The dress was put on. The twirl was shakily given.

'Don't forget to tie up the bow around the neck.'

'I have... it's tied.'

'I don't think so. I don't think it's tied tight enough...'

25

Kate pulled the sliding glass door closed behind her, relocked it with her pick, and stared at Lucas, shaking her head. 'You can't be here,' she said. 'I'm calling it in. You have to go.'

'No way,' he said. 'I'm not leaving you on your own. Whoever did that is still around. Still on this site. And you could be next on the list.'

'Look, it's broad daylight. I'll be fine.' She gulped. She did not feel fine. She'd seen some nasty crime scenes but none of them had been so personal to her. Within twenty-four hours she had found the bodies of two of her old friends in the most ugly, bizarre dioramas of death. 'Honestly, Lucas, I *cannot* drop you into this — not again. I'm just going to tell them I was worrying about whether Bill had really gone, and I broke in to check. Which is the truth. There's no reason to involve you. It'll only get complicated.'

'Look, as soon as you report in you're going to be bogged down in procedure for hours,' he said. 'And there may not *be* hours before... before this killer kills again. Or gets away.'

She groaned into her palms, caught between the need to

race away with him and hunt down their killer... and the need to report in and get the Suffolk coppers on the scene. She had always respected procedure. Always clung to its secure framework as much as possible... well, until she'd met Lucas Henry last year.

She reached a decision. She walked away from the chalet and waited until they were on the main path through the site to call the number for DS Stuart. She prayed it would go to voicemail and her prayers were answered when it did. 'Hi, DS Stuart..? It's Kate Sparrow. Um... I don't know if you're aware of this but one of our number — Bill Lassiter — left the site last night. At least... it seems like he did. We checked with reception this morning and his car's gone, but I'm worried because we haven't raised him since. He hasn't answered his phone or his texts. Could one of your guys get into his chalet? It's number 158. Just to... put our minds at rest that he really has gone..? I knocked and tried the door and there's no reply, but even so... if your guys could check and let us know I'd be grateful. Thanks. I'll see you at two.'

'Well, that'll explain your prints all over the door handle,' said Lucas as Kate ended the call. 'Just hope we didn't leave any traces inside.'

She squeezed her eyes shut for a moment and shook her head. 'Everyone leaves a trace... but we might get away with it. Especially if we find this bastard. So, let's get on it. Where do we go now? What's Sid telling you?'

Lucas stood, suspending the blue glass stopper and focusing. Kate tried to piggyback on that focus, without much success. She was fizzing with adrenaline and anger and fear; her heart pounding, ready for fight or flight. Should she be phoning all the others? Warning them? But that would mean she would have to tell them the truth about Bill... and she'd just set up a lie with the Suffolk police which her friends would surely blow open later on when they were interviewed. She knew they were sticking together, so they ought to be safe, surely? And she was in no hurry to give them yet more horrifying news.

It also hadn't escaped her attention that in DS Stuart's position, she might very well start to view the woman who'd discovered both crime scenes as a prime suspect. It wasn't unknown for a killer to present themselves as an innocent, stumbling upon the body. *Shit.* They needed to get this bastard fast, before she got hopelessly entangled in someone else's case.

'We need to go,' said Lucas, raising a pale face to hers, green eyes wide. 'We need to go NOW!' He began to run towards the northern end of the site, and she chased close behind, heading past the playground and the children's theatre and on towards another block of chalets.

Oh god, whimpered a voice in her head. Because she recognised the route they were travelling from last night — the path, the block, the numbers — Lucas skidded to a halt outside Talia's chalet. Talia shouldn't be here! She should be with the others, not alone. But everything about Lucas's face told her that Talia was in there.

'TALIA!' she screamed, wrenching at the door. It didn't move, but she thought she saw movement behind the net curtain. 'TALIA!' she screamed again, fumbling her metal pick into the lock and working it open with trembling hands. It seemed to take forever but at last she heard the click, over the pulsing of her own blood through her ears, and felt Lucas grab the handle and pull it open.

A gust blew out the curtain and she fought past it and ran into the room. At first, she saw nothing and for a second she tried to believe that Lucas had been wrong, and Talia was safe with Craig and Nikki. But then she saw a foot extending from behind the sofa.

Her friend lay on her back, eyes closed. She was wearing an ugly yellow dress; some kind of nylon monstrosity with white daisy flowers stitched down the front. The words 'I'm sorry" were scrawled across it in red felt tip, and the 1980s bow at the neckline was pulled tightly around her throat, cutting viciously into the flesh. Kate abandoned her fears of crime scene contamination and ripped at the bow, sobbing her friend's name and pressing for a pulse at the side of her bruised neck.

'She's alive,' said Lucas, his hand on her shoulder but his eyes fixed on the back end of the chalet. 'Call an ambulance. I have to go after whoever did this. We've just scared the killer away through the back window.'

'Talia!' called Kate, patting her friend's cool cheek. 'C'mon, baby, wake up!'

Lucas left at speed and she didn't try to stop him as she fumbled for her phone and dialled 999. 'Ambulance! Right away! My friend's been strangled... she's only barely breathing. Please hurry.'

She sounded, in her own head, like so many taped distress calls she'd heard over the years — on the edge of screaming panic. She *had* to get a grip. She put the phone down, on speaker, and continued to give her location while she shifted Talia's limp body into the recovery position, keeping a palm to her mouth to feel for warm breath. There was some. Talia *was* breathing... but how much damage had been done to her? How long had her brain been starved of oxygen?

She sat back on her heels, holding on to Talia's hand and trying to work out what to do. Her professional brain seemed to have deserted her. The police would be here any minute, because the emergency dispatcher would have automatically alerted them, and some were already on site. She had promised she would stay here until the ambulance arrived but, as Lucas had said, the moment the police got here, she would be grounded. They would check in on Bill and find him dead and she would have to decide whether to confess that she'd been into that crime scene too and not reported it... and all the convoluted reasons why. She would have to involve Lucas *again* and it was going to take hours and hours, if not days. She might even get arrested.

And meanwhile, Craig and Nikki were at terrible risk. She should call them right now. Warn them. Except she didn't have their mobile numbers. They just hadn't stayed in touch that way. They were friends on social media and used that to message each other. She was just about to resort to Facebook Messenger when she heard the static beep of a two-way radio and was brought sharply into focus. What was she going to do now? In the distance, she could hear the muted whoop of an ambulance siren.

'Police!' called out a young female voice — not DS Stuart's, Kate was certain.

'In here!' she called, and two uniformed officers arrived at the open patio door. They entered at speed, kneeling next to Talia and firing questions at her.

'Her name's Talia,' Kate said. 'She's still breathing. Look...' She put her hand over her mouth. 'I'm going to be sick. I have to...'

She got up and stumbled to the bathroom, pulling the door shut behind her while the two officers dealt with the casualty. The paramedics were probably just seconds away, now, and the PCs would guard Talia until they arrived.

Kate made retching noises and ran the taps. Then she eyed the high, narrow letterbox of a window already wide open above the bath and took a deep breath. This was one of those times when being small and lean was going to be a blessing. Thirty seconds later, leaving the taps running full blast to cover the noise, she wriggled across the window sill, over the frame, and squeezed through the tight gap, dropping into the cover of some rhododendron shrubs.

And now what? Where the hell had Lucas gone? She didn't have the benefit of instant dowser satnav, so she had to find Craig and Nikki right now. She crept away through the rhododendrons, urgently thumbing a message to them both. **Where are you? Really URGENT! Tell me where you are!**

She edged deeper into the boundary shrubs and worked her way down the site, in the direction of the pavilion, guessing they might be there or maybe back in the restaurant.

A minute passed with no reply and then, from Craig, a recorded audio message popped up: 'We're doing the *Famous Five* thing again!' he said, puffing slightly as if he was walking fast. 'Talia's meeting us down at the bunkers when she's got her jeans on. Didn't you get her text? She's bringing sandwiches and ginger beer from the restaurant. For old time's sake before we go home. Get yourself down here, Sparrow!'

Kate tried to call via Messenger but it didn't connect. So she recorded an audio message herself, panting her reply as she ran. 'Craig! DON'T go to the bunkers! DON'T! I don't think that text was from Talia. She's been attacked. She's going to be OK but whoever got her is coming after you too. STAY on the site and DON'T go anywhere near the bunkers! CALL ME as soon as you get this!' She reeled off her mobile number, cursing herself for not taking the trouble to share it with them as soon as they'd all met up again.

She continued her race along the perimeter, dodging around trees and shrubs but staying in their shadows as much as she could. She could hear more sirens getting closer and pictured Suffolk's finest now on full search and arrest mode, combing the site. Her behaviour now would seem at best erratic and at worst, downright guilty. She called Lucas but it went straight to voicemail. She left another short-of-breath message. 'I'm out. The police are with Talia, but I got out of the bathroom window. Where are you? I'm heading for the bunkers on the beach. I think that's where the killer's sent Craig and Nikki. Please get there! Get there as soon as you can!'

And then, as if to provide the soundtrack to her escalating fear, there was a shrill, hooting alarm. Across the holiday village, all the outdoor speakers were relaying a strident repetitive hoot and the message: 'THIS IS NOT A DRILL. THIS IS AN EMERGENCY. ALL HOLIDAY-MAKERS MUST GO IMMEDIATELY TO THE SPORTS FIELD MUSTER POINT.'

The message went on, again and again, along with the chilling cold war–style hooting, and a cacophony of panic began to build in the air.

Kate had been mentally flailing around as she sprinted for the beach, clutching at straws, telling herself that no murderer could attack in broad daylight on a busy beach. But that beach would be emptying now. The Buntin's holiday camp had its own speaker system on high poles set into stony stanchions; six of them across its designated beach area. As she reached the path, she was met by several families worriedly clambering up past her, clutching buckets and spades and inflatables. She did not see her friends among them.

The holidaymakers glanced at her but didn't try to

dissuade her from racing along the path to the shore. 'It's all a bloody false alarm, I'll bet,' muttered one dad.

And he was probably right, she realised. It was false alarm for everyone on this site today, except the ex-Blue-coats who should never have come back.

26

Backflip Barney was cycling around the stage in the children's theatre at top speed, on a bicycle no bigger than a shoebox, to the shouts, cheers and gurgling laughter of forty or so children.

Ellie wanted to cry. What a hellish week this had been, and it didn't look like it was going to improve any time soon. Nettie had run back into the theatre just in time to stand at the back with her and nod meaningfully. 'They're on their way,' she said, close into Ellie's ear. 'They think it could be him. They asked me if he'd been here seven years ago, when Martin and that other dead Bluecoat were here, and I said yes. I've always thought he was dodgy.'

Ellie closed her eyes. She didn't blame Nettie. This was all so scary and yes — Barney *was* a little suspicious, the way he acted. He was the classic awkward loner... all the more so because he was a good-looking young man, and should have been cocky and lapping up all the female attention. He didn't do that, though. He kind of lurked, always slightly ill-at-ease unless he was on stage with all his glitter and props. The lights in his caravan were on at all hours. He didn't really mix with anyone. She'd even heard that he had a horribly domineering mother managing his career and that *really* screamed 'Norman Bates', didn't it? So yes... he *was* suspicious, if you thought that kind of behaviour meant dodgy.

So why, as he finished up his children's show with uproarious applause from the delighted under-elevens, was she getting the instinct to warn him — to tell him to gather up his props and flee?

She heard the crackle of a two-way radio and saw Phil, the deputy chief of security, loitering in the lobby with two uniformed officers. They were being discreet, obviously. They weren't about to rugby tackle Backflip Barney to the ground in front of a bunch of kids. She turned back and stared wretchedly at Barney, and at that very moment he looked at her and clocked her expression. She gave the tiniest shake of her head. He couldn't have seen the police but maybe he was picking up that radio static. He finished his final bow and, sweeping up his miniature bike and a case of other props, he retreated at speed to the small dressing room just off the wings on stage right.

The second he'd disappeared, Phil and the officers walked swiftly through the audience, across the small, low stage and into the wings in pursuit.

'CRACKERS!' yelled Nettie, waving her hands. Half the audience turned away from goggling at the policemen and shouted, 'CRACK! CRACK! CRACK"

'SNAPPERS!' yelled Ellie, grinning past her dismay for Barney. Her team yelled back, 'SNAP! SNAP! SNAP!'

'Time for BINGO!' yelled Nettie. 'Aunty Ellie's just getting out the bingo cards and away we'll go! Grab a pen, everyone!'

As the kids scrambled to get their pens, Ellie ran

through to the backstage area to get the cards but also to find out what was going on. As soon as she arrived in the dim light of the wings she could hear the two-way radios going again.

'He's escaped out the back,' one of the coppers was saying. 'Out through a window. We're in pursuit but we need eyes across the whole site. OK — we're looking for dark, curly hair and light stubble, six foot two, IC1, wearing a silver shirt and black and silver striped trousers when last seen. Approach with caution.'

Then alarms started sounding all over the site and everything spiralled into a fresh level of hell.

———

BARNEY COULD RUN FAST. He could unicycle even faster, especially as the path down towards the caravan and the coast was on a slope. It had been worth slinging the unicycle through the window first, even though it had slowed him down by three or four seconds. Normally, a fast dash through a holiday village on a single wheel and saddle would have caught a lot of attention but right now the holidaymakers were tearing out of the pavilion, the pool and the chalets and making for the big sports field behind the adventure playground — the muster point for fire alarms and bomb scares. With the blaring of the siren and the mild panic of managing their kids, most of them barely blinked as he slipped between them all, travelling against the flow, angling the wheel and the saddle with the fluid expertise of someone born to it.

He'd had dealings with the police before — what traveller hadn't? They didn't tend to go well. He was an odd person and your average copper didn't take to odd. He knew it was only a matter of time before he found himself getting helped into the back of a patrol car, and there was just one thing he needed to do before that happened.

Because his chance might never come again. He'd waited seven years for this. Seven years of thinking about it. Seven years of wondering how things might have been if he hadn't ever met that particular bunch of Bluecoats. If he hadn't met Kate Sparrow.

It had taken a lot of mental preparation for him to finally express himself. This time tomorrow, his last chance to do that would be gone. So, evading capture for these last crucial hours instead of tamely handing himself over... it was worth the risk.

He was almost at the caravan before he realised they might be waiting for him there and so he flipped left across the grassy lane between two chalet blocks, narrowly missing a mother and toddler. He angled right again, navigating the familiar alleyways, like a live *Pac-Man* arcade game. The mother had shrieked but he hadn't slowed down. He was going to finish what he had started. Whatever it took.

———

'LUCAS?' The young man stepping out in front of him was undoubtedly Francis. He'd been six or seven the last time Lucas had seen him, but there was no mistaking the Scandinavian colouring and the way he wrinkled his brow, just like Kate.

'Need your help, Francis,' puffed Lucas, grabbing hold of the lad's arm and dragging him along against the tide of worried holidaymakers. 'Kate's back in the chalet with her friend Talia. Someone attacked Talia. They killed Bill too.

The police are here but I haven't got time to tangle with them. I'm chasing down the killer.'

Francis ran alongside him, face creasing with shock and fear. 'What the *fuck?!* Is Kate all right?'

'She's fine... I think,' said Lucas, because, as ever, he was never entirely sure of himself when it came to Kate. 'But I'm getting the feeling I need to be on the coast. I think that's where this killer is heading. And I don't think he's finished yet. Have you seen Kate's other friends..? What are their names..?'

'Nikki and Craig,' said Francis. 'Shit... I haven't. I don't know where they are, but they were supposed to be sticking together.'

Lucas felt a ping in his jeans pocket and hooked out his mobile. A voice message had come through from Kate. He pressed it close to his ear as he ran on alongside Francis, his knee singing out painfully every other step.

'I'm out,' came Kate's message, breathy and urgent. 'The police are with Talia, but I got out of the bathroom window. Where are you? I'm heading for the bunkers on the beach. I think that's where the killer's sent Craig and Nikki. Please get there! Get there as soon as you can!'

He snapped the call off and slowed down a fraction, grabbing Francis by the arm. 'That was Kate — I — WAIT! Sshhh!'

The path was suddenly clear; the holiday crowd now funnelled away to the sports field by the ongoing alarm and the eerie, repetitive recorded voice. Lucas stopped and held Sid in his fist, allowing the pendulum to drop and spin and swing. 'He's close,' he said. 'He's around here and he's moving fast. Stick with me.'

They cut across one of the smaller toddlers' play parks and down a narrow alley between two chalet blocks. 'Left,' said Lucas, feeling the pull and the buzz of Sid, and the patterns of something ugly and violent pouring along like a malevolent river between the blocks. 'Stay behind me. Right behind me.'

Francis did, but he murmured: 'I'm a brown-belt in karate and taekwondo. You don't have to protect me.'

'If I don't, your *black*-belt sister will kick me into next week,' Lucas muttered back.

There was a flash of silver and then another blur of blue. A guy in a blue jacket suddenly shot into the alley turn ahead of them, and there was a crash and a cry and the silver man sprawled into view.

'THAT'S HIM!' hissed Lucas.

'Which one?' hissed back Francis, picking up speed behind him.

'Fuck it — I don't *know* — they're both moving too fast!' Lucas felt his abilities spin uselessly as the two figures twenty metres ahead disentangled themselves and departed in different directions. 'It might be *both*... I'm going for the guy in blue,' he puffed. 'Can you follow the guy in silver?'

'Yes,' Francis puffed back.

'Don't tackle him — just keep tabs. Call for help if you see any police,' Lucas threw back over his shoulder as he pounded on after the guy in blue. Francis grunted his reply and was gone from view immediately. Lucas consulted the fast-flowing patterns and chased on, only seventy per cent certain he had the right quarry. If he'd got this wrong and Francis ended up tackling a cold blooded killer... but he pushed that thought away. He had to trust his instincts on this. That guy in blue was heading for the shore and so was Kate, somewhere off to the east of the site. She might already be on the beach, but his target was cutting across the farmland above the low cliffs. Both were heading for those derelict bunkers.

He needed to run faster.

'POLICE! STOP!'

Lucas spun around and groaned as two uniforms came running at him from a side alley. *Shit! Not again!* He didn't have time for this.

'I know where the killer is heading!' he yelled, in the vain hope that they might believe him and just run along with him.

'STAND STILL! PUT YOUR HANDS IN THE AIR!' yelled one.

The other one produced a whine. A high-pitched whine that he remembered far too well. If he wasn't mistaken, he was just about to get his third encounter with a police issue Taser. He would be unable to move or speak for at least five minutes.

Fuck that! Lucas did a U-turn and ran back the way he'd come.

———

THE FIRST THING you learned as a circus performer was how to fall over. Do it wrong and you were apt to break bones or knock yourself out. Barney had been falling as expertly as Charlie Chaplin since he was six.

So when he collided, out of the blue, with some guy whom he just had time to vaguely recognise in their split-second crash, he was able to roll and get back on his feet before the unicycle had even hit the ground. He grabbed the toppling saddle and was up on it and away again before the other guy had even stood up. He made a calculated U-turn, realising that his best bet now was to get back to the top of the site and along the edge of the car park, and out through the perimeter before he could be caught. He could tell them later that he'd simply gone off on a jaunt along the coast road, keeping out of the way while the Buntin's staff handled whatever emergency they were dealing with. It had nothing to do with him. Yes, he had abandoned his props in the children's theatre. It was no big deal. He had another gig in the ballroom that evening, and it was much easier to carry his kit straight over there than lug it all the way down the site to his caravan and then lug it back again. And the silver stage outfit? Well, he was an eccentric. He didn't always notice what he was wearing.

Of course, he knew he was a suspect for Julie's murder... but *they* didn't know that he knew that. He sped on through the narrow alleys and up to the top end of the site, dodging around a corner twice in succession when he spotted uniformed officers moving quickly along, heads sweeping left and right, two-way radios in hand. He could give himself up, of course, abandon his plans. It was inevitable they'd get him in the end. But he just couldn't bear to. Not yet. Not when he was *this* close. He had to show her. He had to.

He cycled quickly along the top of the car park where the staff were asked to park, their cars inconveniently far from the pavilion, and found the gap in the hedging he'd noticed before. He shot through it and out onto the road, turning a sharp left and pedalling on at speed. He would do a wide arc and get to the coast further down.

It was working well. He felt in control in a way which would be baffling to the average person watching him speed past, balancing on a single wheel, post and saddle, arms slightly raised for balance.

Then he was hit from the side by a mustard yellow Ford Capri.

27

K ate tore along the empty beach, sending pebbles skittering left and right as her flat-soled sandals pounded into the shingle. She felt her phone vibrate and grabbed it from her pocket to see the number she recognised as DS Stuart's. She didn't answer. She would call back the second she found Craig and Nikki, but until then she needed to focus; she couldn't be worrying about a battalion of suspicious East Anglian bobbies on her heels.

AND WHERE WAS LUCAS? He was the backup she really needed. Had he heard her message? Had he already dowsed his way ahead of her and found her friends... safe and well... or dead? The beach had never, ever seemed so long. She could now see the first bunker, tipping slightly into the sand and pebbles, the endless eroding pummelling of the sea slowly taking away its foundations. Above it hung the low-level cliff and above that, folds of brooding grey cloud. She yelled her friends' names as she pelted towards the bunker but heard nothing back but the sea, the gulls and her own heavy breathing and shingle scattering.

AT LAST SHE reached the slanting structure and threw herself inside it, to be hit in the face by the sharp stink of stale urine. The chamber was barely big enough to accommodate six people, standing, and it was dark, very dark. Just a shallow slit of light fanned in through the letterbox opening where the World War Two weaponry would once have been positioned, many decades past. She flipped her phone torch on and threw light around the walls, her belly clenching at the prospect of finding a corpse propped up in the corner. There was no corpse, but something glinted on the floor. Something that looked like a wine goblet. She crouched down, breathing hard, and found a large hourglass. It was new — shiny — and the last few grains inside it were still falling. She estimated that it had to have been put in place sometime within the last ten minutes. She cursed herself for having no latex gloves or plastic that she could pick it up with. It would have to stay put. She flashed the torch around the walls again, highlighting a fresco of graffiti. Between the old daubings of genitalia and obscenities she saw a gleaming red rendering of two words:

SAY SORRY

GOOSEBUMPS WASHED over her as she recalled the note from Martin on the sanitary towel, from Julie on the lard packet, from Bill on the flipper and, most recently, from Talia on the yellow dress she'd been forced into. She approached the

words and put out a finger, dreading what it would meet.
But before she could contaminate the evidence, her nose
told her this was not blood — it was some kind of acrylic
paint. She recognised the smell from Lucas's art studio back
at his bungalow in Wiltshire. *Lucas.* Where the hell was he?

SHE DUCKED out of the bunker and glanced left and right.
She could see nobody on the beach or up along the grassy
edge of the low crumbling cliffs. She sprinted on towards
the next bunker, just visible beside a recent cliff fall further
down the beach. As she ran her mind buzzed with confusion. *Who* was demanding apologies? And *why?* Like Lucas
had said, what the hell had they done?

THE NEXT BUNKER was more upright, but half buried in the
silty sand that regularly washed down from the stones of the
cliff, along with heavy rain or the ingress of high tides. She
ran in, steeling herself against the worst, phone torch
already lit and flailing around the concrete walls. Pebbles
crunched and something like a tin tray, probably an abandoned barbecue, flexed with a metallic twang beneath her
foot. No bodies, but another display of fresh graffiti across
the older scrawlings. Red words, daubed bigger and more
violently around all of the walls.

SAY SORRY.
  Say sorry.
  Are you sorry?
  Too late!
  Too late!

Too late!

'FUCK!' she screamed, spinning around and yelling at the walls as if they could answer her. 'WHY?! WHY SHOULD WE BE SORRY?'

HER ANSWER CAME with a sudden hiss and rattle. It hit her on the scalp and rained down across her bare shoulders. She dodged to one side, and stared up at a stream of sand pouring down through the centre of the low concrete ceiling. 'What the hell?' she breathed.

'I WANT YOU TO KNOW SOMETHING,' said a voice, low down at ankle level, 'of how it will be at the end. This is your taster. The practice run.'

SHE DROPPED to her knees and peered past the sandfall towards the door, but nobody was silhouetted in its warped frame. Instead, she spotted a pinprick of red in the corner and realised she was hearing a recording, or perhaps someone talking through a remote device. Her torchlight found wires connected to the half buried metal panel she had trodden on. As the voice went on she guessed the recording had been triggered when she stepped inside. Maybe the shower of sand, too. She'd better hope nothing else was about to go off.

·　·　·

'WHO ARE YOU?' she yelled at the red light, in case this was a live transmission, and someone was listening to her.

'YOU SHOULD HAVE SAID SORRY,' went on the voice. Male and tinny through the cheap silver device propped up against the wall. Vaguely familiar? Maybe. 'You should all have said sorry. But you left it too late. Seven years too late. You're sorry now. You're sorry now. You're sorry now.'

THESE LAST THREE words carried on, looping around. The sand trickled to a halt and Kate recalled the earlier words in the message. *'The practice run.'*

SHIT! She hurled herself back outside and along the beach. There was one more hut, a good half kilometre down the shore. She did not like the shape of this story. It was some warped version of *Goldilocks*. In hut one, a small shower of sand inside the timer. In hut two, a bigger shower of sand. What was waiting for Nikki and Craig in hut three? Was she already too late?

SHE FUMBLED WITH HER MOBILE, pulling up Lucas's number and pressing CALL, praying that he would answer and tell her he'd found them in the nick of time and had the killer pinned to the floor, knocked unconscious or dead.

WHO? *Who?* Who the HELL was it?

28

L ucas lay still on the roof of a Buntin's holiday chalet, trying not to breathe.

Dodging away from his pursuers, allowing Sid to guide him at speed, he'd soon realised he was hemmed in and needed another option. Half a dozen deck chairs had been left flat and folded alongside the end wall of a chalet block, offering him that option. He had taken a leap of faith — literally — and used the stacked wood as a step up to the low, gently sloped tiles. Three seconds later he was flat on his back and out of sight, and not a moment too soon.

Below him, he heard hard boots striking the paving slab alleys. 'Suspect on foot,' puffed a male officer. 'Answers to description but wearing different clothing — jeans and a black leather jacket.'

Lucas groaned silently as he finally made the connection with the silver man on the unicycle. It was that guy he'd seen outside the cocktail bar last night; the one who had looked a bit like him. Now he knew why the Suffolk police were so hot for Lucas Henry — mistaken identity. But if silver man was a prime suspect, had he sent Francis after a killer after all?

'We're getting the drone up,' came back another voice, tinny though the two-way.

Shit. He wasn't going to get much time on this roof then. He didn't have it anyway. As soon as the officer had moved along far enough, he slid to the edge of the roof, knocking a decade of lichen and moss growth off as he swung back down into the alley and turned back towards the coast. He had lost five minutes at least, but he'd have lost a good five hours if those Taser-wielding officers had caught up with him.

Keeping low and focused on the vibrations, he reached the edge of the park and pushed into the hedging and out the other side, onto the edge of the long, molehill-pocked meadow.

As he ran for the distant curve of the coastal cliff, Lucas realised the shifting of soil and sand and grit in these parts had been whispering a story to him for the past two days. Sometimes the patterns he was chasing were part of a much bigger picture — something he'd been getting shown for maybe hours or days before he truly focused on it.

The sink hole; the way it had opened up, the land dropping down into the cavern below with a sigh that seemed like relief... a release of tension held in check for *decades*. Something waiting to be resolved; to find its settling point; its resting place.

This had *meant* something and maybe, if he hadn't been busy rescuing those stupid teenagers from their own folly, he might have picked it up then and acted sooner. It wasn't that dowsing foretold the future — he was no clairvoyant — but it did sometimes give him a warning. The patterns of frequency, the whirls and lines of fourth-dimensional energy, the almost audible hum and crackle of it all... these suggested the shape of things to come, like weather forecasts on the radio. If you were paying attention — and properly tuned in — you could learn a lot; plot a better course across the hours ahead.

But he had been obsessing about Kate... and then getting distracted by sex. Not until this morning, when Sid had conveyed the sense of more land slipping, away to the south east where he knew Kate was, had he started to wake up.

Now, as he chased after the killer of at least three people, it all connected up. The slip and the slide and the dizzying panic. Was it just inside him? Or was he properly tuned in now? He could just make out a distant figure, maybe a half kilometre away — a blurred shadow on the cliff edge. As the sky darkened it was getting harder to see. It might have been a scarecrow or even a footpath signpost, but Sid was certain this was their quarry. Lucas ran on, trying to ignore the sharpening pain in his knee, which had been comprehensively injured and rebuilt within the last few months.

He hoped Kate *had* called in backup from the police. Despite her fear of being grounded when she most needed to run to her friends' rescue, *he* did not want her anywhere near this guy. Because he was also picking up an almost pyrexial level of madness in the streams of energy billowing back through the air between them. He could sense there would be little point in reasoning. Kate was capable, highly trained and fit, but there was some terrifying instability crouching on that cliff — both human and mineral.

His phone went off in his back pocket, and he snatched it out and picked up the call from Kate.

'It's the bunker!' she yelled, between tearing gasps,

running as hard as he was. 'The last bunker of three. Are you there?'

'I'm on my way!' he gasped back. 'Kate — stop! Don't go any further!'

'I can't stop! Get there, Lucas! Just get there!' The call ended and he knew there was no hope — or time — to change her direction and her velocity. He felt like he was already witnessing a car crash.

———

As soon as he opened his eyes to see the young man leaning over him in horror, Barney recognised the fair hair and the well-defined features. 'You're Francis... Kate's brother,' he burbled, on his back in the grass verge on the opposite side of the road.

'How do you know Kate?' demanded Francis. 'Are you stalking her? Are you planning to murder her?'

'What?' Barney sat up with a wince and said. 'No, of course not! I just wanted to show her my tattoo!'

'You what?' Francis stared down at him, pale and shaken.

Barney pulled up the sleeve of his silver shirt and showed Francis the calligraphic black wording encircling his pronounced bicep with a Celtic bracelet design. It read: *You are always enough.*

Francis hunkered down and read the words, screwing his face up in confusion. 'What has this got to do with my sister?'

'It's what she said to me, seven years ago,' Barney explained. 'Um... can we get in your car and park up, and I'll explain? I'm a bit visible here and I think the police might be after me for Julie's murder.'

'*Did* you murder her?' demanded Francis, narrowing his eyes and clenching his fists.

'No. But I'm the pikey in the caravan.'

Francis considered this and nodded. 'Yep — see your point.' He glanced around warily, clearly considering whether he should yell for help. Then he looked back at Barney and seemed to properly read his expression. 'OK,' he said. 'Get in.'

Barney threw the unicycle in the back seat, wincing at the pain in his elbow, which had taken the brunt of the fall. He'd rolled pretty well but a sideways shunt with a Ford Capri would test even Charlie Chaplin.

'Are you... injured?' asked Francis, as he jerkily engaged first gear and drove fifty metres or so along the road to a leafy lay-by, out of sight of the Buntin's camp gate.

'I'll be OK,' Barney said. 'I know how to fall.'

'I wasn't intending to run you down,' Francis went on. 'It's just the clutch is a bit slippy.'

'OK. I believe you.'

'So... I've got to go... but what about this tattoo... and what Kate said?' asked Francis, starting the car and immediately stalling it again.

'Should you be driving this thing?' asked Barney.

'Not really. Look — tell me what you're talking about,' said Francis. 'Or I'm just going to drive back in there and hand you over to the cops. Even if you're innocent, you can't just run away, you know.'

'Fine — relax,' said Barney. 'I met Kate when she was here as a Bluecoat seven summers back. I tend to leave my caravan down the end by the Bluecoat chalets, and we met, and we sort of hit it off.'

Francis stared at him, still wrestling with the old gear stick. 'She never mentioned you.'

'Maybe not,' Barney said. 'But even if it didn't mean much to her, what she did meant a lot to me.'

'What *did* she do?'

'She took me shopping.'

Francis blinked, leaving the car in neutral. 'Look... you're going to have to give me more. And speed it up. I've got to be somewhere.'

'Right... well, when all the other Bluecoats were taking the piss out of me and treating me like pond life, your sister was the one who came to see me and got me talking, and then called the others over, telling them I had brilliant stories to tell about my days travelling with the circus and the fair. She... she made them *see* me. As a person. Someone interesting.'

Francis nodded. 'Yeah... that sounds like Kate. So... where did the shopping come in?'

'I had no fashion sense. I was only eighteen and I'd never had a relationship with anyone but my mother. And my mother was a nightmare; really controlling. I'd never had a proper childhood and I didn't have a clue how to be a teenager. I lived in manky tracksuits and circus gear, and I looked like a weirdo. I *was* a weirdo. But your sister talked to me like I wasn't and so, every week when I came by, we'd just chat. It was just... normal and nice. And then one day, when all the Blues were taking the piss out of my clothes, she offered to take me into Lowestoft and help me buy some gear that would make me look a bit more like I belonged to the 21st century.'

'And then what?' said Francis, looking sceptical. 'Your life changed overnight? You turned into a cool guy and all the girls wanted you..?'

Barney grinned. 'Not overnight, no. You can't shake off a whole lifetime of weird just like that... but it was a start.

I looked better. She even got me to go to a good hair-dresser to sort out my bubble head of curls. I learned about *wax*. But... I took her advice. I didn't change *me*... I just changed the picture frame *around* me, and things got easier. I got more confident. A year later I even got my first girlfriend.' He grinned at the memory. 'That didn't work out *at all*. A year after that, I got my first boyfriend. And that *did* work. We're still together. I even came out to my mother when I was twenty-one and she just had to deal with it.'

He turned to look at Kate's brother, pointing to the tattoo. 'She probably doesn't remember saying these words because it wasn't a big deal to her, being nice to someone like me. But it was a big deal to *me*. I got this tattoo four years ago, when I came out. And I've never forgotten Kate and what she did for me. When I heard they were all coming back for a reunion I knew I *had* to see her and thank her. That's all.'

Francis paused for a moment and then shoved the car into gear. For a second, Barney thought he was going to drive him back into Buntin's and call for the police after all, but no, the car pulled out awkwardly into the road, away from the gate, and stalled again.

'Kate's in danger,' Francis said, desperately struggling with the ignition and the clutch. 'She's heading for some old bunkers on the beach and so is this psycho who killed Julie and Bill and Martin. I need to get there.'

Barney went cold. 'Wait... you mean... Martin was *killed*? And Bill, too..?'

'Yep. And he's going for all of them. He attacked Talia... but she's still alive.'

'Get out,' said Barney.

'What?'

'Get out and let me drive! I know a farm track down to the bunkers.'

'You're not insured!'

'And you *are*? Don't tell me you've passed your test!'

'You're right,' said Francis, already opening the door. 'Get in! Drive!'

29

As she reached the third and final bunker, Kate felt a belt of nausea and panic. She tried to call upon her professional armour; she was a capable police officer, fully trained and excellent at self-defence.

But if she'd learned anything over the past half a year it was that nobody is ever fully trained *enough*. She was about to enter what was very probably the murder scene of two friends. She stopped a few steps away from the slanted, broken concrete entrance, taking a moment to survey what she was about to run into. This hut was more damaged than the other two. The local council had boarded it up and screwed metal warning signs to it, but someone always came along to wrench the boarding away and enter the dank, dark hut for a laugh. The latest board lay tilted against the wall. Lumps of concrete, fallen off the roof, wallowed in the shingle next to it.

The cliff looming above was a good two metres higher here than further along the beach and part of it had collapsed over the end of the bunker some time ago, burying half of the 1940s structure in sand and grit. She

walked a wide arc around to the far side, watching for a
figure crouching in its shadow. She could see nobody there,
or above on the cliff. Only dark clouds rolled low across it,
ready to release rain at any time. She took a deep breath and
then called out, 'CRAIG! NIKKI! ARE YOU IN THERE?'

There was no reply. Not a sound above the sea and the
gulls. Even the siren back at the camp had stopped now. She
approached the doorway, wishing she had Lucas and Sid to
dowse what was in there. The mandatory stink of old urine
met her nose as she drew closer. 'Craig!' she called again.
'Nikki!'

Nothing. She took another lungful of air, held her
breath and leaned in, shining her torch into the fetid gloom.
At once, the light picked out eyes. Wide, staring, shining
eyes. She jolted in shock, even though there couldn't be
much to surprise her in this. But the eyes were not fixed and
cold... they were very much moving and alive. Nikki and
Craig were sitting up against the far wall of the bunker.
Their mouths were tightly gagged with some material and
their hands were behind their backs.

But they were alive! She held back from rushing in.
Exhaling slowly, she shone the torch into every corner of the
bunker. It was twice the size of the other two and she would
need to venture much further in, away from the beach and
what might come for her along it, but there was nobody
inside and nobody outside that she could see. With luck the
next person here would be Lucas. Maybe the killer had
finished... maybe this was all of it.

She didn't believe that. He'd taken way too much trouble. But she had to release her friends and get them out.
What if there was an explosive device buried in the detritus
across the slanted floor? Nothing would surprise her. There
was no MO you could trace with this guy... throat-slitting,

drowning, strangling, shooting, lard, frogs... it was any method to fit his twisted narrative, and she still had no idea what the story was.

She stepped in carefully, hugging one wall and keeping clear of any potential pressure plates in the centre. Nikki whimpered and rolled her eyes. The phone torch beam flashed across more red paint. Thick and tall this time. One message stretching the length of the opposite wall.

You should have said sorry.

What did they do? What did they say? She had a mental flashback of the many sessions of bitching and gossip, and heedless name-slinging and casual, light-hearted bullying that had gone on. She hadn't really joined in... had she? She recalled trying to make them all play nicely... what about that time with Backflip Barney..?

Oh shit. Not Barney! He was here! He had tried to talk to her earlier on the beach.

She reached the corner without setting anything off. *No. Surely not Barney?* The guy was a bit odd, but he was good-hearted. She couldn't believe he would do this. Yes... her friends had royally taken the piss out of him, but they'd all come around in the end, hadn't they? They were mostly nice to him once they'd got to know him better.

'Are you attached to anything electrical?' she whispered to Nikki and Craig. 'To any devices?'

Craig and Nikki shook their heads. Closer to them, she could see that their wrists were handcuffed to some old piping that ran down the back wall. She guessed they must have tried hard to pull against it and failed to budge it an inch. These old bunkers had been built to last.

'Are you hurt?' she whispered, setting her phone torch-light against the wall and reaching behind Nikki with her metal pick.

They both shook their heads again. She could take off their gags, but she needed to keep things quiet; to hear what might be going on outside. 'Was it Backflip Barney?' she whispered again. They shook their heads.

'Do we know him?'

In the torchlight they looked at her and then at each other, eyebrows raised in uncertainty and confusion. And fear. A lot of fear.

'It's OK,' she murmured, working the metal pin. 'I'm going to get you out of here. And my friend Lucas is on his way to help. He'll be here any minute.'

At that point she heard movement outside and her adrenaline surged, feeding both fear and hope. There was a thud and the light from the doorway vanished. She swung around, ready to see someone standing there, blocking it. But the light was gone completely. She realised, too late, that the discarded boarding had been put back into place.

She hurtled across to throw herself at it and shove it out onto their foe, but before she could reach it there was a gritty crunch. Something heavy had been pulled against the stout wood panel.

'STOP RIGHT THERE! POLICE!' she bawled, launching a flying kick at the door. But although it juddered, it did not shift. She rebounded back onto the pebble and litter-strewn concrete floor, knocking the breath out of herself. She was up a moment later and trying again, but even as she launched another kick she heard more grating noises and grimly realised that this, like everything else, had been planned. If she'd paid more attention she might have realised that the slabs of concrete beside the bunker had a purpose. She had assumed they had randomly fallen... now she knew there was *nothing* random about what was happening.

A hissing sound caught her attention, and she grabbed up her phone and shone the torchlight up to the ceiling to see another column of falling sand. And then a second. And then a third. Thicker and heavier sand, falling through from gaps she had not noticed. A red light blipped in the far corner of the hut and a voice played out of it.

'Say sorry,' it said.

———

'*WHAT FOR?*' *yelled the muffled voice.*

He smiled. He might as well have written the script for all of them. They had all said and done precisely what he had imagined they would say and do, during the many weeks in which he had planned and rehearsed and visualised each and every scene of his revenge play. Ever since he'd seen the name — Talia Kingston — on the bookings system and realised she was bringing all seven back. Every last stinking one of them.

'You don't remember me, do you?'

'I can't even bloody SEE you!' yelled Kate Sparrow. 'How the hell am I supposed to remember you?'

'You've met me this weekend,' he said. 'You looked right at me. You said my name. You asked for my help... and even then you didn't recognise me.'

'Wait... stop this bloody sand,' she choked. 'I can't hear you properly. It's blocking the signal on this radio device.'

'No it's not,' he said. 'I can hear you and you can hear me, because that's exactly what I planned. I want to hear you all, right to the end. I'd like to see you, too, but the video doesn't work in the dark. Audio will have to be enough.'

'Oh, for fuck's sake — just tell me who you are and why you're doing this! What the hell did we do to you?'

*'It wasn't what you did to **me**,' he said. 'You weren't nice to me, but I could live with that. It's what you did to Tessa.'*

———

LUCAS COULDN'T SEE anyone on the cliff top now. There were lines of stunted trees and wild grass, all curved with the prevailing sea breeze, but no sign of anyone among them. Sid, though, was zoning in on the killer and by now there was no doubt. The guy in silver whom he'd sent Francis after wasn't dangerous. That was one small consolation.

It didn't outweigh, though, his overriding certainty that Kate was in severe peril. He could sense — and see in his mind's eye — her scared and angry patterns knotted up with the killer's. The killer wasn't scared. He wasn't even angry. Every frequency that spun away from him, like spider threads on the wind, was iron grey and iron hard. Bitter grief and vengeance were the only drivers working within this individual. He didn't care about being caught. In fact, Lucas realised, he fully *expected* to be caught. The only thing he feared was losing his liberty before he had finished the job.

Lucas ran, powering through the ever worsening pain in his bad knee. He was dimly aware of Francis somewhere off to the west, with someone else, also moving fast. But not fast enough. There was so very little time now. He estimated he could reach the cliff inside a minute if he could keep up this pace, but it might be too late for Kate and her friends. The sensation of slipping land rolled through him again. He felt as if, at any moment, he might be running on air.

Above him, to the north, he could both hear and sense a high-pitched buzz. Glancing over his shoulder he made out a black speck, moving too steadily and purposefully to be a bird. It looked as if the police had got a drone up. That was good news... maybe. Or maybe it would only hasten the murderous plans of the man on the cliffside.

For that's where he was — halfway down the short, crumbling and tumbling slope that led down to the shingle. And he had metal tubes with him... guns? Maybe. But bigger than that. Slipping... land was slipping... darkness was engulfing the three life forces inside an old, old box that could only be one of the bunkers.

———

'MIKE,' said Kate, realisation dawning. 'Mike on security.'

'Well done,' said the voice from the corner, the pinprick of light pulsing with each intonation.

'You... you were Mickey back then, weren't you?' she said. 'I thought there was something familiar about you... but you're much bigger now. You were a skinny lad back then; you must have put in a lot of time at the gym.' She wasn't trying to flatter him; she was thinking aloud and hoping, of course, to distract him from drowning them in sand.

Because the sand was not letting up. At first she had thought it might genuinely be another landslip, and the sand finding its way in might peter out. But now she could hear a clanking and realised that it was being funnelled in deliberately, maybe through piping or guttering of some kind.

'What happened to Tessa?' she asked as the sand poured on, forming dunes around her feet.

'*Don't* you say her name,' he snarled. 'You're not fit to say her name.'

'Come *on*, Mickey!' she yelled. 'How can we be sorry if

we don't know what for? We were idiots back then — we
didn't think about anyone but ourselves. We're older now.
We'd get it this time. What happened with... your sister?
Was it your sister?'

'She came here for *fun!*' he yelled, emotion in his voice
for the first time. 'To hang out with me and have *fun*. And I
wanted her to be proud of me, so I'd told her you were all
my friends. But you weren't, were you? You didn't have any
time for me at all, any of you. You couldn't be bothered with
me... or with my little six-fingered sister.'

Kate heard Nikki make a yelping sound and glanced
around to see startled recognition in her eyes. Bill had been
talking only last night about Little Mickey and his six-
fingered sister.

'We heard you all talking,' he said. 'We were in the next
chalet. You lot always went up a hundred decibels whenever
you were pissed. We heard *everything* you said about us.'

Kate winced, recalling the girl now, awkward and lumpy;
a pale thing with wispy hair and blotchy skin, clinging onto
her brother's arm. A flashback of Bill and Nikki came to her,
both doing a skit about Mickey and his little sister while
they were all lounging about in Craig and Bill's chalet. She
recalled Bill throwing in all the mandatory Norfolk
inbreeding gags, choking with derision about the awkward
way Tessa walked and the strange lump on the outer edge of
her hand, which they decided was a stunted extra finger. Bill
had come up with the Six-Fingered Sister name and also
insisted that Tessa and Mickey were genuine Norfolk
inbreds because he'd seen their webbed toes. *Oh god... the
frogs... the glued-up feet!* Kate shivered as she made the
connection.

She remembered she hadn't enjoyed it then, watching
Talia and Craig explode with laughter. She had *tried* to make

them nicer — but they were pissed and silly and exhausted from having to be so upbeat and cheery with all the punters for a twelve-hour stretch. If she was honest, she had giggled a bit too, because Bill had natural comic timing and clever mimicry, and it was hard to resist. Of course, none of them had known the targets of their spiteful comedy were listening in.

Martin, tanked up on JD and Coke, had joined in the fun. The girl had fixated on him, like so many did as he strode around the pool in his lifeguard trunks and vest, tall, ripped and good-looking. He'd told them he had asked her to leave the water. Something had happened... what was it?

Oh *fuck*. The note on the sanitary towel. *Now* she remembered. 'I had to get her out before she turned the water pink,' Martin had spluttered into his glass. 'She was getting her fuckin' period and she hadn't worn a tampon.'

His words sliced through Kate's mind, still vivid seven years on, because she had felt caved in with pity for the poor girl, who hadn't been more than fifteen at the time. Imagine being hauled out of a public pool and asked to leave because you were bleeding into it. The horror was palpable then and it still was now. *Shit.* She was starting to get it.

'I'm sorry, Mike,' she called up, while testing the blocked door again and reaching the sinking conclusion that she could not shift it on her own. 'We were thoughtless little pricks, all of us. Is that why you made Martin write on the sanitary towel? Because of what happened in the pool? To get revenge for your sister?'

'Oh — you picked that up, did you?' he sneered. 'With your special detective powers?'

'People forget the stuff they do,' she said. 'Especially when they're ashamed of it. They blot it out. We weren't much older than your sister, were we? We were all hardly more than kids.'

'Even after the pool,' said Mike, 'she kept trying. She so wanted to fit in, you see, because she thought you lot meant so much to me. She was wrong. SHE was the only one who mattered. But she kept trying. She said Julie talked to her. She went to one of Julie's classes and Julie gave her advice. Julie said she could be quite pretty if she just *lost a bit of weight*.' He spat out the last five words with a dark venom and Kate closed her eyes and shivered, picturing Julie with her throat and mouth choked with cold lard.

'That's when she stopped eating properly,' Mike said. 'That's exactly the day she started to become anorexic.'

'Oh god, Mike, I'm sorry,' said Kate. She meant it, too.

'Why should *you* be sorry? *You* didn't tell her she was fat, did you? *You* didn't take the piss out of her clothes, either. That was Talia. Talia saw her in the bar with me, wearing her favourite dress. The yellow one. Oh, she made a big fuss of it — nearly had us both fooled. And then you came in and she gave you a sneaky look, which she thought we didn't notice — but we could see it in the mirror in the bar. She was just taking the piss, as usual. It broke Tessa's confidence in two, that did. Do you remember that? Do you remember the dress? You might have seen it today. It looked better on Tessa, don't you think? Tessa looked beautiful in it. Talia looked like a fucking whore.'

'Oooh, shit,' murmured Kate, hearing the fraying sanity in his voice and losing hope that she might reason with him and end his vendetta. She sank down in a drift of sand which was now covering the legs of Nikki and Craig, and started feverishly working away at the cuffs behind them. There was nothing else she could think of to do.

Craig was making distressed noises about Talia. 'She's

alive,' Kate said to them both, sensing a little give in the cuff attaching Nikki to the pipes. 'We got there before he could finish her off. She'll be OK.' She just hoped neither of them would ask about Bill.

'It could have been all right, you know,' went on Mike. 'Because she kept trying, my little sis. She didn't give up, because she wanted to show me she could be part of the gang. She didn't know that I was never *in* your gang — I just pretended I was.'

'What happened to her?' Kate asked, although she was beginning to guess.

'You were meant to meet her,' he said. 'You said she could come along on one of your stupid little trips along the beach, checking out the bunkers. Do you remember, Kate?'

And now Kate *did* remember. It had been one of those throwaway things you say to someone who is on the periphery of a group, listening in, anxious to be included. Mike — or Mickey as they'd known him back then when he was just a Bluecoat, like the rest of them — had been there with Tessa, listening in to the chat but not really taking part. Kate had been in the cafe next to the amusement arcade, on a break with Talia and Craig, if she remembered rightly, and also Mickey and his sister. Craig had suggested a tour of the bunkers and the cliffs, with snacks and drinks, on their half day off. They'd set the time and the meeting and agreed on it and she, noticing the close attention Mickey and Tessa were paying to these plans, had said, 'OK... let's all meet on the beach at eleven, then.' She had included them in her glance-around. Because she was being kind. Stupidly kind, as it turned out.

She hadn't gone. She'd got a migraine not long after and had needed to go and lie down in the chalet. But Nikki and Craig and Talia had gone. So, it later turned out, had Mickey and Tessa, trailing along in the wake of the others and generally cramping their style. At least that's what Talia had said later, when she'd come back to the chalet, waking her up and making excuses for what they'd done. Because they'd trapped Mickey and Tessa inside one of the bunkers 'for a laugh'. Only, it then turned out that Mickey hadn't been in the bunker. It was just Tessa. What the hell she was doing in there on her own nobody ever worked out, but Mickey had gone off to take a piss around the corner when they had, in a fit of giggles, dragged a bit of detached wooden safety boarding and slab of old concrete across the doorway.

When Tessa realised she was trapped, she became hysterical. Very quickly. Sand, apparently, had fallen through the cracks in the bunker and she had believed there was a landslip and she would be buried alive.

They'd got her out after only a couple of minutes. That's what Talia had told her. But Kate, even at the time, had wondered about that. It wouldn't have surprised her if they'd run away and left the poor girl for her brother to find. Later that day, Tessa had gone home to Norwich and Mickey hadn't spoken about it again.

Neither had she. And she should have. She should have checked in with him and found out how his sister was. She should have apologised for them all at the time, instead of sweeping it away because she felt guilty and awkward and ashamed.

'What happened on the beach that day,' she said. 'It was horrible. I really am sorry.'

'Why? You weren't there,' he said. 'You didn't do it.'

Kate felt a ping of metal and one of Nikki's wrists came free of its cuff. The metal chain was wrapped around the pipe, though, and she needed to get it unwound. The sand was coming in thicker and faster than ever. It was clean and fine. She could only imagine Mike had shipped several bags of it across the field and stowed it somewhere up the top of the shallow cliff, among the low, windswept trees, along with some metal drainpipes or guttering. She heard a clunk and a deep grating, shifting noise and felt fear grab at her throat. The weight from above was affecting the worn old concrete, already weakened and split by decades of storms and landslips. There was every chance they would all be crushed by a cave-in, if they weren't choked with sand.

'So... what did *I* do, Mike?' she asked, raising her voice above the incessant hissing of the fine sand showers and the increasingly panicked noises from Nikki and Craig.

'Nothing,' he said. 'Absolutely nothing.'

She saw his point.

30

Lucas crept through the twisted limbs of a line of dwarf pine trees, hearing voices above the hiss of the sea and the cry of the gulls. Sid was thrumming against his chest, warning of instability in all directions. The crumbling cliff was ready to go at any time and so was the crumbling mind of the man crouched three or four metres below him.

He stared down, recognising the burly frame of the security chief he'd seen around the site, who was emptying a sack into an open-topped metal chute, sending sand funnelling down through broad cracks in the roof of the old concrete bunker. There was no doubt in Lucas's mind what the endgame was. Whoever was inside that bunker was going to be engulfed in sand or maybe crushed by concrete, because the tension in the old World War Two construction was positively screaming through his dowsing senses. The land just above it wasn't much more stable, straining under the weight of the security guy and his sacks of sand, and the metal shute he had rigged up. Lucas was aware that his own weight was adding to the danger. Clinging onto the branch of the tree, he could sense the way its roots had loosened over time and become brittle and frail. He couldn't be sure it would hold his weight if he swung from it.

His base impulse was to jump the guy from behind, but to do so risked catastrophe for the three life forces he was reading inside the bunker. One of them, he registered grimly, was Kate. *Shit, Kate! Why do you have to put yourself in these situations again and again?*

He crouched, frozen with indecision, aware that the damaged psyche just below him was unlikely to be talked around. Whoever it was, the pain they had experienced over many years — most acutely two or three months ago — was directing this scene. Anger and vengeance were all this man was clinging to. Without it, he would be empty and spent.

There was no killer more dangerous than a killer with nothing to lose.

'She wouldn't want you to do this,' he said, acting on instinct. His words were buffeted by the breeze and a flurry of rain spattering across the cliff edge, but the man looked around, taking off his cap to reveal thin, greasy hair. He wasn't old — around Kate's age — according to Sid, but he looked a good decade older.

'Who the fuck are you?' said the man. He did not shift his position and the sand continued to funnel down onto and into the bunker.

Lucas grasped Sid and dowsed the man as intensely as he could. He was not a psychic... but energy patterns helped him out and his lucky guesses often struck home. 'Whoever you lost,' he said. 'Your... sister?' The man didn't argue, and Lucas nodded. 'Your sister. She wouldn't want this.'

'Maybe not,' said the man. 'But *I* want this. As you can see.'

'Do you really want them dead?' Lucas went on.

'Because... if it's punishment you wanted to give out, you've done it. You've taken their friends from them and you've put them in a state of terror. Maybe that's enough.'

'It's not enough. I want all seven of them and then I'm done.'

'Even Kate? Did Kate hurt your sister?' Lucas was hazarding more guesses here, but his instincts were rarely wrong. He could not imagine Kate ever knowingly hurting an innocent. Kicking the balls of a guilty man, yes, but picking on a young woman — never.

'I did think about sparing Kate,' the man went on, almost conversationally. 'Because she was probably nicer to Tessa than anyone else. But it's not enough to be nice. It's not enough to stand by when others are doing wrong. They crushed my sister's confidence... they caused her panic attacks and her anorexia, and they didn't give it another thought. They never said sorry. So I *made* them sorry.'

'When did you lose Tessa?'

'In February,' the man said, a catch in his voice. 'I spent seven years trying to make her better and I failed. She just hated herself. And it was those fucking Bluecoats... the self-anointed *Magnificent Seven*... who were the death of her. When she died, she weighed less than five stone.'

'That must have been awful,' Lucas said.

'Oh no! It was just what Julie had *told her to do*! I told Julie that before I strangled her; told her that Tessa had lost *loads* of weight, just to be accepted. Stones and stones of weight. I told her that before I poured lard down the skinny bitch's throat.'

'Mike!' The tinny voice emitting from the guy's two-way radio was Kate's. Lucas felt his insides crunch up in hope and fear. She was still alive — so were the other two — but the unusual movement of the man, with his sacks of sand

and the metal guttering, were putting an intolerable pressure on both the bunker and the bank of unstable sand, grit and flimsy root networks above it.

'Please... can you stop the sand now?' Kate said. She coughed and then went on: 'You've made us all sorry now. You've done what you set out to do. Come on, Mike! I don't believe you really want it to end like this.'

'Shut up, Kate,' he said. 'I don't want to hear from you any more.' And he switched off the radio and hurled it down to the beach, where it bounced and broke apart. He reached for another sack of sand.

'Mike... I'm not going to let you do that,' said Lucas.

'Try and stop me,' said Mike, turning and pulling a handgun from a holster under his Buntin's security blazer. Lucas was pretty sure it wasn't standard issue for a holiday camp. It looked like the real deal and was probably how he'd managed to get Nikki and Craig into the bunker. Sid was fairly certain it was loaded, too.

So here it was — Kate and her two friends were trapped and drowning in sand. The man attempting to kill them was armed and determined. And even without him, the crumbling promontory beneath them was screaming its intention to collapse at any moment. What the hell was he going to do?

———

THE SAND WAS at waist height. Nikki was now free, and she and Kate were grappling through the growing drifts to release Craig. He'd managed to push himself up against the wall into a semi-standing position, his cuffed wrists as high as he could raise them behind his back so Kate could pick the lock, but her pin wasn't finding the way in. Sand was blocking the keyhole.

'This can't be happening,' sobbed Nikki, shining the torch beam from Kate's phone onto Craig's cuffed wrists. 'I can't believe this is happening.'

Kate ran her hands up and down the semi-submerged pipes, trying to find a weakness. Her fingers located a bubbling, rusty texture on the metal and felt a slight give. She abandoned the pin and dragged the cuffs to the weak point. 'We're going to have to pull him,' she said to Nikki.

A fresh deluge of sand hit them as they grabbed Craig's shoulders, putting a foot up against the wall behind him, and pulled. Craig screamed as the cuffs cut into his wrists, the noise thin and dull against the incessant hissing. But the pipe pulled away from the wall and began to bow out. A few more seconds of dragging, screaming and trying not to inhale sand, and finally there was a dull twang and the weak point gave. They all tumbled headlong into the dark dune surrounding them.

Craig's hands were still pinned behind his back but there was no time to try to free him. The buckling of the pipe had done nothing for the stability of the bunker and once again there was a gritty, shifting groan above them. It was no longer possible to run at the door. Kate didn't believe Mike had enough sand to literally bury them all, but she did believe there was enough weight building up on the roof above to collapse the whole bunker. She could hear more twangs in the metal piping, which told her there was way too much movement. If the ceiling caved in they were going to be crushed to death.

'Come on!' she yelled. 'We have to push together!' She waved her phone torch towards the blocked door. 'I can't move it on my own — but all three of us might.'

Choking and gasping, Craig and Nikki waded across with her. There was another metallic yelp as another pipe buckled under the strain. Kate felt, rather than saw, one of the broken slabs of roof tip inwards.

'NOW!' she screamed. 'We have to get out of here NOW!'

———

'SHIIIIIIIT!' cried Francis, as Barney shifted violently into third gear and drove them along the bumpy, rutted farm track, heading for a field which ran along the low cliff top.

'That's your mate, yeah?' called Barney, expertly avoiding the worst of a deep hole in the centre of the track. 'The dowser guy?'

The figure clinging to the low branches of a stunted cliff-side pine was definitely Lucas. 'Yeah!' yelled back Francis. 'He must have found them. Where's the killer, though? I can't see him.'

'Wherever he is, your mate's got backup now,' said Barney, sending the Capri hurtling off the track and onto the lumpy turf of the field with no attempt to brake. In fact, he went up a gear.

'I'm not sure this car can take this!' Francis warned. 'It's pretty old and—oofff!' The words were knocked out of him as the car bucked and rode the uneven grass.

'It can take it,' said Barney. 'I've been driving since I was twelve. I know what I'm doing.' He went on to prove this by getting them right to the edge of the field, within sight of the beach, and then handbrake-turning sideways on to the stretch where, further along, Lucas was crouched, focused on something happening below.

As Barney jabbed the accelerator again to get them closer, the Capri did its party piece.

LUCAS GOT READY TO JUMP. Mike was holding the gun firmly and pointing it back at him with his left hand, while the right hand was hauling another sack of sand towards the guttering. This was more than the structure could take. It was going to collapse in the next ten seconds if any more sand hit it.

'You can't stop me,' said Mike, feeling for the opening of the sack and getting ready to nudge it over with his knee. 'Give it up.'

'The police are watching everything you're doing!' said Lucas. He could hear sirens and sense officers now running — and maybe driving — towards their location. 'They've got a drone up, look!'

Mike gave the drone, hovering fifty metres above them, a cursory glance. 'Good,' he said. 'Justice should be seen to be done.'

That might have been the moment — that microsecond when the killer looked up — but Lucas missed it. He needed something to distract the guy, to wrong-foot him for a second or two.

There was a deafening gunshot.

The report sent seabirds screaming into the air, and Mike jolted and looked behind him. 'It's the police. They're going to take you out!' Lucas warned him. There was another bang and this time Mike actually looked spooked, as if he'd suddenly remembered he *could* get shot — and that maybe he didn't want to die. His eyes scanned the sky as if he thought the drone was armed.

Lucas realised it was now or never. That roof could not take any more sand. He leapt on top of Mike, angling himself, even as he was airborne, so that he would slam the man against the bank and not onto the roof of the bunker.

He struck Mike's arm as he landed on him, knocking the gun away down the cliff. They both crashed into the steep bank. Mike was briefly winded but soon started fighting back, aiming to push his attacker backwards onto the roof of the bunker. Even amid the bloodrush violence of their struggle, Lucas could see and sense the roof cracking and tipping inward.

'KAAAAAATE!' he screamed. 'GET OUT OF THERE!'

Mike rolled out from under him, dragging Lucas sideways and gashing his cheek against an outcrop of stone. Lucas fought against his instinct to violently repel his foe, aware at every moment that he could not risk either of them landing on that roof. He wrapped one leg around Mike's knee, hooking him in close and hugged the killer close with his spare arm.

Mike shoved himself back, took Lucas by the shoulders and bashed him repeatedly against the cliff wall. With every thud, earth, sand and stones ran out in torrents. Lucas knew this whole promontory was disintegrating under the pile-driving force of the two men fighting on it. It was going to go at any moment, and Kate and her friends were still entombed beneath them. He was all out of ideas and hope.

Then Mike jerked and his eyes rolled up in his head. The pounding ceased and his arms fell away. A second later, as Lucas slumped, winded, against the cliff, Buntin's Head of Security started levitating.

Lucas gripped a network of roots and stared up, open-mouthed, at the man's black work boots as they floated past his head. He tracked this surreal spectacle with his eyes and made out two strong arms in silver sleeves, a metre above his head. There was every chance, Lucas thought, that he was concussed and hallucinating. That, or Mike had just been stunned and collected by an alien equipped with a tractor beam.

―――

BACKFLIP BARNEY WAS EXTRAORDINARILY STRONG. Francis had every chance to notice this as he clung to the young man's buttocks and thighs, feeling the tension in every muscle, tendon and sinew of the athlete's body while a feat of staggering physicality occurred.

After abandoning the backfiring Capri, Barney had flung himself out of the driver's side door, grabbed something from the back seat and run to the edge of the cliff.

'ANCHOR ME!' he bawled, flinging himself belly-down and Francis, shaking and stunned, had run after him and thrown himself on the guy's legs to pin his lower half to the ground. There was a fight going on below and Francis recognised the shout of warning to Kate. Lucas was down there with the killer.

Barney hadn't said another word. He had something shiny in his right hand. Francis had just enough time to recognise it as the post and saddle of the unicycle before it was swung down in a swift and brutal arc. He *heard* the saddle connect with someone's skull and then felt the swift and accurate surge, drop and grab as Barney collected the man by the head and pulled him up over the cliff.

Slewing around on his chest, the circus performer ended his trick with a flourish, slinging the stupefied man across the grassy edge of the cliff. Francis released his grip and rolled onto his side as Barney leapt up and dragged the body away from the edge, which was crumbling fast.

'Lucas!' yelled Francis. 'He's still down there!'

Barney crawled back to the edge, grabbing one of the tree branches to anchor himself, and held out one arm. A few seconds later he had hauled Lucas up onto the trembling lip of the land.

'Back! Get BACK!' yelled Francis, snatching a hold of the two of them and dragging them away into the field. 'It's going to go!'

———

'ON MY COUNT! All of us at the same time — same level!' shrieked Kate, shining her torchlight on the mid-section of the solid wood panel. 'Give it everything you've got!'

They rushed the door as one, shouldering it painfully. Nothing.

'AGAIN!' screamed Kate. They gave it all they had. There was a crack as the wood splintered around the weight of the concrete slab on its far side. The slab shifted but did not tip. The old wooden board, though, was cracked in two, and she was able to punch the top of it away. Light flooded through the slim gap. It was just wide enough to climb through.

She boosted Nikki up first, driving her through the ragged opening with as much velocity as she could manage at her awkward angle.

'GO!' said Craig.

'No — YOU GO.' He was skinny and light, and she womanhandled him through, glad that Nikki was there to catch him, as he still had no hands free to save himself.

She felt, rather than heard, the collapse.

———

BARNEY THOUGHT he might not be able to manage that night's show. He had wrenched his arms quite severely... and he suspected he'd shortly be in police custody, no matter how much evidence there was that he hadn't been involved in this murder spree. He wondered if he had accidentally killed Mike, the security chief, though. It was possible he'd broken the guy's neck.

He got to his feet, feeling as if he was on the inflatable castle back in the kids' adventure playground. The ground was shaking and bouncing.

Mike lay on his back, close to the edge, unconscious and maybe dead. They should try to drag him back onto the safer ground... but then the earth gave one last shudder and fell away, taking the security guard with it.

———

MICROSECONDS WERE in play for Kate now as she shot through the gap, Nikki swiping at her shoulders and tugging her into the open air.

A bright blade of pain shot though her calves and she wondered whether she would ever see her feet again. A thundering rumble was rolling around her, from the collapsing bunker but also the cliff face above. Stones and grit were flying. Nikki was screaming. Natural and man-made structures were roaring, surging, cracking, flailing and falling.

Kate threw her arms up over her head and blinked out of the world.

31

L ucas had always known his past was a circle. The intense trauma of his mid-teens was riven through his very bones. He fancied a magnetic resonance imaging scanner could probably see the shockwaves in his femurs, his tibias, his ribs, his skull... like the hairline cracks left in rocks by seismic events.

Some people said what didn't kill you made you stronger. He didn't subscribe to that. You could grow a tough shell, but when the framework that held you up on the inside was rocked and cracked at so young an age, could it ever be as strong as before?

That day on the crumbling Suffolk coast proved to him, once again, that the past, like Halley's Comet, was back once more, swinging by on another close orbit, full of evil portent, threatening to finish what it had started when he was fifteen.

As the gritty groan of the landslip subsided, he could hear only a bass hum of all too familiar dread inside his head. He was dimly aware of Francis and the silver-shirted guy trying to stop him, but he pushed them away and stag-

gered to the collapsed edge of the field. In a rising cloud of
displaced sand and dust he could see a stew of broken
branches and roots, lumps of earth and rock, and the long,
flat edge of what had once been the roof of the bunker. It
was caved in and half buried in sand, pebbles and organic
matter.

The path down to this wreckage was untrodden by man;
freshly opened earth, webbed with abruptly denuded roots.
He could see a black work boot protruding off to the right of
the bunker. If Mike wasn't dead yet, he soon would be;
barely a trace of life force was there.

Lucas did not pause to consider the stability of this new-
born cliff face; he'd already sensed it was sound enough to
withstand another year or two of east coast erosion. He half
climbed, half slid, down to the front end of the bunker — or
what little remained of it beneath the landslip. His heart
was crashing painfully in his chest, but he seemed to have
forgotten how to breathe. Kate was here, somewhere...
buried... buried alive.

He made himself stand still, inhale and close his eyes.
Filtering out the myriad people now approaching the scene
at speed, he brought Sid out and let the blue glass stopper
hang from his fist.

'It's Kate,' he told it, aloud, as if that would help. 'Be
precise.'

There was a drone buzzing overhead and shouts from
the Suffolk police, no doubt arresting the silver-shirted guy
and Francis. He had to block them out before they got closer.
There might be only seconds before it was too late for Kate.

Sid spun, twisted to a figure of eight, then swung back
and forth, indicating the plane and orientation. Lucas
angled with it and walked with light tread until Sid pulled
down and halted, straining at his chain. There was a broken

wooden board with a WARNING — DO NOT ENTER sign spray-painted on it. It was pinned down at an angle by lumps of concrete, sand and stone from the cliff.

Lucas knelt down and felt beneath the board. His hand found hair. He gulped. Putting Sid in his pocket, he pushed the board up with enormous care, causing a small avalanche of detritus. Kate lay on her side, her arms up around her head, one elbow bloody and raw. There was a drift of shingle over her face and for a moment Lucas was back in the quarry, staring down at the dead-eyed visage of Zoe, buried in a rocky grave. The bass hum in his head went deeper, louder. He felt himself sway as his senses did a slalom of horror.

But the eyes were screwed up shut, not fixed and staring. Kate shuddered and coughed and opened them. He let out a cry of relief and dropped his face to hers, seeking evidence that she was really breathing. He felt the warmth of her exhalation and heard her mutter, 'Shit. Have I still got legs..?'

'Don't move,' he said, stroking her gritty hair. 'Stay still. We'll get you out of there.'

'Nikki? Craig?'

He glanced along the beach and saw her two friends, huddled together by the shore, looking catatonic with shock.

'They're OK. You got them out.'

'Mike? What happened to him?'

'You don't have to worry about him,' said Lucas.

She gave a long sigh. '*Get away from it all... have a little break... that's what they said. Forget all the murder and have some fun.*'

———

THE SAND in the timer was nearly gone. He knew there was very little left.

But there was still the final reckoning to be done. Tessa was kneeling by his side, wearing her favourite yellow dress, looking young and well again. 'You did all this for me?' she said.

'I'm not finished,' he grunted, moving his limbs and noting that although they were screaming in pain, they were still **able** to move. Grit, stone and sand avalanched off him as he slowly sat up. He could hear the drone somewhere above, and police radios and chatter on the field and further along the beach. Had he finished off the last three? Had the bunker folded them into its concrete embrace and crushed them? If he knew that for sure, he could join Tessa in the next life with satisfaction.

'Don't worry now,' said his sister, smiling tenderly at him. 'Just come to me.'

'Not...' he grunted, pulling a block of stone off his left leg, '... yet.' His eye was drawn by the gleam of metal a short way along the crumbled cliff. Something he'd brought with him earlier. Something he wanted to get back.

'You've done everything you needed to do,' insisted Tessa.

But no. He could hear voices. He recognised one of them as she said, 'Mike? What happened to him?'

Just the other side of the bunker. Right there. Kate.

'Let her go,' said Tessa. 'She didn't try to hurt me.'

'She didn't try NOT to hurt you,' he whispered, getting to his hands and knees and crawling through the pain, crawling for that bit of metal.

———

KATE TRIED WIGGLING HER TOES. Her left ankle complained but all ten toes appeared to be in working order. 'Come on,' she said to Lucas. 'Just lift the board up, will you?'

'Kate — don't move! You might have broken something!' warned Lucas.

'Lucas - move it or I will!' she said, with a reassuring belt of energy. He leaned over with a frustrated sigh and carefully shifted the board a little higher. Before he could stop her, she had wriggled out and was scrambling upright as the broken board, losing its human underpinning, splintered further under the weight of the broken concrete.

He grabbed hold of her as she got to her feet. 'Jeezuz, Kate! What if you've damaged your spine or something?'

'I'm fine!' She could see Nikki and Craig — alive, if not exactly well, and felt a surge of intense relief. She'd got them out. She'd saved them from being buried alive. She could also see police approaching along the shore and hear the reassuring two-way radio chatter. It was over.

In the periphery of her vision, a figure staggered away to the right of the collapsed bunker and stumbled down to the water's edge and into the grey surf. Kate spun around, sucking in a lungful of air. 'It's HIM!'

A shot rang through the air and Nikki screamed. She and Craig dropped to the pebbles, clinging together, a sitting target for the madman sloshing through the waves towards them, screaming, *SAY SORRY! SAY FUCKING SORRY!'*

Whatever damage the collapse might have done was forgotten as a red mist of rage swept around Kate. Shoving Lucas away as he tried to restrain her, she ran down the beach, directly towards Mike. He was taking aim at Nikki and Craig again, screaming torrents of unintelligible words. One side of his head was dripping with blood and his balance was clearly out as he lurched around in the shallows.

But the aim still looked pretty true as he went to take

another shot. Kate screamed, 'MIKE! YOU FUCKER!' and he spun around and fired at her instead. The shot went wide, but only just. She felt the heat of the bullet as it tore past her. Up on the cliff, a loudhailer voice bellowed, 'ARMED POLICE! PUT DOWN YOUR WEAPON! PUT DOWN YOUR WEAPON OR WE WILL SHOOT!'

But Mike, she knew, was past caring. As she closed the last few metres between them, he was laughing and steadying his gun arm with his left hand. Her left foot found a lump of stone and she launched off it, calling on her countless hours of training in the dojo as she swung up her right foot and aimed for his face.

The sole of her sandal connected with his jaw at the same moment the gun fired. The pair of them toppled into the sea. She landed on his chest and drove the heel of her hand into his face, pressing him down under water. On land, she would have held him there but even now, while fury flooded through her at what he had done to Martin, to Julie, to Bill and to Talia, DI Kate Sparrow took over and a second later she wrenched him back up above the waves, spluttering and feeble. The water around them was blooming blood and for a moment she wondered if she'd been hit... again... before realising it was his head wound, releasing bright rivulets of red across her hands as she gripped him by the ears.

Energy seeped out of him along with the blood. His eyes opened and stared glassily up at her. He looked utterly drained. Kate could hear Lucas splashing towards them and the drone buzzing overhead as Mike moved his mouth, whispering something to her. She leant in and caught his last few words.

'Tessa...' he breathed, as a string of bloody drool slipped from the side of his mouth. 'Tessa... liked you... the best.'

32

'Barney Bagnall, I am arresting you in connection with the murder of Martin Riley, Julie Everall and William Lassiter, and the attempted murder of Natalia Kingston. You have the right to remain silent—'

'It wasn't him!' yelled Francis. 'He just bloody saved a guy's life!' It was hard for Kate's brother to get the words out, though, face down on the ground and getting his hands cuffed behind his back while another officer was reeling off *his* rights.

At a similar angle in the grass, Barney managed to give him a crooked smile. 'Welcome to my world,' he said. He was fairly relaxed, all things considered. He knew this would be sorted out as soon as Kate and her friend came back up from the beach. Then a couple of gunshots went off and his belly tightened in fear. There was no mistaking *those* for a backfiring Ford Capri.

He and Francis were left nosing the grass as the officers dumped them, handcuffed and sprawling, and tore off to the edge of the cliff.

'Shit! Kate!' hissed Francis.

But Barney heard someone shout 'Suspect down! Suspect under control!' and felt a wave of relief. On the beach there was a genuine suspect for the police to focus on... and it wasn't him.

———

AROUND SEVEN OFFICERS witnessed the final scenes of Kate's struggle with Mike. This was helpful when she finally got off the beach and onto the field where an assortment of police and paramedics had gathered, and found her brother cuffed and face down in the grass.

'For fuck's sake, get those off him!' she had commanded, in a voice that belied how wrecked she felt. 'And him!' she pointed to Backflip Barney. 'Neither of them should be cuffed. They're witnesses, not suspects.'

The Suffolk police did not appreciate her directions but happily, footage from the drone was now playing out on screen in the senior officer's patrol car and so how the last half hour had unfolded was evident. As soon as she'd been declared 'fit enough' by the medic, Kate was able to join the small group and watch the tangled fight on the cliff between Lucas and Mike, then marvel at the way a silver-shirted Barney had suddenly arrived on the scene and taken a swing at Mike with the saddle end of his unicycle, before hooking him up through thin air.

She put her less injured arm around Francis, now freed and drinking a cup of water, which periodically trembled in his hands. 'Thank god you got Barney to us when you did... and... you know... hung on to him.'

Francis turned to look at her, narrow-eyed. 'Are you saying that my part in all this was just to heroically clamp myself to a guy's arse?'

'Nobody could have done it better,' she said. She knew there was every chance that Barney and Francis had together made a huge difference to the outcome. Mike must have been at least semi-concussed by the bash to the head, and then further by the landslip. With his sense of balance wrecked, his firing had been off-centre and she — and Nikki and Craig — were all still here to tell the tale.

She shivered as she saw again the way his eyes had gone fixed and glassy while she held his head between her hands. Watching him die had affected her more than she was letting on. She had never been more relieved to hand over to another crew. Gary was going to be very pissed off. Not only was a block of chalets now out of commission — the whole beach would be a no go area for the next forty-eight hours at least. Buntin's Lakefield Holiday Village just couldn't catch a break this season.

She walked back to the ambulances, where Craig and Nikki were being treated for shock and minor injuries. Craig, wearing an oxygen mask, lay on a stretcher, his eyes closed. His brow had a nasty welt from a blow dealt with Mike's gun. Apparently the Head of Security had made Craig cuff Nikki to the pipes and then struck Craig half-senseless, so he could cuff him, too ,without a struggle.

Nikki was sitting nearby, getting a graze on her leg cleaned. She looked grey with exhaustion.

'You'll be OK,' said Kate, kneeling down beside her and taking her hand. 'It'll take some time... but you will be OK.'

Nikki nodded. 'Did we really drive that man to kill us?' she murmured. 'Did we really do that?' Tears leaked out of her eyes, painting thin streaks of mascara down her face.

'His sister died,' said Kate. 'I think that just broke him. He needed someone to blame.'

'And he blamed us,' said Nikki. 'And you know what...

we weren't… we weren't *blameless*, were we? All those things he said to me and Craig when he had us at gunpoint… about all those horrible things we said about his sister. They were true. We *did* say them. We just… we didn't know she heard us.'

Kate nodded. 'I know,' she said.

'But…' Nikki sniffed, then winced as the medic applied antiseptic spray to her wounds. 'We *did* know about leaving her in the bunker. It was just a joke… but it was a horrible joke. We did that. We left her stuck in there. For a laugh. What kind of people would do that?'

Kate shrugged. 'Immature people. Idiots. Kids.'

'And now look what's happened,' said Nikki, shaking with repressed sobs. 'Kate… I'm sorry. I'm so, so sorry.'

It was a relief when they were taken off to hospital to join Talia. Kate was running out of things to say to make her friend feel better.

33

'He was perfectly placed to plan it all,' DS Stuart told her the following day, switching off the tape in the interview room. Kate had given a basic statement the day before but she'd been shocked and exhausted so her fully detailed account of the whole Buntin's experience had been commuted to this morning. She outlined everything she could think of, simultaneously trying to remember to keep her elbow off the table. It stung painfully whenever she rested it without thinking. Other grazes and cuts were stinging all over her too, but she knew she was lucky to be alive.

'He used the security camera system to track you all,' went on Stuart. Her tone had shifted to informal, and Kate realised she and Upton were sharing off-the-record information... as a professional courtesy. They seemed to have forgiven her for going somewhat rogue on them.

'So he knew when Julie was alone — Bill and Talia, too,' Stuart went on. 'You're supposed to be able to control the cameras from the chalets, for privacy. They get switched on at the chalet end when parents go off to party and leave their kids under surveillance by the Sleep Tight team.'

DS Upton rolled his eyes. 'Jesus — after Madeleine McCann you'd think people wouldn't be so trusting. Imagine if he'd been a paedophile.'

'I think being a psychopathic murderer was quite bad, too,' said Stuart, wryly.

'Well, he got what was coming to him,' said Upton.

Kate said nothing.

'Anyway,' Stuart went on, 'He hacked the system so he could take control of those cameras as and when he wanted. Not long after killing Bill he sent a text to Talia from Bill's phone, asking her to meet him alone at her chalet, saying he'd come back and needed to talk about Nikki. He obviously knew all about Bill and Nikki together in the night, too.'

'Bloody hell,' murmured Kate, shivering as she realised they must all have been spied on.

'Take a look at these,' said Upton, sliding some large colour prints in front of Kate. They were shots taken inside Mike's staff chalet. One wall was plastered with images of his sister and the others were dedicated to the seven Bluecoats he held responsible for her death — with assorted photos from social media and even some press cuttings about Kate's recent adventures in Wiltshire.

'He clearly had you all in his sights as soon as he learned you were coming back for your reunion,' said Stuart. 'Seems as if that was his trigger, so soon after the death of his sister. And he knew all the tricks, like setting off the alarm to get everyone away from the beach where he'd planned his finale. Somewhere on the CCTV tapes there'll be footage of him taking all those sacks of sand and bits of guttering down through the site, heading for the beach. There's film of him buying frogs from a pond and aquatics centre in Ipswich. We're still picking through it all, but it looks like he planned it down to the smallest detail.'

'I think it was all he had left,' said Kate. 'Once his sister was dead, he was just running on revenge. I don't think he cared about being caught at the end of it, as long as he got all seven of us. It was all for Tessa.'

'Well, start to finish, it's looking like one of the fastest serial killer cases we've had,' said Stuart with a sad smile. 'There are even photos of the murder scenes on his phone and his laptop. Pretty safe to say there was nobody else involved.'

Kate nodded. The perpetrator was dead. The evidence was clear. It would be tied up relatively swiftly in the coroner's court. She wondered how much of the background to these murders would come out in the press reports. She had no doubt the grisly details of the murders would sell a lot of papers and drive an absolute frenzy of clickbait... but would the full story of what had happened seven years ago ever make it out into the media? None of the Magnificent Seven had committed a crime... but they had all been complicit, to some degree, in driving one woman to starve herself to death and her brother to commit multiple homicide.

'You won't have to repeat everything you've told us today at the inquest,' said Stuart, surprising her with a glance that held quite a bit of insight. 'The families of Bill Lassiter, Martin Riley and Julie Everall... it's going to be hard enough for them already. Put simply, the guy had a grudge against you all because he wasn't part of your crowd.'

Kate nodded. None of them spoke further about Mike's motivation for what he had done. She guessed she could make the decision later about how much she wanted to say.

Of course, Talia, Craig and Nikki might speak about

their part in it all, too... but she doubted it. It wasn't that they wouldn't feel it; they just weren't the types to go for the whole *mea culpa* line in public. They were... it was hard to say it even to herself, but it was true... more than a bit shallow. The way they had all regressed to their catty laughter and thoughtless piss-taking that weekend told her that seven years hadn't matured them much.

So if anyone spoke up for Mike and Tessa, it would be her. Maybe. Maybe not. Guilt was a terrible thing to carry but perhaps, for the sake of grieving relatives and traumatised friends, she would have to put that dull grey stone in her emotional backpack and just take the weight for the rest of her days.

34

It was the quietest Sunday Ellie had experienced at Buntin's. After the shocking events of the day before, the place had emptied. Buntin's had either refunded all the guests or given them transfer tickets to other sites around the country, where they could decamp and continue to have some fun without the distraction of forensics tents, police cordons and the occasional body bag being stretchered past.

She had been right about Martin's death all along. It didn't make her feel much better, but it was something. The Bluecoats had been offered counselling, and a week off. About half of them had taken up the week off but she, in common with the other half, had opted to stay and just have a bit of downtime before the fresh intake of families arrived next Saturday — those that hadn't already seen the news and cancelled (and apparently there were surprisingly few drop-outs). By then, the whole village would be empty of police and the chalets deep-cleaned. The bookings team would not be offering up the murder scene accommodation for rent.

Gary was quiet and withdrawn whenever she saw him wandering around the site, with or without the investigating officers. She had never challenged him about the accusation against Martin and probably wouldn't. The poor guy had enough to deal with. The new lifeguard had arrived, as well as a new security lady who looked like a world class wrestler and was most likely not a psychopath. Ellie shivered at the memory of her last conversation with Mike, in the security hub with all its screens. She'd heard he'd used his position to efficiently corner his victims, having tampered with the cameras so he could watch them inside without permission. She and Nettie had scoured the Bluecoat chalets for evidence of cameras, a lump of Blu Tack in their fists, ready to outwit spy technology with a blob across a lens. But there were no cameras inside the staff chalets.

Backflip Barney drove past, caravan in tow, as she sat on the steps of the pavilion with Nettie. Nettie had the grace to look ashamed. Barney's heroic actions down at the landslip had got out. 'He saved that guy who Mike was attacking... with a unicycle,' muttered Nettie, shaking her head. 'And I had Barney down as a psycho.'

She stood up and ran to the open window of Barney's Land Rover as he slowed down.

'What's up?' he asked, pausing with the engine on idle.

Nettie leaned in and Ellie, wandering across to join her, heard her say, 'Look... I'm sorry, OK? It was me who told the police you were... suspicious. It was me who got them onto you.'

Barney sighed, resting a tanned forearm across his steering wheel. 'You're not the first to go in for a bit of trav-eller-bashing,' he said. 'Won't be the last, either.'

'I really am sorry,' said Nettie. 'You're a bloody hero, apparently.'

'Ah,' he said, grinning. 'But would I ever have been there to help if you hadn't got the police to hunt me down?'

'What..?' Nettie wrinkled her brow. 'You mean... me stitching you up actually saved lives?'

'Don't push it, Nettie,' said Ellie, as Barney snorted and pulled away.

'I'm going to be better,' said Nettie, as they settled back on the steps, enjoying the sun on their skin. 'I'm not going to be so prejudiced.'

'Really? That's good then,' said Ellie.

'I'm even going to be nice to the guy in our local Paki shop,' said Nettie.

Ellie dropped her face into her palms.

35

Lady Grace Botwright brought Lucas breakfast in bed. A bed she had *not* climbed into the night before. When Lucas had arrived back late in the evening, bruised, scratched, and exhausted, she had immediately switched to maternal mode. 'You're not driving home tonight!' she'd told him. 'Get to bed, now!'

He had shared sketchy details of the day's events while she tucked him in and pressured him to finish the soup and roll she had brought him. Afterwards, she had commanded him to sleep and, observing that he was already working on that, left.

Now she was back with another tray. 'How did you sleep?' she asked, setting it down on the bedside table and checking his forehead for signs of fever.

'OK,' he said.

It hadn't been. He had been wiped out, so he'd fallen asleep very fast, only to be tipped directly into the darkest pits of dreamland. He couldn't get the image of Kate buried under the board and concrete and shingle out of his head, even during REM. And it kept morphing into the image of

Zoe, all those years ago, her dead eyes staring up through the rocks she'd been entombed in.

He'd woken up at around three, sweating and fighting with the duvet. He'd had to walk around and drink some water to get his heart rate down to something approaching normal. He knew he had to cut himself some slack after his cliff-face fight with a psychotic killer, and the shock of seeing Kate buried alive and then shot at. Not to mention finding the dead black dude with frogs in his mouth... Who wouldn't have a touch of PTSD after that?

Eventually he'd felt able to settle back into his pillows — and then the phone had buzzed beside the bed. Number withheld. His heart had leapt back up to full jackhammer as he'd answered it. He didn't wait it out this time, he just said, 'Speak! What's the point if you don't speak?!'

And then he'd heard a gasp at the other end, and once again thought of Kate. But it *couldn't* be Kate. Kate had called through on a different number and anyway... why on earth would she be messing with his mind like this?

'Lucas.'

Oh fuck. He was still dreaming.

'Lucas...' There was a long gap and then the line went dead.

It had been another hour before sleep finally reclaimed him. Now, he wrenched himself back out of it and sat up. The smell of scrambled eggs and toast made his stomach growl involuntarily.

'So...' said Grace, putting an extra pillow behind him and placing the tray on his knees. 'You've helped to put an end to another murder spree with your lovely detective friend. But did you get a chance to have that frank conversation with her? I'm guessing not.'

He shook his head, shovelling down a mouthful of hot,

fluffy egg on thickly buttered toast. He swallowed and then said, 'We were both taken away for a massive debrief. And checked over for injuries, of course. Nothing serious for either of us this time... which makes a change.'

She touched his bruised face. 'You still took quite a pummelling.'

'You should see the other guy,' he said, and then closed his eyes and shook his head. 'Bad joke. Other guy's dead.'

'But *you* didn't kill him,' she said, pouring coffee into a bone china mug. 'You have nothing to reproach yourself for... apart from not speaking to Kate about what's on your mind. So, I'm hoping you have made plans to do that.'

'Yes,' he said. 'We're meeting up next week, back in Salisbury. It's time.'

'Good,' said Grace, dropping a lump of Demerara into the coffee. 'Get it all out of your system. Say everything you need to say. Get it off your chest. It's the only way to move forward.'

Lucas struggled to swallow his next mouthful. He had plenty to get off his chest... but he suspected it was only going to move him backward.

Could anyone ever escape their guilty past?

————

'Sorry about your car,' Kate said, as the Ford Capri was winched up the ramp of the RAC truck. The police had cleared them to take it away, but its speedy journey across the lumpy field had cracked the chassis and it was unsafe to drive.

Francis sighed. 'I wish I could tell everyone it was me doing the stunt driving... but it was Backflip Barney. I did crash into him earlier, though,' he assured her. 'Knocked him off his unicycle.'

'Bravo,' she said. 'That was bound to get him onside.'

After the police had released them the previous evening, they'd got a cab into Lowestoft and managed to bag a room each at a budget hotel. Neither of them fancied trying to sleep back at Buntin's. Now, following her off-the-record briefing with Stuart and Upton that morning, she was back in practical mode. She had hired a car, and they had returned to collect their belongings from the chalet and oversee the recovery of Francis's pride and joy.

'Well, I wouldn't *normally* drive at someone on a unicycle,' Francis went on. 'But I thought he might be planning to kill you at the time. He was behaving like a total weirdo.'

She sighed. 'That's just Barney. He *is* a total weirdo — but a lovely weirdo.'

'If you tell him that, he'll probably get it tattooed on his *other* arm.'

'What..?'

'Oh yeah... you need an update. Ah — no problem. Here he comes now.'

Kate spun around to see Barney strolling across the field towards them, his car and caravan parked up at the edge of the gravel track, close to the road. He grinned as he got closer and waved his right arm before clutching it to the shoulder of his left.

'Ah yeah...' muttered Francis. 'That'll probably be where he got hit by my car.'

Kate found herself grinning back as something like relief flowed through her. She had only thought about Barney being the killer for long enough to dismiss it, but it was good to be proven solidly correct. She held out her arms and Barney, after pausing and looking endearingly awkward, ambled across and allowed the hug.

'Sorry about my brother trying to run you over,' she said.

Barney flicked a glance at the Capri, now being secured on the flatbed of the RAC truck. 'I hope I dented its body-work more than it dented mine.' He rubbed his arm again. Francis dug his hands in his pockets and bit his lips together, guiltily.

'Are you OK?' Kate asked. 'I haven't had the chance to thank you for knocking out Mike yesterday. You and Lucas — and Francis,' she grinned toward her brother, 'you won us enough time to get out of that bunker. You saved us.'

Barney shrugged again. 'Group effort,' he said. 'And... I owed you.'

She wrinkled her brow. 'Why? Francis was saying some-thing about... a tattoo?'

Barney pulled the sleeve of his sweatshirt up over his left bicep. There was a graze and a bruise on his upper arm, but encircling the blue, purple and green was a beautiful Celtic–style ink bracelet with lettering. She tilted her head side-ways and read the words.

You are always enough.

She had a sudden flash of memory. She had taken Barney into town. The other Blues had been taking the piss out of his clothes and his hair that week, and she'd said, 'He just needs a bit of styling, that's all. Give him a break.'

And then Talia had said, 'Well — go on then. Style him. I bet you can't make anything out of *that*. I mean, god... look at that those joggers! Look at that little orphan Annie haircut.'

And then Nikki and Bill had chimed in, daring her to go and proposition Barney; to convince him to go into Lowestoft and buy some decent outfits. In the end Bill had shouted, 'Oi! Backflip Boy! Kate wants to get you out of those clothes.'

Barney, doing some work under the bonnet of his Land Rover, had looked quizzically at Kate, unsure how to react. So, she had shot a look of poison at the rest of them and marched across to the young man, taking a deep breath.

'I'm sorry about them,' she had said. 'They're a bunch of tossers. They take the piss out of everyone, and I just said... I just said I could maybe help you... choose some clothes. If you fancy it.'

He had wiped his hands on a cloth and said, 'Why? Why do I need more clothes?'

And then she had laughed and shaken her head, and said, 'Because you're — what — nineteen? And you're dressing like your granddad! Come on! I've got the morning off and so have you. Drive us both into town and I'll help you. You've got money, yeah?'

And to her amazement... he'd said yes.

Three hours later, when they'd driven back in, parked up next to the Bluecoat chalets, and got out, everyone came bursting out to see what transformation she had made. And their jaws had dropped. Barney was wearing Levi's 501 jeans and a soft denim shirt, Converse trainers on his feet. His hair was cut so well he now looked like a member of a boy band, rather than a character out of *The Simpsons*.

He'd learned fast and thoroughly. She'd told him to go back to the same salon every month and to stick with the styles and colours she'd picked out for him. And looking at him today, she could see he had remembered and worked with that advice ever since.

But it was the words that clearly meant the most.

'You told me I was enough,' he said, staring down at his arm and going a little red across his handsome face. 'After the clothes and the haircut, and all the Blues being so impressed, you came up to me the next day, on your own and you said... you said it didn't matter what I wore or what my hair looked like, not really. It might help me fit in and feel more comfortable... but in the end what mattered was that I had to be myself. And I had to know that... I was enough.'

She smiled, feeling her throat constrict. God, she was emotional these days.

'I'm really glad I was able to help,' she said. 'That you let me.'

'It turned things around for me,' he said. 'It made a difference. So... I got the tattoo done a few years ago. Jason, my other half — he loves it. He agrees with you. He says I am *way more* than enough. Sorry if I freaked you out, chasing you down. I just wanted to tell you... show you... and say thanks. That's all.'

She smiled at him warmly as he nodded and then walked back to his vehicles, skirting the RAC truck as it carried the Capri across the field. She hadn't been able to say anything because she knew she would just squeak. She was on the edge of tipping over at any moment.

She'd had a phone call with Talia, on a drip in Lowestoft Infirmary, an hour earlier, and had struggled to hold it together then, too. 'Shit, Kate,' Talia had croaked. 'Never thought we'd piss someone off so much they would literally try to kill us.'

'Yeah, well, it's a long story,' Kate had replied. She knew Mike's sad, broken tale would come out soon enough. She didn't have to deliver it to Talia herself. Either way, Kate was pretty sure Talia would get through it. She was made of tough stuff. Hopefully Craig and Nikki were, too.

'Bloody hell — who knew my sister was such a

paragon?' Francis was marvelling as they followed the track back to the hire car. 'Inspiration for a tattoo, no less! Can the Pope beatify you if you're not Catholic?' When she didn't answer, he gave her a brotherly nudge and added, 'Well done, girl.'

Kate felt something inside her drop. 'I didn't do so well for everyone,' she said, her throat constricting. 'In fact... I did so, so badly, I don't know if I'll ever forgive myself.'

Because not everyone who'd tangled with the Magnificent Seven had come out of it as well as Barney, had they? She thought of poor Tessa, in her awful yellow dress, sitting in the bunker, hoping to be included and instead being bullied and joked about by some stupid, thoughtless young people who should have known better. She pictured Tessa being embarrassed by Talia, dented by Julie, publicly shamed by Martin, privately mortified by Bill and his brutal comedy turn... and let down by Kate Sparrow, who should have stood up and shouted STOP, but didn't.

She felt something crumple inside as she grappled with her failure. Then, finally, she began to cry. And once she'd started it was very, very hard to stop. Even though she was seriously freaking out her brother.

Could anyone ever escape their guilty past?

36

A skylark was spiralling up into the hazy blue, a speck, identifiable only when its joyous song rang through the warm air.

Lucas had suggested Pepperbox Hill, and on this morning in early summer it was a sound call. Peaceful and quiet. The pleasant walk along the ridgeway would be a distraction... for a while. Kate parked up and set out along the path, taking in the soft greens and yellows of the valley below and the silver braids of the River Avon as it wound its way towards the northern edge of the New Forest. The spire of Salisbury Cathedral was just about visible on the western horizon.

She found Lucas after a couple of minutes, sitting on a weathered wooden bench, taking in the same view. His biker's jacket was slung over the back of the seat, and he was stretching and yawning, his toned arms visible in the short sleeves of a dark blue T-shirt. His jeans looked freshly laundered. He was tidier than she'd seen him in a while, the beard trimmed back to fine stubble, the loose waves of his dark hair looking freshly washed. It made her uneasy. She couldn't quite manage the idea of Lucas sprucing himself up for her. Every meeting they'd had over the last half a year had been under circumstances of stress, tension and knife-edge necessity; she was pretty sure neither of them had given a thought to their personal presentation up until today.

She'd be lying to herself if she tried to claim her own attire had been given no consideration. Like him, she was in jeans and a T-shirt, but they were among her favourites. Her tan, faux suede jacket was also something she might select for a casual date. She hadn't gone the whole hog and put make-up on... well, other than a little mascara and a touch of lip sheen.... because this was not a date. This was very far from a date.

Lucas didn't look at her as she joined him on the bench. He cupped his mobile in both hands and stared down at it. 'I keep getting these calls,' he said.

'Well... that does sometimes happen... with a phone,' she said. 'It's a glitch they've never fixed.'

He made a noise which was not quite a laugh. She became aware of how tense he was. Well, good. So was she. At least they were at level pegging.

'These calls,' went on Lucas. 'I thought they might be from you.'

She tilted her head, perplexed. 'Well... yes. I have called you.'

'But not from a withheld number,' he said. 'Not in the middle of the night, just to hang on the line, silent and breathing.'

'Oh,' she said. 'No. I can promise you I've never done that. Normally I just yell accusations down the phone at you.'

He nodded, and clutched at the outline of Sid, under his T-shirt.

'What are you trying to tell me, Lucas?' She gulped, suddenly convinced that she did not want the answer. Suddenly certain that this was a very bad idea.

He glanced at her, his eyes shadowed and uncertain too. 'Sometimes,' he said. 'You remind me of her. And other times I'm reminded that you're nothing like her. Nothing like her at all. You...' he reached out a hand and stroked a strand of hair from her cheek. '...you are so different.'

She breathed in slowly through her nose. Her pulse was pounding through her ears and she wanted it to stop. Wanted it to calm the fuck down. Wanted to have control. Lucas smelled... like Lucas. A mix of warm leather, a faint grassy aftershave and something else... probably just the washing powder he used, combined with the warmth of his skin. Honestly, they had not spent enough time together for her to know his smell. It was ridiculous. But she felt it wrap around her as she sat there, close enough but not close *enough*. Shit. *Stop it. Stop it, Kate. This is not appropriate.*

'How do you remember her?' he asked.

She looked away down the valley. 'It fades over time, doesn't it? The detail. She was... a classic big sister, I guess. I looked up to her. She was cool and pretty, and she had great friends. She was everything I wanted to be. But... I annoyed her. I was too young to really be in her world. She hated taking me out with you and Zoe, when Mum made her. Normal stuff, really. Didn't mean she didn't love me.'

He nodded. He opened his mouth to speak and then closed it again. 'She *was* cool,' he said, at length. 'And pretty. They both were.' He gnawed on a fingernail; the first time she'd ever noticed him do that. She felt the prickle of unease go up a gear. 'But she could be mean to you too. I remember that. I remember her telling you to get lost quite a lot.'

Kate felt a sting of defensiveness. He was talking about her sister — his friend — who was dead. But at the same time, she knew he was speaking the truth. Mabel had often been mean to her. She would walk away and hide from her, when they were out and about, sometimes leaving her crying and alone for half an hour before she reluctantly returned, eyes rolling. At home, she refused to let her little sister play with her stuff or try on her clothes or make-up. In fact once, when she discovered Kate had been in her room without permission and tried on a couple of tops, she had gone into her little sister's room and destroyed one of her art projects; drawings of wildlife Kate had been really proud of. Mabel had then put the ripped up pieces under Kate's quilt so she would find them when she went to bed. Kate had been distraught, but Mabel had never apologised.

'I'm not trying to be unkind,' said Lucas. 'But I think people tend to talk about victims of crime as if they were angels. Nobody's an angel and Mabel wasn't one either.'

Kate wondered where this was going. She decided to cut straight to it. 'Lucas... what happened that day? What happened in the quarry? Do you know?'

He got to his feet, staring along the path to the north. 'Walk with me,' he said. 'It'll be easier if I don't have to look at you.'

Oh fuck, whimpered a voice inside her head. *Oh fuck. No, Lucas. Don't tell me.*

They walked in silence for some distance, the view occasionally screened by trees and shrubs. The valley below wore that silvery green sheen unique to the month of May. Birds flew. Tiny cars travelled the skinny thread of the A36. A red tractor slowly worked its way across a field. So much life happening all around them, oblivious to Kate Sparrow and Lucas Henry and their dramas. Her mouth was dry. She could hear his boots crunch, his slightly laboured breathing, the faintest chink of the long steel chain around his neck as he gripped Sid, now outside his T-shirt and in his right fist. Was he dowsing something? Was he... was he *taking* her somewhere? He had suggested this place, hadn't he? A coldness settled over her. Maybe there was something to see here.

She fought the urge to turn and run. The disquiet of not knowing... the nagging at the back of her mind... the unsettling wrongness/rightness about her attraction to him... she could live with that. She didn't *need* to get the answers to the questions which haunted her dreams and tickled the back of her waking mind. She could just leave now and forget about it. Maybe.

There was nobody else here. The car park had been empty, apart from Lucas's bike. It was a weekday in term time but she would have expected to meet dog walkers and joggers somewhere around here. It seemed they had all gone elsewhere today. Was she safe? She was ninety-nine per cent sure that she was. But that still left a single percentage point of doubt, didn't it?

Lucas took a steep path, winding down off the ridgeway to a lower part of the beauty spot, where a thicket of trees clung to the hillside. Grasshoppers sang in the sun and the peaty scent of the lower slopes rose up on the light breeze. Kate felt her breathing quickening and she squeezed a small slug of plasticine in her jacket pocket, trying to ground herself.

'Lucas,' she said. 'Are you taking me to see... something?'

He only nodded. He did not look at her. She felt her phone, in the other pocket, and her thumb brushed the redial button while her mind spun with indecision. The last number she had called was to the station — to Chief Superintendent Rav Kapoor. Her boss had recently decided to champion Lucas, after experiencing first-hand the evidence — and the benefit — of the dowser's talent. He had gone as far as discussing with her the option of putting Lucas on their regular police consultant list.

She had called Kapoor this morning to update him on the events in Suffolk, before DS Stuart could do that for her. Kapoor had been shocked at her bad luck in getting the long weekend from hell at Buntin's, so soon after her other tribulations. He'd urged her to take a week off to recover, and then given in when she'd said time off was the very last thing she needed. She'd be back in tomorrow, she told him. She had just one thing to do today.

Now she wondered if she'd be seeing Kapoor sooner. *No, Kate... no!* called her inner voice, the voice of a ten-year-old who had utterly trusted the boy who was now the man clambering down a steep path beside her, gripping a lump of glass which might or might not be leading them both to something too terrible to imagine.

'Lucas, I'm not feeling very comfortable with this,' she said, finally pushing out words that had to be the understatement of the year.

'Me neither,' he said. He flicked her a glance and then stopped, resting his right hand on the trunk of a slender birch tree and taking a deep breath. 'You *are* like her, but you are *nothing* like her,' he said, again. He reached out and ran his left hand over her shoulder, pulling her closer to him. For a long moment she stood, caught in a riptide between fear and desire, watching his mouth and wondering what it would feel like on hers. She could feel the warmth of his breath reach her lips.

'It was never like this,' he said. 'Never felt... like this. God... she was so manipulative. She could make you do almost anything.'

'Sounds like you didn't really like her that much after all,' said Kate, coldly, stepping away.

'No... you don't understand. I loved her. Kind of. I loved them both.' He looked at his feet and his face coloured up.

'What are you telling me, here?' demanded Kate.

'I was just a kid,' he said. 'I was fifteen, and a stew of hormones and terror. Mabel... she was really confident. She wanted... she wanted sex. She wanted to know what it was like.'

Kate felt a wave of nausea. 'So you showed her, did you?'

His reaction was somewhere between a laugh and a sob. 'She showed *me*. I was fucking useless at it. What the hell did *I* know? I did my best, but it was all fumble and panic and over within a minute. She just laughed. And it *was*... laughable.'

'So... you got mad..?' Kate's words came out in a whisper.

'What?' He squinted at her, shielding his eyes with one hand as a shaft of sun hit the side of his face. 'Mad? Angry mad? *No!* No — I was embarrassed. Just... sick with embarrassment. And then Zoe...'

'Did she join in? Did *she* start teasing you as well?' Kate could picture it all too easily. She thought she really might be sick.

'She was kind,' he said. 'She felt bad about the way Mabel had laughed at me. Mabel told her everything... like sharing the details of her last shopping trip. Told her everything, right in front of me.'

'Right there in the quarry?' Kate asked, lightly.

'This was before that day,' he said. 'A week or so before that day. And however bad I was at it, she still wanted to try again. She told me that, next time we were all on the downs again. She wanted to see if I could improve. Only... I *didn't* want it. I mean, she was sexy as hell, but she was... cold, you know? I knew I couldn't take it, if I failed again. And then Zoe...'

'What? What about Zoe..?!' Kate heard the edge creeping into her voice. She sounded like she was back in the Salisbury nick interview room, sitting next to DS Ben Michaels, taping this conversation while they both took turns at coaxing the truth from their suspect.

'Zoe stuck up for me,' he said. 'She told Mabel not to be a bitch and then we walked home together. We left Mabel on the downs and we went back, and when we got to my house, out of nowhere, Zoe kissed me. She told me she loved me. She was everything Mabel wasn't. She wasn't sexy and controlling but she made me feel OK about myself and honestly, when you're fifteen and your mum's a drunk and your dad's vanished and nobody really seems to give a flying fuck about you, that counts for quite a lot.'

Kate held her breath. She was losing the thread of this. Where was it going?

'So... you had both of them on the go,' she said, channelling Michaels, who would certainly have put it like that. 'You were getting into a little threesome.'

'No,' he said, shaking his head and raking his left hand through his hair. 'No way. I was trying to get *out* of a threesome. I didn't want it. I loved them both and I knew this was going to mash up our friendship, but it was already blown apart and I didn't know how to handle it. I said we all had to talk. The three of us. I wanted to get back to where we used to be. I wanted to stop it all. I just... wanted it to stop.'

Kate's throat felt like it was filled with concrete. She had heard this so many times. The standard cry of the abusive man in the interview room, while a woman lay cold on the slab in the mortuary. "She screamed and screamed, and I just wanted it to stop." Or, "She laughed at me and I had to make it stop." Or, 'She was leaving me; I had to make it stop."

She became aware of Sid, spinning below Lucas's fist. 'Where... where is Sid taking us?' she said.

'Down here, I think,' said Lucas. He moved on down the narrow path, barely more than an animal track now. Beneath the trees it was muffled and quiet, with moss and lichen covering much of the ground like a green carpet.

Kate followed, her belly set like iron, wondering whether she was actually *here*. This whole thing was so, so hyperreal, she wouldn't be even a bit surprised to wake up from it, her body drenched in sweat and tangled in the sheets, panic ebbing as she realised it was just another nightmare.

A fallen oak lay decaying in the lowest part of this sleeve of green. It had to have been there for a decade or two. Lucas moved slowly down the slope towards it, holding Sid out on a steady arm and pausing every few steps to watch the way the pendulum swung. Eventually he dropped to his knees and stared at the underside of the log. His face, when he lifted it to Kate, was blanched and mask-like.

'There's something here,' he said.

37

He was here, on his knees, because of the last silent call. At just after 2am, he had woken to the buzz of the mobile on the bedside table and snatched up the device to see the familiar *number withheld* notification as it vibrated in his palm.

'Hello,' he'd said.

Once again, a long silence, although he could sense the caller on the other end. 'Speak to me,' he'd said; a medium channelling a ghost.

Still nothing but a long exhalation. And then, finally, the words, like a sigh of air around a door. *'Lucas. It's time to dig me up.'*

The call ended before he could respond, but it had done its work. Here he was, a few hours later, kneeling by a fallen oak tree, Sid spinning in his hand and Kate staring at him as if waiting for the jump scare in a particularly disturbing horror flick. She was right to prepare herself. This wasn't going to be pleasant for her.

Lucas took a moment, knowing his world was about to spin wildly out of control in a matter of minutes. When he revealed what was here, Kate might never look at him the same way again. Because she *had* begun to look at him the way he knew he was looking at her.

Once or twice in a lifetime, if they were lucky, a person could meet someone who would put a match to the dry kindling in their soul. Someone who would light up their world from within.

As soon as she'd come marching into his old bungalow, waving her ID and demanding his help last year, Lucas had recognised Kate as a match bearer. She certainly had turned the heat up. The physical attraction was palpable, and he was pretty sure it wasn't a one-way thing. It was doomed, of course. Aren't the best romances always doomed? In the last few days, though, he'd begun to wonder if, once they'd talked out everything they could, there might be the faintest chance that this could work.

And then the call.

'It's time to dig me up...'

Even though he knew it was almost totally hopeless... or maybe *because* he knew it was almost totally hopeless, he had held her back for just a minute, up on the hillside, before committing to speak his sorry tale. He had pulled her closer, breathed in the scent of her, felt the heartbeat inside her, *known* that the attraction was mutual, even if she was wrestling with it. Would that be enough to sustain him after today? It was all he had.

He hadn't needed to bring her here, of course. He didn't need to tell her *everything.* He could edit the story for her like he'd edited it for the police when he was fifteen. After all, he hadn't exactly lied. He'd only not mentioned a few things that they might have found... interesting.

But that call...

'It's time to dig me up...'

There was so little chance for him and Kate now. It was a tiny, tiny sliver of chance. But if he didn't show her what Sid was pointing at now, his own guilt was going to destroy even that chance, so hey. Here they were.

She looked incandescent; her face pale and luminous as if lit from within while her eyes fixed on him, waiting. He could sense the tension in every muscle and sinew of her; her belly was taut and clenched and her limbs were a microsecond's notice away from leaping into fight or flight. She'd never been more beautiful, and he had never been more wretched before her.

Lucas reached into the damp peat and moss beneath the fallen tree and drove his fingers in deep.

38

Kate was battling with a sense of unreality once more as Lucas began to dig under the fallen tree. What the hell had he found? Oh god. She didn't want to see this. She didn't want any of it. Why had he brought her here and told her his sorry tale of *wanting it to stop,* and then forced her to stand and watch while he excavated their shared past?

Because this, surely, was what it was. The brutal loss of two teenage girls nearly seventeen years ago, which had blighted both their young lives and remade each of them in different shapes... forever a little twisted as they grew older... was playing out again, here, now.

Was this where Lucas Henry finally confessed?

She had been stamping on that tiny seed of doubt for months now. Everything she sensed in Lucas fought with the notion that he might be guilty of bludgeoning a girl to death in a quarry and burying her remains... and then taking the other one elsewhere and despatching her, too. She could not see it in him. She could see conflict and repression, though. Plenty of that. And who knew what a young man, boiling with testosterone and sexual shame, could be capable of? Who knew what *anyone* could be capable of in the heat of the moment? One rash, fatal over-reaction... she well knew that the most normal of people could suffer this. She had helped to convict several such hapless individuals of manslaughter over the years.

But *two*? A crime of passion or accident or confusion... that could happen once. Anyone could believe it. Not twice, though. You couldn't haplessly kill *two* people and put it down to tragic bad luck.

She glanced up the empty hillside. Had she made the right choice? So many choices she'd made recently had led her into catastrophe. *Oh god.* Lucas was elbow deep in decayed leaf litter now and still going, Sid dangling once more around his neck; the little friendly helper who pointed the way to death.

Lucas stopped abruptly, exhaled slowly, and then lifted his face to hers. An unreadable expression was on it. He tugged something out of the hole beneath the fallen tree and it wound around his grimy fingers, dyed with woodland dirt but still just about discernible as originally pink with white elastic.

Kate felt her knees begin to give way and grabbed hold of a low branch close to her, drawing in a ragged breath.

'This,' croaked Lucas, his brow suddenly wrinkling, 'is not how it looks.'

She recognised the bra. The little butterflies of lace along the top of the cups were caked in mud but she remembered it clearly. Mabel liked to stroll around her room in her underwear and Kate had always longed to have bras like her sister's, with little matching bikini knickers, instead of the babyish vests and pants she still wore. When she'd suggested she might have the bras Mabel had outgrown, her big sister had hooted with laughter. 'You've got nothing to put in them!' she'd hooted. 'Just a couple of pimples!'

Not long after, Kate had abruptly inherited *all* the bras and the knickers and the tops and the skirts and the shorts and the jeans and the dresses.

But she would never wear any of them.

Lucas went back to digging, the filthy bra hung on a stubby dead branch that stuck out of the log. 'There's more,' he said and then dragged out another piece of elastic and cotton, like a blackbird hauling a long pink worm from the soil. Kate heard static and hiss and a rush of something rumbling like a train out of Waterloo, which might very well have been her soul departing her body.

Lucas turned around again, sweat, or maybe tears, marking a grimy track down one side of his handsome face. He held up the matching knickers, closed his eyes, and then said, 'Kate, this is not what you're thinking. Let me explain.'

And then she snapped. She was on him and throwing him onto his back before he could utter one more poisonous, sick, polluted word.

'Lucas Henry!' she yelled, flipping him over with a kick to his flank and an elbow to the side of his head. 'I am arresting you for the murder of Zoe Taylor and Mabel Johanssen.'

'Kate! STOP!' he cried. 'Listen to me first!'

'You do not have to say anything,' she choked, grief flattening her words and tears welling in her eyes.

'Kate! There isn't much time. They're coming. You HAVE to listen to me!' bawled Lucas, fighting back as she pulled the cuffs off the back belt loop of her jeans and swiped his wrists together.

'But it may harm your defence,' she sobbed. 'If you do not.... you *fucking bastard*.'

'I'm not... I'm not, Kate. You don't understand,' he said.

There was a crashing sound above them, and several dark figures came plunging through the trees. She had been deeply conflicted about thumbing that redial button, but she now knew it had been the right thing to do. She was hollowed out with shock and grief and simply did not have the strength to hold Lucas down and get the cuffs on him while he struggled to be free.

'POLICE! STAY DOWN! RAISE YOUR HANDS!' bellowed one of her colleagues, and Kate let go and staggered away from him, falling backwards into a thicket. Lucas did not stay down.

'STAY DOWN!' repeated the officer. 'YOU ARE SURROUNDED. WE ARE ARMED AND WE WILL SHOOT IF NECESSARY!'

Lucas vaulted over the fallen log, leaving the underwear hanging on it, and scrambled away into the thick undergrowth. Kate sagged into the thicket and allowed the armed response team to chase past her in pursuit. She was vaguely aware of the black-clad figures streaming by while her eyes rested on those muddy bits of material, hanging limply on the log like the world's saddest lingerie display. Was Mabel under there, too? Were her remains decomposing beneath the soil? Until this point in her life, Kate had always cherished a tiny flame of hope that Mabel might still be alive. No matter how often her mother told her to let go and accept that Mabel was never coming back, she hadn't ever quite let go. Seeing this evidence before her now, Kate felt that flame gutter and die, taking some part of her with it.

'Kate!' A face loomed in front of her. The creased features of Superintendent Rav Kapoor and, next to him, her detective sergeant, Ben Michaels, looking strained and angry. 'Are you all right?' asked Kapoor. 'Are you hurt?'

She shook her head. 'I'm fine,' she lied.

She pointed to the evidence. 'Mabel was wearing those the day she disappeared. Lucas just brought me here and dug them up. He told me more about what happened that day.'

Kapoor nodded. 'We have a recording of much of what you said to each other,' he said. 'Not great quality through the phone connection but our tech guys should be able to tease it out.'

Kate nodded and watched while Ben walked across and began to take phone camera shots of the log and the underwear, careful not to tread too close to the burial site. Soon this whole area would be tented, lit, and excavated.

She already felt her sister gone. A void was tearing open inside her. But what made her feel sick to her very soul, was the grief she felt clawing through that void. Not for the loss of Mabel, but for the loss of Lucas.

'I think,' she said, in a voice as thin as parchment, 'I want to go home.'

*Y*ou *should have waited. You should have given me the benefit of the doubt.*

Lucas paused, his pen hand unstable as the boat hit a swell. It also didn't help that his wrist was bandaged and sore, possibly sprained, from falling heavily as he'd outrun the Wiltshire Police one more time. Just holding the pen was painful. He guessed he was about mid-Channel by now. A glance through the window revealed only a vast expanse of grey sea and grey horizon.

How could you think I would kill Zoe and Mabel? How could you? What does your copper's instinct tell you, Kate? Don't you go with that any more?

He felt fury and hurt fizzing through him as he wrote. Although he could understand, too. He had not presented his story in the best light, had he? He should have told her everything he knew well before they had gone to Pepperbox Hill. Sitting in a cafe, in a place of safety. He had clearly overestimated her instinct to grasp that he was no threat to her. But then, after the hellish weekend she had just been through, how could he expect her to be sound and steady in her judgement?

Her bitter expression as she'd launched at him and flipped him brutally onto his face was something that gave him chills to remember. And he remembered it roughly every thirty seconds. Part of him had considered giving up; allowing her to cuff him and take him in, and interview him under arrest. She would have had to listen to everything he said and weigh it up like the professional detective she was.

But it was the others crashing down the hillside that ended that idea. He'd been in the not so tender care of her Salisbury colleagues before. He didn't really blame them for Tasering him — twice — but he knew *they* blamed him for leaving them stranded in a bog one time, while he'd done a runner. And for showing them up by beating them to the resolution of two cases with his dowsing talent. With the possible exception of the chief superintendent, they all loathed him.

Instinct kicked in as he sensed DS Michaels and other unfriendly officers heading for him with a lot of hate in their hearts and quite a bit of firepower in their holsters. So he'd run. Once again using Sid and his own adrenaline-driven dowsing instincts to get him away before he could be captured.

Because there was only one way to make Kate believe he was not a killer, and he needed to be free to do that.

I am not running away, he wrote on. *I am running **to**. I am determined to find out what happened in the quarry that day. Because I really WASN'T in the quarry that day. I did not kill Zoe. I didn't do anything to Mabel.*

I am going to find the answers and then I am coming back to show you, Kate. I am coming back to show you.

ABOUT THE AUTHOR

AD Fox is an award winning author who lives in Hampshire, England, with a significant other, boomerang offspring and a large, highly porous labradoodle.

With a background in newspaper and broadcast journalism, AD also spent a memorable summer working at a holiday camp on the east coast of England when she was 19 - which she maintains was the making of her. Probably. Although she's still scared of kids in swimming pools.

Younger readers will know the AD alter ego as Ali Sparkes, author of more than fifty titles for children and young adults including the Blue Peter Award winning Frozen In Time, the bestselling Shapeshifter series and Car-Jacked, finalist in the national UK Children's Book of the Year awards.

For more on AD Fox, including blogs and updates, visit www.adfoxfiction.com

ALSO BY A D FOX

available now on Amazon

HENRY & SPARROW book 1:

THE DYING DOLLS

HENRY & SPARROW book 2:

DEAD AIR

and HENRY & SPARROW book 4:

DEATH CIRCLES

(available Summer 2021)

and for a free copy
of the Henry & Sparrow prequel novella

UNDERTOW

go to www.adfoxfiction.com

ACKNOWLEDGMENTS

Deep and heartfelt thanks to Beverly Sanford (editor), Nicola Sparkes (vital insights provider) and Sarah Bodell (police procedure guidance). Also to Neville Dalton, Mr Backstop, whose extraordinary eye for detail has saved me from ignominy!

Warm appreciation also goes to The Collective, who have really helped to keep Henry & Sparrow rolling by keeping their creator focused on the bigger picture. You know who you are!

And, of course, Simon Tilley, whose late night observations have been brilliantly helpful... even when semiconscious...

Printed in Great Britain
by Amazon